PRAISE FOR THE MARKED SON SERIES

"Lush emotions, vivid characters, and a world rich with history—I didn't want this journey to end."
ESSA HANSEN, AUTHOR OF *NOPHEK GLOSS*

"Stunning. The world building is some of the best I've ever read, and the main character, Akrist, has left me with a permanent ache in my heart. Set in a brutal, often merciless world, the story kept me breathlessly turning pages to the very end. Clear your calendar, because you won't be able to put this one down."
JULIE ESHBAUGH, AUTHOR OF *IVORY AND BONE* AND ITS SEQUEL, *OBSIDIAN AND STARS*

"A compelling story like none other, told in an incredibly crafted world."
DAN VADEBONCOEUR, CO-HOST OF THE MEDIA NERDS PODCAST

"This is recommended for anyone who is sick of waiting for the newest Game of Thrones book, because seriously. That's taking a while."

A LOVELY LITTLE BOOK BLOG

SHELLY CAMPBELL

VOICE OF THE BANISHED

THE MARKED SON
BOOK TWO

DARK LITTLE BIRD

ALSO BY SHELLY CAMPBELL

Under the Lesser Moon

Gulf

Knowledge Itself

Making Myths and Magic: A Field Guide to Writing Sci-Fi and
Fantasy Novels

Love you all, but this one's for me.

Content Warnings: Violence, non-graphic sex, physical abuse, mental abuse, child abuse, sexual abuse, animal cruelty, suicide, self-harm, kidnapping, mental illness, blood, death.

Cover design by James T. Egan of Bookfly Design.

Map by Allison Alexander.

ISBN 978-1-7388568-2-4 (softcover), 978-1-7388568-3-1 (e-book)

Published by Dark Little Bird Publishing

Cochrane, Alberta, Canada

www.shellycampbellauthorandart.com

THE STORY SO FAR

A KRIST WAS A FIRSTBORN son (a daeson) and a pariah of his stone-age tribe. When he befriended Tanar, another eldest boy from a different tribe, they discovered the awful truth: daeson were sacrificed during the dual moons' eclipse—a holy event that took place every twelve years—in an attempt to appease the goddess Nasheira and win back her dragons.

Tanar escaped before the sacrifice, abandoning Akrist to face his fate alone. But on the night of the eclipse, a dragon saved Akrist by scarring his chest, marking him as a Speaker—a holy leader among his people. His camp was torn over his fate. Many insisted Akrist should still be sacrificed. Arsu, the sister of the camp's Speaker, particularly wanted him dead. But the elders agreed to a compromise: Akrist's sacrificial status was annulled and he renounced any claim to leadership.

Wrought with guilt over the deaths of the children he couldn't rescue, Akrist vowed to save the next generation of eldest sons. Twelve years was plenty of time to mobilize a mass escape, but also long enough to forge bonds with his estranged family and to fall in love. As the moons closed on each other again, Akrist, his pregnant mate, Yara, and the daeson of his camp prepared to flee, but Arsu framed him for the murder of his beloved aunt on the night before their planned escape.

Arsu convinced the tribe that Akrist should never have been left alive—that he would always be a daeson. His tribe castrated and abandoned him alongside the next generation of damned sons, but Akrist survived. Giant, scavenging wurms, attracted by the smell of blood, found Akrist in the wilderness. One of the creatures imprinted on him when it felt the dragon's scar on his chest. They were suddenly connected; Akrist could sense its emotions and learned to communicate with it. The bond deepened as Akrist healed and the wurm grew.

When the wurm cocooned, Akrist protected it from danger, including from other cannibalistic wurms. One night, he awakened to a knife at his throat. His estranged childhood friend, Tanar, had found him and meant to kill him. But at that moment, a dragon emerged from the cocoon, knocked Akrist's attacker aside, and saved him. She spoke to him through his thoughts and introduced herself as Nardiri, one of the golden guides of the sky.

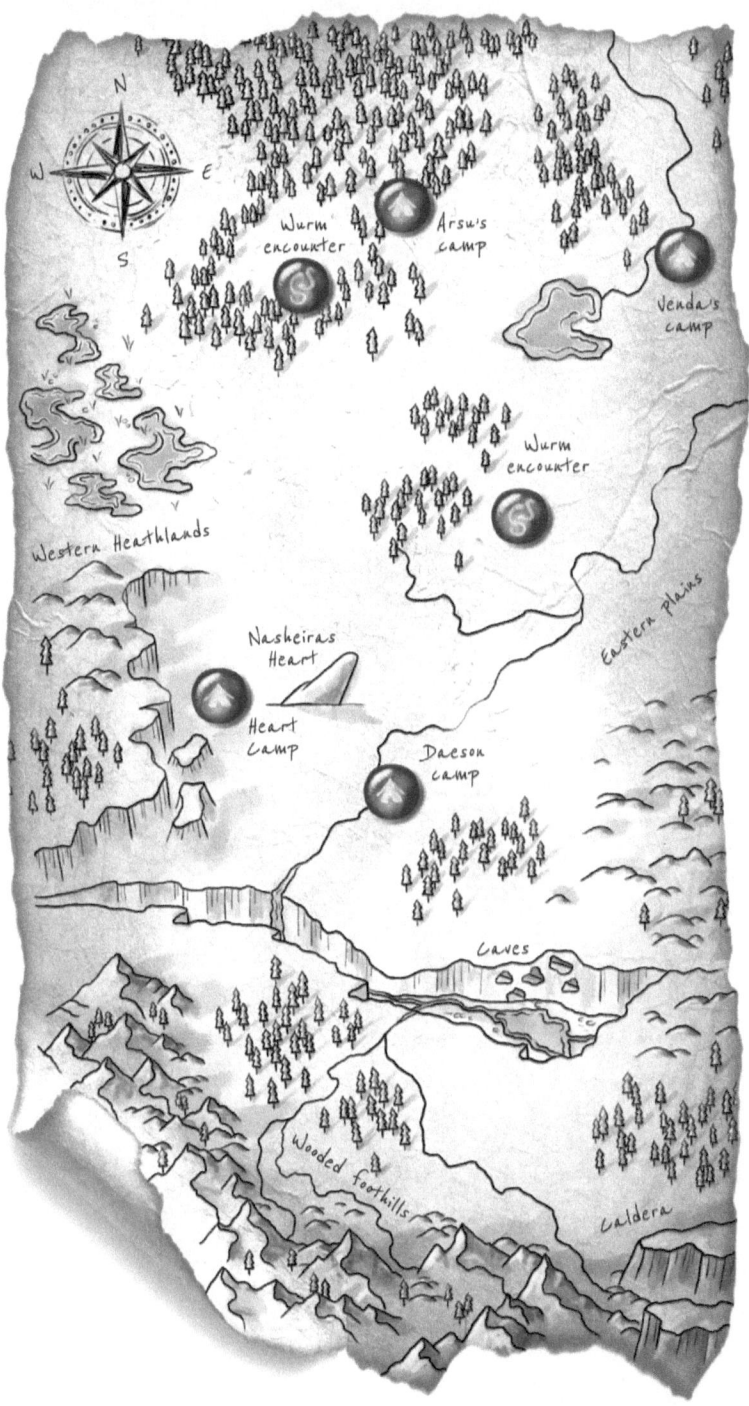

PROLOGUE

NASHEIRA HAD TWO SONS. She created them herself, the first out of soil and the second out of sky. She named them Pau and Yurrii. Pau of earth hated Yurrii of sky, who floated amongst the stars, while Pau curled like a slug in the dirt.

Nasheira told him that, although his little brother had the company of constellations, Pau could breathe life into soil.

Pau was jealous. He shook his earth and spat poison about him, so that no life could grow. Yurrii shined the light of his sun down, cooled Pau with his rain and shaded him with his clouds, but Pau hated him and still would not let life grow.

So, Yurrii took pity upon his elder brother. He told him that if he would allow life to grow, if he created a human whose feet walked on soil and whose fingers touched sky, Yurrii would travel through the fingers to the feet and take Pau's place in the ground. Then Pau could travel through the feet to the fingers and have Yurrii's sky.

Pau agreed.

He grew a human woman on his soil, but when Yurrii came through her fingers into the ground, Pau killed him. He pushed his brother's body out of the ground, into a great rock that became the moon. Now Pau owned both the earth and the sky, and Yurrii was entombed.

Nasheira saw what Pau had done, and she took him and trapped him in a moon beside Yurrii, and said, "My first son, you shall never again grow the seed of life on this barren rock." Then she took a pebble from Yurrii's moon and a pebble from Pau's. She planted the stones in the human woman's womb and the woman birthed. Out of Yurrii's stone grew a golden angel of the skies, a dragon to guide and protect in Yurrii's memory. Out of Pau's stone grew a monster. A wurm. It would forever remind people of Pau's evil.

Pau was the first daeson.

PART ONE

"GUIDE"

CHAPTER ONE

HUNTING WITH A NEW dragon was like dancing with a partner whose missteps could kill you. Nardiri, a golden-scaled dragon, had emerged from her cocoon ravenous, with an instinctive capacity to kill. On her second hunt, she dismembered a large ox as easily as I pulled apart a cooked rabbit.

It wasn't the kill that stymied the young dragon. It was the chase.

This morning, she'd pounced too early toward a herd of harek, scattering the armoured pigs before she could grab one. We searched for more prey until well after sunset.

There are seven of them. Nardiri shared her sight so that I could see the huddled forms under the silhouette of a towering tree. Two weeks we'd lived together as bonded man and dragon, and I still wasn't used to her words filling my head. When she'd been a wurm, her thoughts had reached me only as emotions—streaming across my consciousness in bright colours. Sharing my mind was taking some time to get used to.

They are called vaiyas, yes? I've seen them in your memories.

Clutched between her forearms as she glided through the night sky, I squinted against the icy wind blasting my numb cheeks. Sickness bloomed in my stomach. Did it have to be vaiyas?

Is something wrong? Nardiri probed.

"No," I croaked. She was hungry, and we'd been searching all afternoon. I wouldn't deny her a meal because her prey reminded me of my childhood—of taking care of the large, reptilian birds that my people domesticated as pack animals. And of Vax, my sweet bird, who had been murdered before my eyes. "Let's land."

We descended. Gnarled branches strained to snag me from Nardiri's grip. She hovered on the wind like a kestrel, keeping her gaze pinned on the wide clearing in which the vaiyas slept. Snow shuddered off nearby trees, sending a cloud of powder into the air as Nardiri flared her wings and extended her hind legs. She kept me held high, pinned to her chest with both forearms. As we closed on the narrow clearing, panic clutched my throat. Her wingspan was far too wide. Thick pechi trees arced upward, threatening to shred gossamer wing webbing, but at the last second, Nardiri raised her wings, and we plummeted the remaining twenty feet. My stomach dropped. I braced for a bone-jarring landing, but the dragon absorbed the impact before depositing me roughly in the deep snow.

"Wait!" I hissed, stumbling on numb feet, but she was already crashing through the undergrowth, a sinuous, unstoppable force. I winced at the thudding crunch of her footfalls and the shatter of dry branches. *You'll wake them all! You'll flush the whole herd.*

The silhouettes in my mind glowed green with life, as Nardiri still communicated mental pictures as basic colours and shapes. They scrambled to their feet and scattered. Blood sang in my ears as I broke into a sprint toward them. As I realised I had no spear, just my skinning knife, something dark and fast whipped toward me, and I ducked. Nardiri's tail sliced through the spot where my head had just been. A spray of snow fanned upward, and through it, I glimpsed a golden haunch. I dodged again as her tail sailed overhead once more.

She growled and skidded to a stop before a towering pine where the vaiyas had recently bedded. Suspended ice crystals winked in the moonlight as the dragon tore a swath of lower boughs from the big tree as though they were twigs, and spat them aside with a snap of her head.

One vaiya lay motionless under her gaze. Its silver-scaled body formed a rounded mound, tail tucked over its feet and long, delicate neck arching gracefully. Even from where I crouched, I saw its dark eyes staring serenely up at Nardiri. It didn't flinch, didn't rise, didn't even blink as those great, gaping jaws dove for it, slammed closed over its top half, and ripped its head from its body.

"Guides," I swore beneath my breath as Nardiri flicked her head up to swallow while the vaiya's body spasmed and geysered blood.

It wasn't my bird. It wasn't Vax. My vision turned red, and I stepped back as Nardiri fanned out her wings, blocking my view.

I staggered at the tearing sounds of her peeling muscle from bone, at the coppery smell of blood. Over the sound of my panting, I barely made out the far-off mourning cries of the retreating vaiyas. I'd learned enough these past weeks to stay still while Nardiri ate. Her predatory drive was still high and any sudden movement on my part could be dangerous. So, instead of backing further away, I tucked my numb fingers under my armpits and clenched my teeth against the icy air until my jaw ached.

Old memories drowned me in their depths. The audience gathering to watch Arsu brand my cheek for a murder she committed. My fingers throbbing from hitting her before I was restrained. The crowd, hungry for the blood of Iva's killer. And then... Vax. Vax, charging in, crowing "Stop." Vax trying to save me. Arsu burying the red-hot spear tip into my sweet vaiya's chest. The warmth leaving his liquid black eye. The sound of my own screaming.

I doubled over, choking. Air squeezed out of my chest faster than I could suck it back in. The image of Vax, impaled and lifeless, merged with the scene of Nardiri decapitating the serene vaiya beneath the tree, and I couldn't keep my head above the wave of panic that followed.

I curled over the crushing weight in my chest for what seemed like hours. The pressure only eased as the skittering noises of night crept back between the trees and Nardiri's whipping tail slowed. I was able to breathe without panting, my limbs weak and watery.

Nardiri fluttered her wings like an excited child before folding them and awkwardly shuffling around to face me.

I'm not hungry anymore, she said happily. A black ribbon of blood smeared up one side of her snout. Moonlight highlighted the arc of the bony crest on the back of her head, her eyes sparkling beneath reptilian ridges.

"I-I know," I stammered.

Her slow exhale wreathed us in fog. I asked, "Why didn't that vaiya run like the rest?"

Nardiri blinked. Whirls of yellow confusion wafted toward me.

I don't know. I just... reached for it.

A memory spilled into my mind, and an involuntary shudder radiated up my spine. I felt through the layers of my clothes for my Speaker's scar, the criss-crossed marking of another dragon's barbed tongue that had lashed across my chest so many years ago, saving me from being sacrificed along with the rest of my camp's firstborn sons.

On that night, when I should have been offered to Nasheira, I had been pressed into the dirt by an unseen weight. The dragon that had marked me hadn't been strong and healthy like Nardiri, but thin, emaciated, her gold scales tarnished in the moonlight. I'd been paralyzed while she raked her tongue across my chest, identifying me as a Speaker for all to see. I thought I had been frozen by fear, but now I wasn't so sure.

Have I done something wrong? Agitated yellow pooled between Nardiri's thoughts as she responded to my distress.

I shuddered. "No."

Our camp's elders had taught us that the goddess Nasheira sent her dragons to mark people who were fit to lead, to *speak* for their people. I'd always assumed that's where the title Speaker came from. But now I wondered if it meant something else, if "Speaker" referred to the ability to communicate with dragons.

I won't eat vaiyas anymore if it upsets you, Nardiri said. Her voice sounded fettered in my head, too small for a creature so big.

"That's not it." I raked my hands through my hair. How could I tell her that I felt woefully inadequate for this, for raising her? Everyone I was close to got hurt. Vax. The daeson. Iva. Yara and our baby. I'd told my mate to flee on the night before my sacrifice. I had feared for her safety. If Yara had run like I asked her to, I'd condemned her to a harsh winter alone while heavily pregnant, and if she hadn't—if she'd stayed with my camp...

Arsu had told me—promised—the awful things she'd let Na-Jhalar do to Yara once I was gone.

We can look for her. Nardiri pushed hopeful green into my head. We can go right now. That always makes you feel better.

"Sweet Nasheira, I don't deserve you." I said, trying to smile and failing miserably. "Let's fly."

Scars

CHAPTER TWO

H OW MANY ARE THERE?"

A swelling morning sun hurtled knives of orange over the treetops below. Mist curled over glittering, frost-backed hills, and a thin column of smoke stretched above a cluster of trees far ahead. The auras Nardiri passed on to me blurred into each other, a green haze of humanity that I could not distill into individuals.

More than ten. An excited hum thrummed through her chest, tickling my shoulder blades as I hung in her grip. *Many more.*

Sweet Nasheira, it could be her. Them. My camp. A sharp ache seeded in my throat and swelled there; it felt like swallowing a boiled egg whole. I held my breath and scanned across the edge of the forest.

There are vaiyas with them. Yellow confusion threaded through the dragon's thoughts as she conveyed the flock of dots. ***They are brighter than the wild ones.*** Green delight uncurled in my mind. ***And they are happy to see me!***

On cue, several garbled greeting calls wafted from the woods. *They are tame—not for eating,* I clarified.

Nardiri huffed indignantly. ***My belly is still full from yesterday, anyway.*** She stretched her hind legs and curled her toes. ***They are not moving toward us. Let's go meet them!***

I touched the scar on my face, the S-shaped brand that marked me as banished. If it was my camp, Arsu would be there.

Words hadn't been enough to describe how badly I wanted Arsu's blood, how I *needed* to make her suffer as she'd made me suffer. During those first brutal days after sacrifice, hard vengeance was what drove my will to live. Nardiri knew that I hated Arsu, that the woman had killed people I cared about, but I hadn't given her more details than that, and she was gracious enough not to prod for more information. I would share my raw memories when I was ready.

Would my camp accept me back, borne in the arms of a Guide—a dragon sent by Nasheira herself? Did I want them to?

I won't let her hurt you. Nardiri's throat swelled, and a blasting call raked over the treetops. ***They know we're here now.***

I sighed. "Thanks for that."

The trilling response of the vaiyas carried across the field. Green dots quivered and threaded through the trees below, but against the glare of the morning sun, I couldn't make out distinct forms.

I want to see them before we land. I pressed a knuckle into the furrow of my forehead. *Can we get closer?*

Nardiri circled the grove as we slowly descended. A succession of snaps announced people crashing through the bushes below. I counted my breaths, but the meditation did nothing to ease the tightness in my chest.

Eight hunters, with spears strapped to their backs, stepped out of the tree line. They all bore faces I recognized. It was my camp.

My brother Jin led the group with his confident, silent stride. My father, Hasev, tall and bearded, was close behind. Cold nostalgia prickled through me at the sight of my family. Behind them came Creb, Barth, Darvie, Nella, and my youngest brother Dero, his face forever pinched in anger. Last of all skulked a wiry woman with a long, sallow face and black eyes—Arsu the snake.

The crooked fingers of my badly-healed hand twitched, hungry for a weapon. Many of my former hunting mates had already dropped to their knees before Nardiri's presence, pressing two fingers to their foreheads in prayer. If we landed fast enough, I could walk right up to Arsu while they all genuflected. I imagined slipping my skinning knife beneath her ribs and twisting until her insides spilled out. She deserved a death as long and messy as the one she'd given Iva.

I could still smell the mix of blood and bile from my memories. Na-Jhalar's laugh echoed in my head, raw and giddy. Arsu had watched while her brother gutted my aunt, my mentor. More than that, she'd orchestrated it. And I had been too late. I hadn't even had time to register Iva's fate before Arsu clubbed me and pressed Na-Jhalar's bloody knife into my hand.

Have we come here to find Yara or to kill the snake? Nardiri's tail thrashed, and I sensed my emotions were spilling into her.

Mother of Yurrii, I needed to cloak my thoughts better. I could not risk enraging Nardiri with my overflowing anger, not when we were about to land in the midst of my family. During the past few weeks, I'd learned that I *could* mask my thoughts and emotions from Nardiri, but it took intense concentration, and I wasn't sure I could summon that right now.

They are afraid of me. Even as Nardiri spoke, Arsu fell to her knees, her eyes widening as she caught glimpse of me, the man she had tried to murder, safe within a dragon's grasp. Her gaze flickered to the ground in apparent terror as she prostrated. But I didn't believe she was truly in awe. The snake always manipulated situations to her benefit.

One of them is receptive.

My head snapped up as Nardiri shed height, dropping closer to the stricken group below. *Which one?*

Just behind Arsu, a man's aura glowed crisper and more brightly than the others.

It was Dero.

I'm going to mark him.

Sweet Nasheira, no. I froze at the memory of my youngest brother's spear pinning me while Arsu dragged Yara from our bedroll. I felt his cruel kick to the ribs after Iva died, saw the sneer he'd worn the night I was cut with the other daeson. He'd been the one to choose the sacrifice site—a goddess-forsaken gully so hidden that there hadn't been a hope of being found by any aeni groups who might have saved us.

You will not mark him. Do you understand? That man is not a Speaker.

He will be if I mark him, she replied sullenly.

Promise me. Not him! I insisted, but Nardiri only huffed, prickling with pink irritation as she set down with a soft crunch.

She folded her wings and lowered me to the ground, then rose up to her full height behind me.

Arsu's eyes trained on me. I adjusted my pack's strap across my chest, acutely aware of the skinning knife within, and stepped forward, scanning the trees for Yara. I couldn't decide if I wanted her to be there or hoped that she wasn't, for her own sake.

Gatherers streamed towards us in the wake of the hunters, eyes wide as they approached Nasheira's emissary. There was no sight of the brown curls I so desperately searched for. I didn't see my mother, either.

Vaiyas pranced through the undergrowth, threading through the crowd, flaring their crests, dipping their heads, and crooning at Nardiri. My old flock. Tears pricked my eyes as I spotted Voti, who was keeping his body between his hens and the dragon even as he whistled to her. So he had become the patriarch after Vax's death. A small lick of pride flashed amongst the wreckage of emotion churning in my gut.

Nardiri tossed her head and burbled ridiculously to her adoring vaiya audience.

"Nasheira's peace with you." Arsu offered the traditional greeting.

I was supposed to answer with *May her Guides mark your skies,* but instead I growled. "Her peace is not with me, nor will it be with you if you don't tell me where Yara is."

Jin rushed forward as though he wanted to embrace me, but he paused, his frantic gaze darting from me to the dragon behind me. "Brother! How..."

Hasev pressed up beside him. My father's big hand reached out and then curled in on itself again. Tears spilled down his gaunt cheeks and into his beard. I refused to meet his gaze. He had stood by while I had been sacrificed. They all had. I rounded on Arsu. "Where is she?"

"Please, Speaker." She held out her palms. As if I would be fooled by the gesture of openness. "We have much to talk about."

Nardiri paced behind me, clicking her teeth and filling me with a strange red hunger that honed my anger like rock striking flint.

Akrist, she vied for my attention, but I ignored her.

"We have *nothing* to talk about." Heat rolled through me, gathering in my limbs.

Arsu's throat worked. "We must offer apologies, Na-Akrist—"

"Do *not* call me that. I am not *your* Speaker!" I roared, reaching for the knife inside my pack. With one swipe I could end her and avenge Iva and the daeson. One swipe, and she would never threaten Yara again.

Akrist! Nardiri's thought twanged into my mind, raw and urgent. *I need to mark him. I can't be this close and not—*
No! I commanded.

Her tail pounded the ground, sending powdered snow flying. The vaiyas hissed. I couldn't dispel my rage. I didn't want to.

"Please." Arsu's voice and hands shook. "Please, we made a terrible mistake." Her head bowed, and when she glanced back up, tears glittered in her black eyes. An impressive performance, and not the first one I'd seen from her. "Nasheira has obviously chosen you for great things. I never thought I'd live to see a Speaker and a Guide together, just like the elders' stories. A hundred apologies would not be enough for how we misinterpreted Her will. Please enlighten us with how this came to be. We will answer any questions you have." Her eyes focused on the dragon behind me, fear and awe naked on her face as she took in the golden splendour of Nasheira's angel.

He needs to be marked! Nardiri's shrill wail filled my ears.

Dero made a choking noise and clasped at his chest.

"No!" I bellowed. "Nobody moves!" Seizing a fistful of Arsu's hair, I whipped out my knife and jammed its point against the side of her neck.

Jin and my father both shouted something unintelligible. Nardiri bugled in frustration.

I ignored them all, tightening my grip until my hands no longer shook.

"You want to know how *this* came to be?" I hissed in Arsu's ear. "This came to be because you killed Iva and framed me for her murder. She was like a mother to me. This came to be because you butchered five daeson and left us for dead. I have you to thank for the dragon at my side." The irony of it brought laughter boiling up my throat, hot and hysterical. I barely stifled it. Suddenly I reminded myself of Tanar; I pushed away the image of his wide-eyed, crazed expression as he held a knife over me.

Dero wailed and tipped over.

Nardiri bared her teeth and darted around me with frightening speed.

"No, Nardiri!"

She cut the connection between us. I dove towards Dero in an attempt to block her—as if I could stop a dragon. An immense weight landed on my chest, crushing the air from my lungs and wedging against my heart. I crumpled, knees loose and feet stumbling. The knife slipped from my grip. My hands reached to protect my face from the impact, but I couldn't lift them. My head cracked against the frozen ground. Pain seared through my mouth as I bit my tongue.

For a panicked moment, I thought Nardiri had stepped on me, but that couldn't be. Through my peripheral vision, I saw her looming over the collapsed form of my little brother. The hunters stood staring, slack-jawed, at the pair. I couldn't lift my head, couldn't speak.

A hand dug into my shoulder and rolled me onto my back. Arsu straddled my chest and pressed my knife against the side of my throat. Her gaze flickered from me to the dragon and back again. "And here I thought you were the one in control. How interesting."

Kill her. Saliva and blood pooled in my throat and frothed my lips. I could barely breathe. *Nardiri, don't let her touch me!*

But Nardiri's mind was closed to me. I strained to turn my head so I could see her, but Arsu encompassed my vision. She leaned in, close enough that her hair brushed my cheek. The knife tip scraped against my clenched jaw and settled in my ear. Arsu liked to play with her prey.

Nardiri! I howled into the void between us, throwing myself against the pressure binding me. White spots sprayed across my vision, and an odd grunting noise rattled up my throat.

"Take this to your death, daeson," Arsu sneered, reaching into her belt pouch to dangle something in front of my face.

I struggled to bring the object into focus.

A hair comb decorated with intricately carved flowers and made of a black ox-horn. I'd gifted a pair of them to Yara.

"Your bitch is dead. She took her own life on the night of the sacrifice. I lit her pyre myself." She stroked my cheek with the comb's tines, then laid it on my palm and clasped my fingers around it.

I couldn't breathe. I couldn't scream.

"Can you hear me in there?" Arsu gripped my chin, nails digging into stubbled skin.

Liar. She was a liar. Yara would never... She wouldn't... Would she?

Hot tears welled in my eyes, rolling down the sides of my cheeks.

Arsu's lips pulled back, exposing her teeth in a terrible smile. "Ah, you do hear." She gently wiped the tears from my face. "Good." Then she pressed the knife into my ear.

NARDIRI! I screeched.

A piercing bawl exploded across the clearing. Arsu froze. People screamed and the ground shook beneath me. Wind and clods of dirt whipped around me. Something slammed into Arsu, batting her aside. Claws clamped around my waist and heaved me into the air. I was a ragdoll in her grasp. The thunder of Nardiri's wings filled the sky.

We flew. Saliva and blood trickled down my chin, but I couldn't raise a hand to wipe my face. I couldn't do anything at all.

Yara cannot be dead. She cannot. Arsu lies.

My crooked fingers still clutched the comb in my hand.

CHAPTER THREE

I'D BEEN BOUND BEFORE, tied up and held down while my own mother cut me. This was immeasurably worse. My own body betrayed me. Although my mind screamed for action, I couldn't move; my lungs struggled within my chest, and my bladder released. Urine dribbled down my leg and pooled in one boot as the ground scrolled by beneath me.

Nardiri winged away from the camp as panic and rage flooded my mind.

Let me go back, Nardiri. Let me go!

If the dragon heard my thoughts, she didn't obey. She let me crash against the shores of my mind over and over as she flew onwards, her wingbeats a steady counterpoint to the intermittent whimpers that escaped my throat.

Nardiri, land now!

Shedding altitude, she banked toward a broad meadow. My stomach clenched as the ground rushed toward us. Nardiri set me down in the snow delicately, like I was a broken thing. Then she released me.

Sensation prickled my limbs. The air felt too cold to breathe, and the sunlight glancing off the snow was blinding. When I groaned, the sound was ear-splittingly loud. Everything was overwhelming, like I'd been dumped back into my own body as a newborn. I rolled away from Nardiri as I felt her trying to reconnect.

"Don't!" I shouted, scrambling back like a fish flopping on a beach. "Stay out of my head!"

Don't be angry.

I wiped blood from my ear with a trembling hand and tucked Yara's comb into my pack. "You *paralyzed* me!"

I didn't mean to. I couldn't control it.

"Liar!" I yelled.

I felt a sensation like a mental shrug. ***I needed to mark him and you wouldn't let me.***

"Dero is corrupt!" I stumbled to my feet and stood on wobbling legs. "He's devoted to Arsu, a woman who used her own drug-addled brother to *murder* my mentor. Now her most devout follower is a Speaker. What a gift you've given her!" I spat.

I could not ignore the pull. You don't know what it's like. Nardiri hissed.

"Do you understand that Arsu almost murdered me while you were busy marking my brother?"

A burst of yellow-tinged fear filled my mind, but I couldn't stop shouting.

"She almost killed me! I couldn't even lift a finger as she twisted a knife in my ear, because of *you*. I had a chance at justice, and you used it to scar the chest of an undeserving, malicious fool!" Turning, I stumbled back the way we'd come.

Where are you going? Her voice was panicked.

"I'm going back!" I bellowed. "I'm going to kill Arsu and find Yara!" I crashed away from Nardiri, embarrassingly aware of my wet crotch.

They'll kill you if I don't come with you.

"Stay away from me," I growled.

Fumbling through my pack, I pulled out the only weapon I had left, a spearhead as long as my forearm. I'd been lucky it hadn't skewered me when I fell earlier.

I'll stop you.

Heart hammering in my head, I turned back to her.

"Is that how this works?" I snarled. "You paralyze me every time I act of my own accord? Reduce me to a prisoner within my own flesh? Because I find death preferable to that."

Nardiri sagged. The yellow in my head darkened into something muddy and grey. I deflected her emotions before they could overwhelm me.

I'm sorry. Her wings quivered.

I fought the urge to close the distance between us and accept her apology. Instead, I turned and walked in the opposite direction, to the stream at the far edge of the meadow. Nardiri said nothing as I washed and changed, but I could feel her eyes on me the entire time. Her fear and sorrow strained against the barrier I'd put between us.

After I had donned a dry set of clothes and my spare boots, I turned back to face the dragon. "I'm going back to the camp, and you're not coming. Understand?"

You can't leave me! Nardiri wailed. She took a step toward me, but froze when I lifted the spearhead.

"Don't come any closer." We both knew the weapon was useless against her, but I didn't care. I pressed the spearhead against my own ribs. "I'd rather die than be controlled. If this is how our bond works, I'll break it permanently."

Nardiri roared. The sound of it thrummed through my chest. The ache of her distress filled my throat. I turned my back on her and walked away.

With every step, I expected to be dropped by paralysis or plucked up by sharp talons. But Nardiri didn't stop me.

My brain ached, stretched from the strain of separation from her, and filled with anxiety about what I was walking into. What if the snake had been speaking the truth? I'd told Yara to run when she had nowhere safe to go. She might have killed herself to spare her and the baby pain.

Something crashed through the brush far ahead of me. I flattened against the nearest tree and cocked my head, listening. Larger than a man but smaller than a dragon—not a wurm.

"Akrist!" A hoarse yell drifted in the wind, overlaying the thumping cadence of a vaiya being driven at full speed. The approaching rider called two more times before I recognized his voice.

Jin, my middle brother and the only person in my immediate family who'd ever wanted to spend time with me. My stomach dropped with a mix of relief and confusion.

Part of me wanted to melt into the forest and let him pass by. Jin had a way of teasing truths out of people. If he sensed that I intended to barge back into our camp and single-handedly kill its leader, he would talk me out of it.

But I couldn't let him careen headlong into an upset dragon either. I didn't know exactly how Nardiri would react to a vaiya bursting out of the woods, but I couldn't imagine a good outcome. Swallowing, I licked my lips, stepped away from the tree and shouted. "Over here!"

The vaiya's footsteps faltered and the animal whistled brightly before Jin shushed it.

Voti tossed his head as he loped toward me. Jin called out and slapped the bird's neck before deftly steering him toward me with his feet. He had a strong seat, which spoke of trust and familiarity with his mount. It made me ache for Vax.

"Surprise!" Voti squealed when he caught sight of me, flaring his crest as he and Jin drew up.

"Akrist!" My brother slid off his mount and dove toward me. Heedless of the spearhead I held, he wrapped me in a back-slapping hug; I only narrowly avoided being impaled. "I'm so glad we found you. Alive and whole, thank the goddess. I was afraid Arsu had...but you're all right." Gripping me by the arms, Jin examined me with bright brown eyes. "And you're traveling with a *dragon*! How did *that* happen?" His nose wrinkled. "It marked Dero."

I shook my head. "Not my choice, I assure you." At his curious gaze, I added, "It's a long story."

He motioned toward a fallen log. "Sit."

Relief at my brother's closeness, fear for Yara, and a sudden desire to tell someone everything replaced my fury. I'd never been good at refusing Jin anything, so we sat.

And I told him. I told him how the wurms had swarmed me and the other daeson, how one had felt the scar on my chest and a bond had been created between us. I told him how the other boys had died, how I had barely survived the winter, how the wurm had saved me, and, finally, how it had woven a cocoon and emerged a dragon.

He listened quietly, his eyes getting wider as the story went on.

"Sweet Nasheira," he whispered as I finished. "Goddess knows I prayed for someone to come save us, but I never expected her to answer like this."

"Someone to save you?" I frowned.

Jin's smile faltered and his mouth hardened. "It's been bad since you left, Akrist."

"I didn't leave. I was *sacrificed*," I hissed.

"I didn't mean it like that. Na-Jhalar is dead." Jin's jaw clenched. "Arsu killed him, I'm sure of it. And she killed a child, Akrist."

"She killed four on the night of our sacrifice." I spoke through my teeth.

He nodded hesitantly. How could I have forgotten that even Jin continued to believe that daeson sacrifices were a necessity. "She killed a baby last week," he said. "An ani joined us to birth her child and Arsu took the newborn while he was still wet." Jin cleared his throat and raked a hand over his face before continuing. "She castrated him right there, while Pau and Yurrii were full; he died of shock in his mother's arms."

My mind filled with the memory of Gideous and Henri's piercing cries in the gully on the night of our sacrifice. The vision of Aella flicking my blood off her blade, the smell of fear, and the sound of wurms chuffing towards us overpowered me for several shallow breaths. I felt my rage returning; biting it down, I enunciated slowly, "And none of you stopped her?"

Jin's gaze flashed, hard and hurt. "What kind of a man do you take me for, brother?"

I couldn't answer him. Words clotted in my throat.

"I was going to come for you, Akrist. Arsu tied me up on the night of your sacrifice. Did you know that?" Tears shone in Jin's eyes. "So I couldn't follow and find you. She tied Aaron up too."

I frowned. Jin's mate held no love for me.

"She kept us both bound hand and foot, slung over a vaiya's back for two weeks while we travelled south." He exhaled shakily and stared down at his fidgeting hands. "It just happened so damned fast. By the time I reached the child, it was too late. His wound was too deep. The look in Arsu's eyes, Akrist..." Jin gulped. "She's convinced that she's enacting Nasheira's will, that allowing daeson to live until the eclipse is what has cursed us. Nobody can stand up to her. She has too many followers. Even Fraesh left. He took his whole family with him. There's nobody to challenge her. Except you."

"She has no fear of me." I brushed a finger over the blood crusting my ear.

"She does. Why do you think she hates you so much? You have always been a threat to her power. She cannot stand against a Speaker with a Guide. Come back with me, Akrist. The camp will surely follow you."

"Where is Yara?"

Jin flinched. Behind him, Voti clicked his beak and hissed at the sudden tension in the air.

"Tell me."

He wrung his hands, and when he looked up, tears were streaming down his face. "I'm so sorry, Akrist. She... she killed herself."

The words pounded all the wind out of me. My legs went slack and the spearhead thunked between my feet as I slid down the edge of the log.

Jin gripped my arm.

"No," I wheezed. "Yara would never... Jin, she would never. Our baby."

"She did it the night you were sacrificed. Stole herbs from Fraesh's stock and poisoned herself. I heard the vaiyas' death call right as Arsu returned to camp."

"No." I felt numb.

"Yara's mother couldn't bear it; she cut her own wrists. We built a pyre for them both and burned them together. That's when Fraesh and his daughters left. I'm so sorry..."

I couldn't tell if Jin said anything else after that. A hornet's nest had split open inside my skull. My insides unravelled. I wanted to cry, to wail, but no sound escaped my lips.

No. No. No. It was the only word I knew anymore.

Akrist? Blue leaked through the widening cracks in my mind.

Jin shouted something.

I fell forward and retched.

Akrist! Nardiri poured into my head.

Take me away from here, I begged. *Nardiri, take me away.*

And the sky filled with gold.

Jin stumbled away from me. Voti froze.

Claws gripped my waist, wide wings flooded my vision and then there was nothing but pale, empty sky.

I had told Yara to escape. And she had.

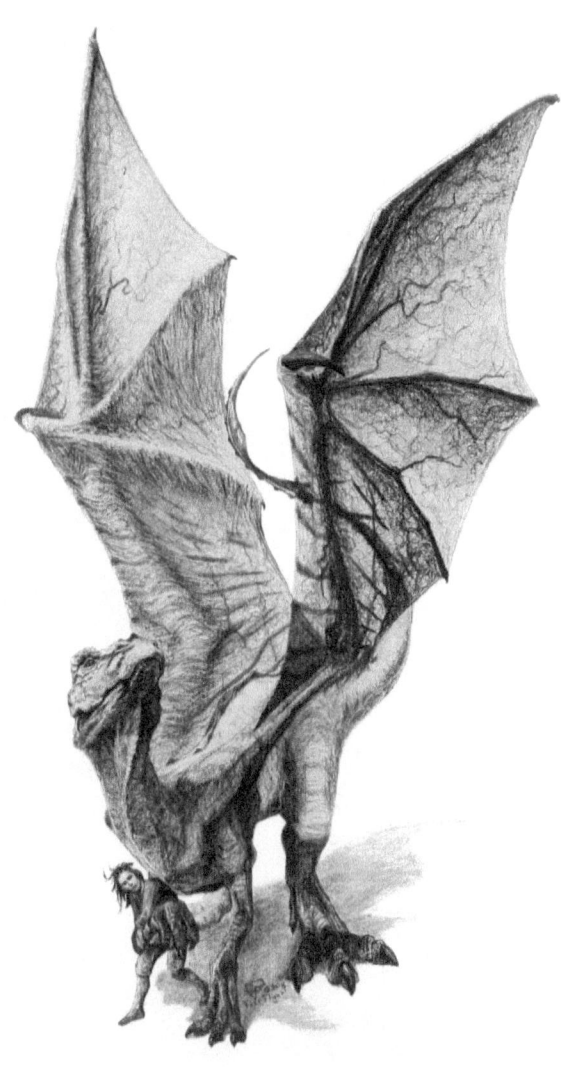

CHAPTER FOUR

AFTER ARSU FRAMED ME for Iva's murder, smashing a lantern against my head and pressing Na-Jhalar's knife into my hand, I had not been myself.

I hadn't been lucid when the vaiyas called out Iva's death, or when I smelled the smoke of her funeral pyre. In waking moments, my brain felt like liquid sloshing in my skull. I struggled to see straight. The world took on a muted cast, and my body felt like it didn't belong in the world.

As Nardiri and I flew away from Jin, I felt the same. Concussed and out of alignment, I couldn't process the thoughts my dragon pressed toward me. Numbness clotted every corner of my mind. A sinkhole opened in my chest and swallowed every emotion until all that remained was my last memory of Yara.

I dissected it, spread it out and pored over every detail, searching for some small clue to invalidate what Arsu and Jin had told me.

"You have to get away," I'd said. She'd replied, *"I know."* Her eyes had been full of tears, but they'd been full of determination too. She'd said she would tell stories to our baby about how brave and strong I was. She'd promised our child would know me.

But vaiyas didn't lie. They sensed souls passing, and they didn't reserve their mourning cries for just their own species, they called when people died too. Jin said he heard the flock's death cry, and he had no reason to lie to me. And then there was the fact that Enna, Yara's mother, had killed herself. She must have seen proof of her daughter's death.

My desperate mind grappled for a reason. What if something had been wrong with our baby? If our unborn child had died, had stopped moving within her, Yara would have been devastated. But no. I shook my head. Her swollen belly had pressed between my knees as we knelt, foreheads touching, and I'd felt our child move on the night before the sacrifice.

Then you can't deny it. One day later, Yara took your baby's life along with her own.

Blackness, cold and sharp as an obsidian blade, lodged between my ribs and drained the last vestiges of warmth from me. Shivers wracked my body.

Nardiri landed. I didn't know where. She silently curled around me and tucked me under her wing.

I lay in the darkness, alone with my thoughts.

What sort of Goddess would let this happen? I'd been born daeson, and perhaps I deserved my fate, but Yara... Yara didn't deserve what had happened to her. Tears welled in my eyes and slipped down my cold, slack face.

She had died because of me.

Days passed. Nardiri roused me only when she left to hunt. Most times she returned empty-bellied and sullenly silent. At night, she curled around me and shared her body heat, but remained otherwise cold and withdrawn. I'd hurt her, deeply. I knew that. What sort of idiot Speaker told his dragon he preferred death over the bond they shared? But I hadn't the energy to speak, much less mend the rift growing between us.

Are you going to tell me what happened? She asked one morning, her thoughts clipped, cold, and devoid of colour.

I blinked up at her, shocked. I had assumed she already knew. Surely a creature who'd had no compunction paralyzing me could have easily eavesdropped when I was conversing with Jin, or taken the opportunity later to dip into my thoughts and see for herself what had broken me.

"Yara died," I croaked.

She stiffened. A dim blue aura reflecting my own grief radiated from her thoughts before she cut them off.

I couldn't tell if the dragon was driving a wedge between us because she didn't want to experience my hurt or if she just wanted to stay angry. Is this who we were now? Two beings grappling with a bond that was mostly thorns, each of us cutting the other deeper every time we reached out? It would be kinder to cut the dragon free of my dead weight, but I didn't even have the strength for that.

At first, when I heard the far-off vaiya call, I assumed it was wild, but when the bird crowed again at closer range, accompanied by an unmistakably human voice, I stiffened.

Nardiri, how many? I scrambled to a stand.

What? She yawned, blowing warm breath in my face.

I'd become too reliant on her to warn me of danger. *How many people are approaching?*

She jerked fully awake. My neck prickled as Nardiri shared her mind's eye and crackling colour filled the landscape around us. Four pinpoints of green light flashed over the hill, downstream of the spring, one vaiya-shaped and the rest human—all of them frighteningly close.

She obviously felt my annoyance.

I was tired.

Clutching my pack to my chest, I swallowed against the naked sensation of being completely unarmed.

Nardiri stood and ruffled her wings. Several of her scales flaked off, something that had been happening more often as she grew.

Guides, I couldn't do this right now. I couldn't face people. What if Arsu had come to finish me off? To Nardiri, I snapped: "You'll not mark any of them and you will not paralyze me. Understand?"

None of them are receptive anyway.

Three people and their pack animal popped over the hillside and stumbled to a stop at the sight of us. Their vaiya crowed a bright greeting call into the stunned silence, and Nardiri huffed in response.

Not for eating. She stated sulkily.

I scanned the slack-jawed group. Colourful ribbons plaited the adult's elaborately braided hair and bright, patterned patches embellished their clothes. These were aeni—wandering people. The trio tottered for a moment before crumpling to their knees and pressing two fingers to their foreheads.

My stomach lurched.

Who are they?

They are aeni—groups smaller than camps who are always on the move. Traders and mapmakers. My gaze fixed on the young boy behind the adults and I shuddered. *And they don't usually travel with children. It slows them down too much. They abandon them in the camps they come across.*

Nardiri craned her neck to peer at the thin boy who was dressed in brown rags—a dull contrast to the bright-coloured ribbons and patches on the clothes of the adults.

"What do you want, Ani?" I asked. I didn't expect an introduction, as they didn't share their names with strangers.

The man's eyes were wide as he took in Nardiri—I wasn't certain, but thought she had grown at least a hand taller in the last week alone.

"N-Nasheira's peace with you." His gaze flicked up toward Nardiri's lethally equipped toes and the golden scales on the ground.

He's so small. Nardiri's focus was still locked on the boy.

He's property. I spoke aloud to the aeni. "Stand. There is no Nasheira here."

None of them rose. With two fingers still pressed against his forehead, the man licked his lips. "We mean no dishonour to Nasheira's Guide."

"He's branded!" the woman interrupted, sitting up. She dropped her hand from her brow and thrust a finger toward the scar on my face that marked me as an outcast, her expression disgusted.

I don't like that one. Nardiri jabbed her snout past my shoulder and barked at her.

The trio yelped and the boy cringed.

"Better an outcast than a slave master," I sneered.

"The boy is no slave," the man said. "He owes a debt."

I snorted. "For what? For being born first?"

A daeson? He is like you! And he's unhappy. I don't think he likes being a slave. We should take him with us. Nardiri trilled.

Though his hair was brown and his eyes were hazel, he somehow reminded me of Gideous, one of the boys who had died at my side on the night of our sacrifice. I'd promised him I'd save him. I'd told Henri, Jule, and Fey the same. But I'd failed them all. I failed everyone I tried to save. My heart battered against my chest and dizziness swept through me. Cold panic clutched my ribs. I couldn't afford to be taken down by anxiety now. Anger was easier to direct, so I pressed a hard smile onto my face as the man added, "He agreed to the terms. But we'd be willing to part with him. For a fair price. Then you can bend him over as much as you like, Outcast."

The oily grin slipped from his face as a low growl purled up Nardiri's throat.

I don't like his smile.

Red thumped at the edge of my vision in time with my drumming pulse. I ached to feel the ani's nose crunching under my knuckles.

The boy is scared of him. Nardiri noted.

The ani's eyes widened and he showed his palms and shuffled back. I suspected he was responding more to Nardiri's growl than he was to the anger on my face. "Apologies. A misunderstanding. You can still buy him if you wish." His greedy gaze dropped to my dragon's shed scales. Aeni didn't consider them to be holy like camps did, but they coveted them all the same. "A nice stack of those should suffice," he said.

Over the man's shoulder, the boy blinked at me and, the fragile hope in his gaze utterly broke me.

I can't save him. Everyone I try to save dies.

Yara would want you to try. Nardiri's thought cut deep into me.

"*Don't* tell me what Yara would want!" I rounded on her, teeth bared. The aeni stepped back in confusion.

Nardiri flinched, and in that moment, I knew. I would fail her too. It was only a matter of time.

Anger and shame choked me. I fled, racing through the forest until the vaiya's forlorn calls ebbed, and thick rage filled the hungry void in my ribcage.

So we just flee every time we meet people now. Is that how it works? Nardiri's words knifed through me. Her shadow rippled over the prairie ahead and I ignored her, concentrating on the rhythm of my feet as they hit the thawing ground. ***You wanted to help that boy. I could feel it.***

"You're wrong," I rasped. Bile churned in my stomach and an icy wind whipped my hair against my cheeks, but it did nothing to ease the heat there.

You still want to help him, but you're afraid.

You know what I want? I squinted up at the dragon. "I want to be left alone."

Nardiri tucked her wings and plummeted to the ground. The grass shuddered as she landed in front of me on all fours, claws carving into the soil. Her narrowed gaze met mine, as cold as jade. ***Then you shouldn't have chosen to be bonded to a dragon.***

"I did not *choose* to be bonded to you!" I bellowed, leaning into her rage.

Her wings sagged and her tail froze. Red bled from her and muddied into yellow confusion. Her posture held all the breathless shock of an animal with a spear lodged between its ribs.

I sometimes forgot how much she didn't remember—that she didn't even know she had been a wurm once. It was a secret I had kept from her, in addition to the fact that tribes regularly killed wurms, because no one knew the hungry beasts turned into dragons. I ran my hand through my hair and turned away from her. "I was tied to a tree and left to die," I said. "You found me, felt my scar, and bonded to me. You helped me survive when I should have died. That is how we met. You think I *chose* this life? I would not have chosen you."

I felt a twinge of regret as the barbed words left my mouth. A shaft of blue pain impaled me before Nardiri snuffed out our connection. Her nostrils trembled, and her muscles bunched as though she were about to take off. Then she lunged for me.

Before I could even try to dodge, a foreclaw snagged on my carry bag strap and it snapped as Nardiri clutched me so tight that my ribs creaked. She launched. I clawed at her forearm and my finger snagged under a scale. The sharp edge sliced into my soft flesh and I winced. "Put me down!" My damaged bag slithered off my chest. I swiped for it, but it slipped through my bleeding hand, bounced off one foot, and tumbled away.

Yara's comb.

"Put me down," I gasped.

The bag landed with a thud in the rapidly receding prairie. I craned my neck to keep it in my sight, but my dragon flew too fast. "Those are my things," I roared. "Take me back, now."

She ignored me, turning back toward the spring where we'd encountered the aeni hours ago.

"Land, Nardiri!" I bellowed.

No. You will tell me what secret you are keeping from me first. Every time I get close to it, you try to drive me away.

"I said LAND!" My bloodied hand throbbed.

Not until you tell me the truth.

You don't get to control me just because you are more powerful. "Am I a slave to you, like that boy was to the aeni?"

Nardiri changed course, settling into a stiff glide. We skimmed past the grassland and around a menacing thunderhead. Red anger rolled off her like fire, igniting within me no matter how I tried to smother it. When we'd passed the tail of the roiling storm, Nardiri landed. She dumped me as soon as we hit the ground.

I tucked into a roll and skidded into waist-high brush. Jagged branches pricked my arms and legs. By the time I scrambled to my feet, Nardiri was already pacing, tail lashing furiously just over my head.

"What's wrong with you?"

She rounded on me, teeth bared, a high growl singing in her throat. *Why didn't you want to choose me? Why didn't you want me to mark your brother?*

"I told you. He doesn't deserve to be a Speaker. He's—"

Why were you afraid when I did it? Her green glare pinned me. *Have you never seen anyone marked before?*

"Of course I have," I blurted.

Before your own marking? Nardiri pressed with a sharp snort.

"Before me? Na-Jhalar was chosen before I was born. Some camps go a long time without a Speaker. I'd only seen dragons from afar."

I knew the secret she was trying to pull from me—what my people did to wurms and why we hadn't seen any dragons during our travels—and it terrified me. She would leave me when she learned the truth, and I would die, weaponless, as I should have in the gully with the other daeson.

I should tell her. I deserved my fate. But I was a coward. I was too selfish to let her go, even as I pushed her away.

Her feet crushed brush into splinters. *Are there any other bonded pairs?*

"I don't know. We hardly ever see—"

Are there any other dragons at all?

"They're rare. There used to be more, but—"

But none of you are choosing to bond? What do you do with your dragon eggs if you don't bond with the hatchlings?

Oh Guides, how could I answer? My pulse pounded at my temples. Blood dripped from my cut hand and I spoke carefully. "We don't have dragon eggs."

Her frustration grew with each hedged response.

You are telling me half-truths.

I exhaled. I couldn't keep the information from her. "Nardiri." I licked my lips. "You were... dragon hatchlings are... large, threatening creatures that eat everything in sight, including humans. We call them wurms. My people don't know that they turn into dragons. They only know that the Guides are disappearing. They think you've abandoned us."

Abandoned? Nardiri shook her head, eyes crackling as she froze mid-pace, breaths whooshing faster. *What do you do with the hatchlings you encounter?*

I was silent. She paused as she put the pieces together.

You're killing us.

I stepped toward her, "I know how it sounds—"

I thought she might lunge toward me, but she sat there, her eyes piercing into me.

All you have thought about since we've joined is killing, and not killing to eat. Killing for revenge. And if we had not bonded, if you hadn't needed me to survive... You would have killed me. She froze before me, trembling, braced on all fours. *Deny it. Tell me I'm wrong.*

I shook my head. "You're not."

Am I the last?

"No," the rough whisper slipped past my lips. I extended my hand past rows of teeth bigger than my arm and pressed my palm against her snout.

She shuddered. Her eyes squeezed shut, and her wings sagged.

"You are the first," I murmured.

Nardiri jerked away and tore our connection out by its roots.

I convulsed and staggered back as she spun away from me and took off. "Don't leave me," I wheezed. "Nardiri, don't."

But she never looked back. I had wanted to be alone, and now I was.

CHAPTER FIVE

I BENT OVER AND clapped my hands over my ears, but I couldn't block the odd rushing sound coming from inside my head. Nausea pulled at my throat and my heart fluttered. No matter how I tried to slow my breathing, it kept gathering speed. *Control yourself.* I jolted upright, shook out my hands and paced, but it was a poor defense for the thick sense of doom choking me.

"Oh Guides." She'd taken something of me with her. Something integral.

I needed to run, to flee, but instead, I collapsed onto the cold grass, panting and twitching. A deep, earnest pain plucked at my chest. Was I dying? *This is what you are without your dragon, Akrist. Pathetic, crippled by fear, and half-mad like Tanar.*

Panic peeled away into numbness. I rolled onto my back and smelled lightning. The storm cloud we'd left in our wake swelled above me, bloated, thick, and brooding. My limbs felt brittle and, even when raindrops pattered the ground around me, I didn't stand.

What is Nardiri feeling right now, without me? I wondered if she was in pain or if she only felt relieved at my absence.

The skies greyed out and rain fell in earnest. I couldn't stand the thoughts filling my head anymore. I had to do *something*, so I stood and sifted through the sticks Nardiri had snapped underfoot until I found a thick branch with a sharp end. It was no weapon, but felt better than being empty-handed. I raised my fur-lined hood and started walking. Despite my overcoat, I was soon soaked through. Hair plastered my face and my shirt snapped coldly against my stomach in the wind. I followed the faint groove of a trail through the soggy grass without any real hope of it leading to game. When the rain eased, the setting sun banded orange between the receding storm and the flat horizon.

And Nardiri didn't come back.

Empty and exhausted, I braced myself to pass the night with no tools to build a fire. *Keep moving. Generate body heat for as long as you can.*

As I walked, every flutter of bat wings darting overhead fooled my senses. In the dusk sky, their silhouettes looked like a dragon from afar. I watched them until my neck ached from the strain and the last of the light bled away. Stars winked overhead in a crisp moonless sky, and I picked my way slowly through the dark grasslands until I came to a dried-out riverbed with a single wooden post pounded into its sandy bank.

Pau had just risen over the horizon, half full. I stared at the moon, holding my breath for several seconds before letting my gaze fall back to the solitary post on the beach. It looked like bleached bone in the moonlight, but was far too straight and precisely placed to be natural. Posts for stretching and buffing hides were carved with flat tapered tops, but this one was mushroomed and splintered from being pounded into the ground. Its long shadow slashed across the desiccated river bed. Under the overhang of the sharp bank opposite, dirty patches of snow huddled, lumpy and misshapen, like wurms waiting to ambush me.

I approached the wooden sentinel slowly, neck prickling, boots scuffing through pebble-strewn sand. It was nearly as tall as I was. Several wraps of tattered rope coiled around its base. My stomach plummeted.

Not a tool. A restraint. A cold shiver seeped down my spine, but I was too tired to run from the memories anymore. Instead, I clenched my teeth, gripped my pointed stick, and closed the rest of the distance to the post. I sat down beside it. My wet clothes clung to me and the night air turned my breath into fog. I couldn't stop staring at the opposite river bank with its dirty band of old snow.

This is the last view they ever saw.

The daeson who had been sacrificed here—their bodies long gone—would have looked out over this river before taking their last breaths. My gaze fixed onto a partially-collapsed hole in the bank, deep in the shadows. A shelf of turf and soil slumped over the bottom half of the opening, but the top half was unobscured and well over two feet wide. A wurm burrow.

Bile stung my throat.

I hear the pop of roots breaking. The tang of fresh-turned soil mixes with the smell of our blood. In the pitch black, large bodies coil through the leaf litter towards us.

Wurms are blind, but they hear and smell well enough. It only takes their stocky tentacles and jawless mouths a moment to pinpoint me and the four boys bleeding out in the dark.

Sound avalanches toward us, eager and unstoppable.

I am the only thing between the daeson and the monsters in the dark. I'm the only hope they have.

If I'd not borne the mark of a Speaker on my chest, the wurm that would become Nardiri would have devoured me and eaten the boys, too. I was sure of that now. She had imprinted when she felt my scar and everything had changed after that. Sweet Nasheira, how had I ruined it all?

I had driven away the glorious, brilliant dragon who had stayed by my side during my darkest moments.

Perhaps I deserved extinction. Perhaps we all did, my people who slaughtered wurms in the name of Nasheira. Convinced of our righteousness, stubborn and certain of our place in the world. And wrong. So very wrong.

Hands tingling, I reached over and brushed sand away from the base of the post. It was packed firmer than I expected, so I used the stick to dig a hollow. In moments, I'd uncovered a buried knot. I followed the rope down and my stick scraped against a hard obstruction. When I pulled back, a sliver of something long, pale and porous glowed in the moonlight—a human bone.

"Shit," I blurted. The stick clattered against the pebbles and I shook out my hands as though they had been burned. *Mother of Yurrii, I can't do this.*

But no one else would build a pyre to send them to Nasheira.

You don't have wood or flint or a fire bow. And Nasheira has no love for daeson souls, a cold voice in my mind snapped back.

"Damn her, anyway." I picked up my stick and wiped my nose with a trembling hand. This was one thing I could do. I could rescue these remains from the disgrace of a muddy riverbed grave amongst the wurms. I could give them a proper sendoff.

So I carefully excavated the entire area around the post, exposing the delicate twin bones of a lower arm, a pair of desiccated hands—ropes still cinched tightly around the wrists—and strands of tiny finger bones, like tapered beads on a necklace. That's all that was left.

I dug further out. The cut on my hand from Nardiri's scale cracked open and seeped blood, but the pain was small and anchored me to my task. I found nothing else until I was several paces away from the post. There, I uncovered a polished wooden handle. Silt sloughed away as I lifted it, revealing a wicked sickle-shaped blade.

Aella had castrated me with a ceremonial blade just like this one. But I could put the flint blade to a different use.

Gingerly, I cut the small bones free of their brittle bonds. I found a large, wedge-shaped stone and some pyrite among the riverbed rocks. Pounding the wedge into the top of the post, I split it into firewood. Then I shaved some strips of wood and unravelled the rope, nestling it against the splintered remains of the post. I struck sparks using the knife's blade against the pyrite, and my pile of kindling started to burn. Feeding the bones to the pyre, I watched as the flames licked at the sky.

I cried, not just for the partial remains of a nameless daeson, but for other bones that lay forgotten. The void in my chest gaped wider until it felt like a bare ribcage picked clean under the sun, filled with nothing but my losses. *Iva, Vax, Gideous, Henri, Jule, Fey. Yara...* I sobbed. *And now Nardiri.*

I loved her, I realized. I loved the dragon like she was my own child. But she wasn't coming back. I had pushed her away, just like my own family had done to me.

Those thoughts kept me company as the callous moons drifted overhead, and I fell into a cold, miserable sleep.

Hours later, something tugged at my consciousness. The moons had both set and the constellations shifted above me, but something celestial and infinitely brighter had stirred me from sleep.

I froze. I couldn't see her, but her soft connection cradled me in its warmth.

"You came," I croaked. Tears filled my eyes. When she didn't answer, I blinked into my dying fire and stammered "I-I found a daeson."

So did I. She stepped into the firelight and set down a boy with tangled brown hair and fragile hope shining in his wide, hazel eyes.

—YARA—

"I love you. I love you, Akrist!" *I'll never see him again.* The thought choked me as Gevi hauled me out of the reeking prison hut. My last view of Akrist was him straining against his bonds to reach me, a feral version of himself; hair matted, teeth bared and eyes full of fire. And suddenly, I couldn't do it, couldn't leave my mate tied like an animal waiting for slaughter, couldn't fathom how I'd ever thought this would work.

"No," I wheezed, digging my nails into the arm around my waist.

But Gevi's grip was unflinching. "If Arsu hears you," he whispered. "She'll kill you too. You and your child both."

My hands, unbidden, dropped to my swollen stomach as we stumbled away from hearth fires into the shadows of the huts beyond. The smell still hung in my nostrils. Vomit, sweat and human waste. It reminded me of Na-Jhalar's hut when I'd been his chani.

I folded and gagged.

Gevi let me sink to the ground. Pebbles stabbed at my knees. I swallowed bile and sucked in deep breaths of clean night air as the man who'd helped me meet with Akrist one last time bent over me.

"I need to go back and stand guard or she'll suspect something," he said. "If you've any wits, you'll run now. You know she'll hurt you if you stay. There's nothing more you can do for him. Run!"

We'd been so close to freedom, Akrist and I. If only we'd fled sooner, perhaps Iva would still be alive and I wouldn't be facing the imminent sacrifice of my mate and the children we'd both vowed to save. Now Akrist was guarded day and night, too weak to run, and I hadn't a hope of stopping an entire camp determined to mutilate their eldest sons. I couldn't breathe. The weight of it all was crushing me.

"Yara, run!" Gevi hissed.

Wiping my mouth, I stood on wobbly legs and trotted away from him.

I should run. But Arsu wouldn't let me. Akrist was right, the woman ached to destroy everything her enemy loved. She'd started with murdering Iva and she would end it with me. If I fled now, she'd track me and bring me back as a plaything for Na-Jhalar, and—I knew this in my bones—she would not let my child survive.

I needed to do better than run. I had to disappear forever and I couldn't do that without help.

My pulse pounded behind my eyes as I returned to Fraesh's hut. Iva's widow was where I'd left him earlier, hunched on the bedroll he had shared with his mate, staring down at his empty hands. His daughters, Baline and Celi, sat on either side of him.

A wretched ache rose in my chest as the healer blinked and slowly looked up at me. Everything he did was sluggish now, like he was wading through mud since Iva died. "How is he?" He asked.

"They are killing him tomorrow. How do you think he is?" My words left me like sparks, harsh, hot and burrowing. Anything to light the fire that had gone out in Fraesh's eyes.

"Tomorrow?" He frowned.

Sweet Nasheira, he didn't even know what day it was. "Yes, tomorrow." I bit down my anger and knelt, my pregnant belly unwieldy and anchoring at the same time. "The sacrifice is tomorrow, and if you don't want to lose us all along with Iva, you need to pull yourself out of the hole you're in and listen to me. We're in danger." I glanced at Baline and Celi. "All of us. As soon as Akrist is gone, Arsu will come after everyone he loves. She means to wipe away every trace of his existence."

"Mother of Yurrii," Fraesh rasped.

"Then we run." Baline spoke up. "As soon as Arsu leaves with the sacrifice procession tomorrow. The wretched snake will be happy to see us gone."

"You think so?" I asked. Baline had protected her little sister and me when we were chani together under Na-Jhalar's abusive rule. I owed her my life, but she was wrong in this and I couldn't afford to be polite. "You're a fool if you think our new leader will let us leave her camp stripped of its only healer and his apprentices. And you think she'll let the woman carrying the child of her enemy just leave? Arsu is many things, but stupid is not one of them. When the moons eclipse, she'll leave guards behind. She won't risk this camp disintegrating while she's gone. We need to do it after, when she thinks she's won and her guard is down. We need a distraction believable enough to buy us a head start."

"Like what?" Celi asked.

I gripped Fraesh's limp hands and squeezed them until he met my gaze. "Like my death." I said. And the fire lit in his eyes.

"What?"

"Arsu wants me dead. So we give it to her. Fake my death. She won't chase a dead woman and it will give you a real chance to run while everyone else is preoccupied."

"Fake it. How?" Celi frowned, but Baline held my gaze with cold steady eyes. She already knew. There was only one reason I would come to a healer with this idea. Fraesh stocked medicinal herbs potent enough to kill.

"Ox's bane and gifen," she murmured, echoing my thoughts. "Slows the breathing enough to mimic death."

"No," Fraesh barked, yanking his hands from mine. His frantic gaze flicked down to my stomach. "An improper dose would kill you and the child both. I'll have no part in this."

"I know, Fraesh." I licked my lips. "That's why I already took it from your stores this morning."

His mouth hung open. Celi blinked and Baline stood, flipping open her father's medicine bag. After rummaging through it, she pressed her lips together and nodded.

"Why?" Fraesh blurted.

"I'll take it with or without you." My voice cracked and tears burned my eyes. "I have no other choice. Arsu *has* to think I'm dead for this child and me to have any chance of living, and you know the proper dosage, Fraesh. Now, will you help or not?"

The healer faltered, his shoulders slumping.

I leaned in. "This is your chance to save the rest of your family. Your daughters. Your grandson."

"You'll come with us?" He raised his head. "A new beginning together. Somewhere safe?"

"Of course." I patted his arm. That was a lie. I had no intention of fleeing with Fraesh's family. I was going to save Akrist.

CHAPTER SIX

S PARKS SPIRALLED AROUND US as the daeson squatted across the fire. His nervous gaze darted toward Nardiri as she settled into a relaxed crouch. He didn't answer me when I asked his name but, when prompted for his age, he held up all of his fingers.

"Ten?" I said, and he nodded. "You are a daeson?"

He looked down.

"I'm a daeson too," I said.

His eyes widened, gaze flicking to my crotch before settling on my brand. Grunting, he traced an S-shape down his cheek before pointing at the sky, then walking two fingers across his open palm.

"You want to know if I escaped sacrifice?"

He nodded and tapped his cheekbone, raising an eyebrow.

"If I was branded for escaping? No. I didn't get away. I—" I swallowed. "Did you escape?"

He winced, clamped his legs together, and shook his head. Firelight flickered across his wrinkled brow.

"Were there others with you?"

He held up two fingers.

I nodded, ignoring the echo of Henri screaming in my head. I held up four fingers. "I'm the only one who survived," I murmured.

The boy pointed to himself and nodded.

"I'm sorry." The words sounded laughably small compared to our losses. "The aeni found you after that?"

Shrugging, he turned his shoulder to me and tucked his hands into his sleeves. He ended our conversation by yawning and curling up in front of the fire, his back to me.

I studied him for several long breaths before scrubbing my neck and sighing.

Branches creaked in the wind overhead. I re-stoked the fire and let it collapse down to rippling coals several times before the dragon broke the silence between us.

Tell me the story. The reason why your people cut all the eldest sons.

I inhaled, and the words poured out of me, just as they had years ago when my father had made me recite the tale every night.

"Nasheira had two sons..."

When I finished, Nardiri was quiet. Levering a stick under a crumbling log, I flipped it before surveying the dragon's frozen face through the sparks. Her hide was pallid in the flickering, orange light. She looked as raw as I felt. "You can read my memories if you like. I have no more secrets from you, Nardiri."

I chewed the inside of my cheek while she turned coils in my mind and poked at all my old memories. A headache pinched behind my eyes.

Firstborns die because you think your goddess is angry at her oldest son for murdering his younger brother and stuffing him into a moon, she summarized.

I pursed my lips, but held her gaze as I answered. *There's more to it than that.*

You slaughter every wurm you lay eyes on, then wring your hands because all the dragons are gone. And every twelve years you butcher your boys in the hope that your goddess will set it all right again? What am I missing? Nardiri's heavy breaths rippled over the fire, flattening the flames.

I squinted at the faint stars above before dropping my chin to my chest. Guides, I felt so wrung out. "We are dying too," I sighed.

Why? The pain and confusion in her voice mirrored my own feelings.

I don't know.

The boy whimpered and twitched in his sleep.

I frowned. "We have to take him back."

No.

We are not thieves.

He is not a possession, she snapped. *Besides, I left them a pile of my scales. They were very happy with the arrangement.* I gawked at her. She preened proudly.

A slow smile tugged at my lips. *You are incorrigible.*

Nardiri huffed, but pleased green threaded through my mind.

I fell asleep propped against a tree. When I awoke, close to dawn, I found myself lying against Nardiri's warmth with my carry bag at my feet. I blinked at it for several moments.

"You found it," I breathed, unthreading the laces on the bag's top flap.

I went back while you slept. It wasn't difficult to find. She boasted. ***It smelled like you.***

I fumbled past my stone lantern, fire bow, sinew, thread, and awl before my hand closed on the evenly-spaced teeth of a hair comb. Pulling it out, I ran my thumb over the carved flowers. My eyes burned and my vision blurred.

It is special to you?

It belonged to Yara. It is all I have left of her. I patted Nardiri's forearm. *Thank you.*

You're welcome. I caught and held onto strands of faint yellow and orange like they were a life line. ***The boy can stay?***

Across the dead fire, the daeson slept curled in on himself, knobby knees against his chest and head tucked so far into his hood I could only see his breath leaving him in even puffs. Even asleep, he terrified me. I had no idea how to care for a child—never mind a mute daeson—but if I returned him to the aeni, he'd always be an object to be traded. No camps would welcome him. And I'd never condemn him to Tanar's wretched, starving fate by forcing him to face the wilderness alone. Exhaling slowly, I accepted the only option I could live with.

When he wakes, I'll ask him if he wants to stay with us.

The boy didn't say yes. He didn't say anything, but when I asked him if he wanted to stay, his eyes brightened. He slapped his chest with an open palm, using his other hand to point at my scar, then at Nardiri. My heart sank when I realized what he'd presumed. "I can't grant you a mark or a dragon. Nasheira chooses Speakers, not me." It felt like a lie as I said it. The goddess wouldn't have chosen a drug-addled Na-Jhalar or my corrupted little brother to lead. She wouldn't have chosen me.

The boy's face fell. His shoulders hunched as he wiped his nose with his arm.

"We can try to find you a camp, if you'd rather." The words sounded lame even to my ears.

He shook his head and locked his knees.

"My name is Akrist. The dragon is called Nardiri. She's quite fond of you."

Nardiri crooned and tossed her head, and the boy's face brightened.

"What can we call you?"

The boy squatted, plucked up a stick, and drew a crude boat and an oversized oar in the dirt. Then he circled the oar and mimicked a paddling motion.

"Paddling?" I frowned.

He snorted and repeated the movement impatiently.

Who would name a child 'Paddling'? Nardiri's thoughts bubbled with bemused green.

"Rowing?"

Nodding, he pinched his fingers together. Shorter.

"Row?"

Wider fingers now.

Shorter than Rowing, but longer than Row.

You are terrible at this game, Nardiri said.

I raised my eyebrow, then turned back to the boy and thought about it before it came to me. "Rowin?"

He nodded emphatically, clapping and grinning. His joy was infectious.

Rowin

Flying was made even more difficult with a second passenger. Rowin was so small that Nardiri alternately worried about dropping him or crushing him in the effort to keep from dropping him.

You are no better, she quipped. *Like trying to carry a wriggling fish.*

You flatter me. I tossed the thought with a wry grin and wiped my cold nose. My legs were numb and my back ached with the effort of holding my torso upright.

Rowin beamed from his perch within Nardiri's opposite foreclaw, legs dangling in the air. His small hands kept drifting away from their grip on the dragon's talons to pick at her scales or cup the wind. I felt myself growing hoarse from hollering at him to hold on.

We need a harness. And for that we need rope. A lot of it.

Can we make rope?

No. I grimaced at the thought of Rowin and I tumbling from the sky due to my substandard work. *Aeni excel at braiding rope, and they are experts at knots. We'll have to seek out another group.* My stomach clenched at the thought, and I caught myself scratching at my scar.

Just act like a Speaker this time and not an outcast.

A snort of laughter burst past my lips. *And you'll act like an angel of Nasheira?*

Indifferent and evasive?

Serene and quiet.

She tossed her head. ***That sounds like no fun at all.***

The aeni group we found was larger than the first, nearly a dozen strong with a flock of four vaiyas. None of the humans were receptive. They knelt as we landed. Their leader, a man with a star pattern decorating the back of his bright jacket, noted my brand.

"W-what do you want with us?"

"To trade." I stepped in front of Rowin to shield him from the stares of the crowd.

"Nasheira sends us a Guide *and* an outcast. What trickery is this?"

"Take that up with the Goddess. I just want to trade." Yanking my neckline down, I exposed my Speaker's mark.

The ani shook his head. "This is a test." He gaped past me at Nardiri. "The Goddess forbids her faithful from treating with outcasts under *any* circumstances."

"She also says to obey the Speakers. I offer dragon scales, and I can tell you where to find every fat harek, gazelle, ox and vaiya for miles around. We can chart a course anywhere you want to go, draw you the finest map, find you other camps to trade with." I lowered my voice. "Or deny us, deny a holy Speaker, deny an angel of Nasheira herself, and see what happens then."

The whole group shifted uncomfortably. One of them, a young man with a blue ribbon braided into his hair, darted a glance from his leader to Nardiri. The leader broke my gaze, fingers twitching. Indecisive.

Now would be a lovely time to frighten them.

Every head craned upwards as the dragon rose to her full height. At my nod, Rowin clapped his hands over his ears as we'd practiced. A wonderful, guttural growl purred through Nardiri's chest before erupting into a throaty roar that belted toward the horizon.

The aeni's vaiyas shrieked and crashed away through the bush.

Something massive smashed down between the leader and me with an earth-shaking thunk. The man tumbled backwards. I blinked as dirt rained around us. It took me a moment to identify Nardiri's tail, its three spikes driven into the ground before my feet, diamond-shaped fluke tapering off to my right. With a snarl simmering in her throat, she wrenched her tail aside. Slabs of clay churned upward. The air filled with the squeal of rocks chattering against each other and the musty smell of permafrost.

Nice touch. My mouth twitched. *You might have warned me.*

It was a spur of the moment addition.

"Wh-what are your needs?" the leader gulped, his dirt-smudged forearm still shielding his face.

Smugness poured off Nardiri in waves. I resisted the urge to roll my eyes.

"Rope," I said, sighing. "We need a lot of rope."

CHAPTER SEVEN

"**W**RONG WAY." THE YOUNG ani flipped his blue-braided forelock from his eyes and glanced sidelong at Nardiri before snatching the rope from my hands. "Loop toward the long end, then push it through like this." I watched his deft fingers. "Leave the tail long. It goes through the second loop. Then pull it through like this. See the tail folds? That's what you want. Bark rope is strong, but if you don't fold the short end back as you tighten, the whole thing unravels." He tossed the finished knot back at me with a half-smile and nodded. "Again. Unless you want to fall."

I would catch you, Nardiri grumbled.

Blue Braid flinched at the half-growl that came from her throat, and I smiled, stretched, and twisted to observe the dragon. "You'd be too slow with that full stomach," I said.

Her great mass was curled languidly a few paces from us, her stomach hide stretched tight as a drum. With her chin resting on the ground and her jaw pillowed by her tightly-wrapped tail, Nardiri's half-slitted eye blinked level with our heads.

Rowin slept against her neck with the sort of comfortable abandon reserved only for exhausted young children with full bellies—head cocked, arms and legs akimbo, mouth wide open.

When I turned back to Blue Braid, he was still gaping at Nardiri—as he had all morning—with undiluted awe and fear.

"What is she saying?"

"That she'd catch me if I fell." I smiled down at the rope, picking at the firm knot.

"Has she eaten enough?"

"She had three of the gazelle. Same as she brought back for you." After the stand-off this morning, the leader and I had come to an arrangement. Nardiri and I had agreed to track the aeni's fleeing vaiyas and coax them back to their masters, as well as hunt for the group.

The dragon had laboured back to the aeni's tents with Rowin and me tucked in her arms, a pair of gazelle gripped in each hind-claw, and an exceedingly full belly. Under the agitated gaze of the aeni, I'd washed Nardiri's blood-crusted muzzle and claws, after which she'd fallen almost instantly asleep. She'd been dozing ever since, immobile enough that Blue Braid had braved an introduction, and brought his leader's end of the bargain: three coils of thick, woven bark rope, two spears, a skinning knife, and a meal of boiled grouse eggs, flatbread, and vaiya cheese for Rowin and me.

"Why didn't she eat our vaiyas?" Blue Braid's question pulled me from my thoughts.

"She knows they are important to you." Pressing a loop into the rope, I used my thumb to thread another one through it. "And she's fascinated by the fact that they can speak." I didn't add that the dragon was also painfully aware of the nightmares I had about Vax's death.

"I think she's quite taken with them, actually." Smiling, I pulled the knot tight. The ani's lips twitched. I handed him the rope as Nardiri snorted, and a short, sharp laugh left my lips.

"It's good." The boy nodded, glancing curiously from me to my dragon. "What is she saying now?"

"That she may not catch me when I fall, after all. I'd better learn your knots quickly, Ani."

It took the better part of the afternoon for me to suitably replicate the three knots Blue Braid had shown me. Two women kept us endlessly supplied with honey-sweetened tea. One of them, the taller of the pair with white-blonde hair, kept eyeing me. I suspected she was waiting for her opportunity to ask for a dragon scale. Aeni did not bestow gifts, not even tea. Every offer was a trade they fully expected to be compensated for.

At one point, Nardiri yawned, and the white-haired ani drew herself up, tipped her head, and extended one hand toward the sleeping dragon. "She is so powerful." Pale, liquid eyes refocused on me, and she dropped her outstretched hand to my arm. "Makes me *quiver*." The last word rolled off her tongue like syrup, and I realized my mistake.

Blue Braid snorted tea into his cup. I held my steaming mug at arm's length, though I couldn't do anything about the tea I had already drank. *Stupid. Guides, you are stupid, Akrist.* The girls weren't vying for dragon scales.

I like them. Nardiri flicked a sleepy emerald gaze toward the aeni pair as they sauntered away, hips rolling.

Blue Braid coughed, tipped his cup, and gulped loudly. He glanced pointedly at my crotch. "You have any interest anymore? I hear some daeson still can after sacrifice, it just takes more effort to..." He coughed again. "Harden up the snake."

I froze. I hadn't told him I was a daeson. I hadn't told any of them.

"He is daeson too, yes?" Blue Braid pointed to Rowin. The boy had woken and was practicing knots too. "I can tell. You both look here when you talk," he pointed to his feet. "Never in the eyes. No matter. It doesn't bother these women. I can tell them if you are interested."

"No." I punctuated my answer by setting my clay cup down hard enough that tea sloshed over the edges. Standing up, I stalked over to Nardiri, lengths of rope trailing from my hand. "I'm not interested."

"Ah." Blue Braid set his tea down too, grabbing the rope I held and wrapping it snugly around the dragon's chest, then twisting a deft knot. "You've promised yourself to just one mate?"

No one could compare to Yara. I had never wanted anyone else. "She died," I rasped. Guides, it hurt to say out loud.

"Sorry." Blue Braid bit his lip. "Is the boy family? A cousin? You saved him?"

"You know," I drawled, tamping my discomfort down with a forced smile, "you pry a lot for someone who refuses to share even his own name."

Blue Braid laughed. Nardiri sniffed, and he jumped and chuckled again, eyes bright, honest, and open as they caught mine. "She smells like a vaiya." He extended his hand, and when my dragon nudged it, he said, "Soft. Thought they'd be hard, bigger scales."

I held out the end of the rope. "If I pass this under, can you grab it from the other side?"

He complied, then stood back to study the dragon. "Where'll you sit? Between the shoulder blades? It's flattest, and your legs could grip over the leading edge. Will that pinch the wing muscles though?"

"I've no idea."

Nardiri ruffled her wings in excitement. *Let's try!*

I straddled the dragon's neck as she pushed up onto her hind legs.

Careful! I winced, slipping back over several hard neck ridges before my legs hooked around her shoulders. I settled into the groove between Nardiri's shoulder blades, gripped the nearest ridge with white-knuckled hands and nodded at Rowin waving madly below. Nearly twenty feet yawned between the boy and me.

Nardiri's muscles shifted, shoulder blades scooping as she arched her wings. Walls of rippling membrane flanked me on either side, crescent midpoint claws nearly touching far above my head.

Don't fly. I gulped.

Don't worry. The shadow of her crest swung overhead as she twisted to blink at me. *I'm too full.* She pumped her wings. Flight muscles bunched and stretched beneath me—once, twice. By the third time, dust and flakes of grass were eddying around us. Blue Braid whooped and shielded his face while Rowin grinned and bounced on his feet.

We finished the rest of the harness within the hour. The two women returned twice to offer us refreshment, but even Blue Braid declined their offer with a polite smile.

"Now tighten it like I showed you," he ordered as I climbed onto Nardiri again, this time with Rowin seated ahead of me. The boy had silently pleaded to climb aboard and I couldn't deny him without insulting Blue Braid's craftsmanship. Besides, I needed to make sure the harness fit both of us before we took to the air.

I cinched the rope belt snug around my waist, then Rowin's, and leaned forward to grasp the pair of handhold loops knotted into the top of the neck strap.

"Mind the slipknot." Blue Braid beamed as he pointed. "If you tie it wrong, it will loosen. If that happens, grab the hand holds."

I chuckled, "I don't imagine there'll be many occasions when I'm not grabbing the hand holds." Unravelling myself from the ropes, I vaulted from Nardiri's back as she crouched. When I turned to assist Rowin, he waved me off and jumped, landing with a stumble. "Thank you, Ani," I said to Blue Braid.

His teeth flashed, and he glanced wistfully at Nardiri. "A pleasure, helping a Guide." His head bobbed back to me. "And a Speaker."

"Ah!" I snapped my fingers. "What do I owe you? What can I offer?"

"No, Speaker." He shook his head, braided forelock flapping as he continued to grin. "You paid with many gazelles already."

"That was for the rope, not your time."

"My time so close to a dragon. Every aeni will be jealous," he insisted, eyes serious and hands clasped together. "That's enough."

"I owe you something, Ani." I coiled the rope in my hand and met the young man's roguish gaze. "Let me repay, if I can."

"All right." He rubbed his ear. "I will take an answer as payment, dragon man. How did you find her?" He gestured to Nardiri, who had already fallen back asleep.

"She found me," I said, "when she was a juvenile. She bonded with me because she felt my Speaker's mark."

The ani's wide eyes studied my chest "I have never seen a young dragon."

Oh, you likely have, my mind rejoined bitterly, overcome by memories of tentacles and teeth and spongy white skin.

"She bonded with you? How?"

"I owed you one answer." I smiled wanly. "And you have it. I do not wish to trade anymore tonight."

He tossed his chin, laughed, and clapped me on the shoulder. "All right, dragon man. Maybe we'll trade tomorrow, yes?" Swinging away, he made for the spiked horizon of aeni tents wreathed in smoke from the hearth fires. "Hey!" He spun to face me, walking backwards as he talked. "You want me to tell the women no more trades tonight?" His teeth flashed, and he slapped his knee.

"Let them come." I shook my head, corners of my mouth twitching with a smile. "Let them come and wake the dragon if they want to get to me."

I didn't think the women would actually have the gall to approach me uninvited. Guides, how wrong I was.

Dusk settled over the aeni camp thick with the smell of roasted meat and the grating hum of insects singing. I'd left a sleeping

Nardiri to relieve myself when the white-haired ani approached me.

"I can offer you more relief than that." She strode brazenly toward me.

"Mother of Yurrii," I hissed, yanking my breechcloth back into place. "Privacy, Ani! Have you not heard of the concept?"

"A Speaker cannot expect much in the way of privacy." She smiled, closing the distance between us even as my cheeks burned. "So many eyes on you all the time. So much pressure. Surely you need a chani? Someone to help you relax."

A chani. Goddess above, the ani didn't want me for one night, she was vying to be my chani—an owned woman.

She reached out to cup my cheek and I caught her wrist delicately and pressed her back. "I appreciated the tea this afternoon. I can repay your courtesy with dragon scales."

"Dragon scales do not interest me as much as a dragon rider."

I raised my eyebrows. "Well, I'm not on offer."

Her teeth flashed in the dark as she shrugged out of her wrap, exposing her breasts. "You are lonely. I think I could convince you otherwise."

"No!" I averted my eyes and cleared my throat. "My answer is no, Ani. I will arrange a fair trade for the tea. Now if you will excuse me. I'm tired. Sleep well." Turning, I left the woman standing in the dark.

Thank the Guides, she did not follow.

I retreated to Nardiri's side. Her wing walled me off from the world. The dragon was awake now, but peaceably quiet. Soft strains of a lone tanbur floated through the still night air, someone plucking its strings in a haunting melody. I turned Yara's hair comb in my hand, utterly exhausted from the day's events. I'd forgotten how draining being around people was.

Rowin whimpered from where he slept beside the dragon. His legs kicked and twitched until Nardiri's soft crooning lulled him back to stillness.

I was too flustered to sleep. The scar on my chest itched and tingled. I couldn't stop thinking about the white-haired woman's bold advance, and earlier than that, Blue Braid's awe. Not just for Nardiri. He'd looked at me like I was Nasheira's favoured.

I wasn't.

I was a pretender. I hadn't even been brave enough to tell the aeni that juvenile dragons were wurms. My world had already banished me once. If I hinted to anyone that my people's sacred creation story was a lie, or revealed that the wurms were not the parasitic spawn of Pau but larval Guides, I'd be branded as a heretic. But even worse than that was the prospect of actually being believed. The ani woman was right. I was lonely, and while the thought of being more alone than I already was shook me, the possibility of tyrannical leaders wielding dragons *terrified* me. I wasn't ready to hand them the key to ultimate power. I hadn't been marked because I was good, but because I was *receptive*, whatever that meant. If cruel, incompetent, greedy Na-Jhalar could be a Speaker, then there was no moral aspect to the bond at all. *I don't deserve a dragon any more than that maggot-filled crust of a man, my broken little brother, or his idol Arsu. I am as selfish as any of them.*

No. Nardiri flicked her head back like she'd just smelled something offensive. *If you were a selfish man, would I have survived after I went to ground?*

I flinched at the memory of the biting, red assault of her insatiable hunger.

A selfish human would have left me.

I picked at the scab on my fingers where her scale had sliced me days ago. *I almost left you, Nardiri, so many times.*

But you didn't, because you are a Speaker.

I lay awake, long after Nardiri slept. The comprehension of how directly my hand had served to mold my Guide floored me. I replayed those last, red-washed weeks in my mind. I remembered collapsing onto cold ground at night, my ribs and the knobs of my spine stretching through sunken skin as I starved to feed the wurm. I recalled marvelling at how my limbs could look so insubstantial yet feel so heavy. Dear Guides, if I'd failed, if I had died outside the cavern she holed up in, Nardiri would have starved before ever becoming a dragon. Without my hearth fire to fend off other wurms, she'd likely have been devoured while she was cocooned and defenseless, and I would have never known what she truly was.

I leaned against her leg. The night wind felt like warm breath on my cheeks, but I shivered nonetheless. I knew that wurms turned into dragons, and I was too cowardly to speak up. Nardiri was wrong. I was selfish and scared. I was no Speaker at all.

CHAPTER EIGHT

S OMETHING SWEET PULLED ME toward consciousness, like a summer sunset. I grew gradually aware of the soft and solid warmth of a body cupping mine. A downy leg draped over my thigh. Cool hands slid past my ribs to skim the scar on my chest while balmy breath brushed the back of my neck. Mortified, I felt myself responding, goosebumps raising on my arms, heartbeat ratcheting higher, warmth gathering at my core. *Oh, Guides.* My breath snagged in my throat.

"No," I barked, grasping a small wrist and flinging it away as I rolled to face my unsolicited company. Sleep blurred my sight. I pushed up on one elbow and blinked several times before the form swam into focus. I fully expected a ghost-white mane of hair to materialise in the night, the ani woman back to collect her trade. Instead, my gaze snagged on tousled, honey-brown curls, and dark, deep eyes.

I opened my mouth to say her name, but my throat collapsed. All I could do was mouth the word. It was *her* round face, long-lashes, and lightly-freckled nose. My lungs pulled for air, and my heartbeat lodged high in between my temples as I sat up and drank in the sight of her. Same achingly soft curves. Same delicate chin. Same birth mark on her left collar bone.

Dizziness swamped me, and I sagged forward, raising a warding hand as she straightened and leaned toward me. The tender smell of new earth and the rich scent of cinnamon enfolded me.

"Yara," I choked. Hot tears pricked my eyes. "How?"

She levered toward me, hip brushing my leg. Guiding my hand to the small of her back, she hooked her cool fingers under my jaw. As she tipped my head up, I breathed her in, trading exhalations.

"How did—" My wet words caught in my throat as I stared down at her stomach—pale, flat, and tight. "The baby?" I realised Yara was unclothed, soft as a budding flower opening to me. How had I not noticed before?

I was naked too. I gulped, staring down at the bare scar twisting down my chest. My ribs expanded like bellows and, further down, a trembling erection rose.

My head snapped up. "Where are we?" I croaked, but could not distinguish our surroundings in the dark.

Yara didn't answer. Her dark gaze held mine as she reached between my legs and gripped me.

I shuddered, stomach slumping. She had not reached far enough to feel the scar, to realise her mate was no longer intact. But it didn't matter. I had recognized this for what it was: a dream. Not flesh and blood... not my Yara.

Dropping my chin, I pulled her hand from my crotch, and slid it upward, pressing her small palm flat against the hollow of my chest. "I miss you." I brushed a curl from her cheek. "So much."

When Yara pressed against me this time, I collapsed into her, wholeheartedly praying that the fall would never stop.

I awoke enveloped by Nardiri's rustling wing, the knob of her ankle digging into my shoulder. It was not yet dawn, and the damp ground was leaching heat from my back. Reality's jagged edge rushed in and, though I held my breath, I couldn't hold onto the fragrance of cinnamon.

That was a nice dream. Soothing green hummed through Nardiri's thoughts.

Stay out of my dreams, please. I crossed my arms over my chest, heaved up a cold wall in my mind, and rolled away from the dragon. That's when I felt it, a lingering hardness between my legs. Frowning, I reached down to confirm it was real and not just some phantom sensation.

"Well, what do you know?" The bitter whisper slipped past my lips. Blue Braid was right; the snake still worked.

Again. You can turn tighter this time. We'd left Rowin on the ground; he hadn't been happy about it, but I refused to test the harness with a child riding along. Besides, after last night's dream, I was in no mood for company.

A rich orange swath of sunlight soaked into my back, teasing mist from the pores of the hills below us. Nardiri banked, and my right thigh mashed into her shoulder blade. The harness constricted, and the leading edge of the dragon's wings dug into the backs of my knees as I squeezed against her. A sharp horizon tilted up to meet us, froths of newly green leaves clotting the treetops. It all rushed by me in a windswept blur, but it wasn't fast enough. I couldn't outfly the image of my dead mate, and I meant to. I intended to push Nardiri until the wind roared in my ears loudly enough to wipe everything else away.

I tucked against the dragon, pressing my chest into the ridge of her neck. My hands wedged themselves further into the gripping loops of the harness. I pushed my next thought out alongside an exhalation that whistled through my teeth. *Tighter, Nardiri. I'm not an egg. I won't crack.*

An egg would sit still, she shot back. **Stop flopping around so much. It feels like you're falling.**

I'm fine. That was a lie. Dabbing a tear-blurred eye against my upper arm, I blinked down at the marbled terrain. *Tighter turn, please,* I ordered.

Her wing listed abruptly. Membrane flared behind us, and my chin cracked against her neck as she executed a hairpin turn. She held the revolution, and the world wheeled like a top beneath us. Flattened against her muscular neck, I took several gruelling breaths before giving her permission to break from the turn.

See? It pressed me right into you. I scanned the meadow beneath us. *Try rolling upside down.*

No. Nardiri trumpeted.

I needed this. Something strenuous enough to choke out the thoughts burning through my head. *I've seen birds do it. Can't you just tuck your wings in and flip?*

I didn't say I'm incapable. The dragon snorted. Her shoulders jerked back. **I said I won't.**

Not at this height. Let's go higher. I squinted, wishing I could see the colour of the air currents through Nardiri's sight, but she'd blocked my access to her vision. *Come on.* I thumped her neck. *You'll have plenty of time to catch me if something goes wrong.*

I do not want to lose sight of the boy. He is alone. We should go back.

I set my jaw. *We're not going back. I want to know this harness holds, no matter what. If you can't do it, just say so.*

Nardiri barked. The resonation thudded up my spine as she pressed away from the ground. Her wings whistled as they tilted to shed air on the next upstroke.

In less than a minute, the spring grasslands had shrunk to a hazed blur below us. My breath streamed from my mouth in cold puffs, and small clouds scudded by beneath my feet. I gulped in icy air, fighting against a sudden feeling of dizziness.

Ready. My stomach tightened.

Nardiri launched upward. At the lowest point of her down stroke, she snapped her wings tight against her ribs, stretched her snout and spun. My stomach crowded my throat as my body shot away from her neck. The harness ropes twanged tight and cut into my legs. I grunted, heaved on the hand holds, and scrambled to hook my feet back under her wings, but we were already righting. I settled back onto Nardiri as she set her wings into a glide and shook her great head. White sparks snapped across my vision and I curled over her back, panting, arms and legs prickling, mind almost empty. The sensation felt frighteningly similar to Nardiri's paralysis. "Again," I gulped.

No! She snapped indignantly. **The air is thin and you are unused to flying. Are you done yet? The red thought seared through my mind. Are you finished flaying yourself for having a dream? Are you done punishing me for the fact that you broadcast it loudly enough for me to hear? I want to go back to Rowin.**

I blinked. Inhalations punctuated my silence, sharp and hic-cup-like. She'd used his name. She rarely used names other than mine.

The harness is crooked, she added. ***Maybe the ani can fix it, so it doesn't twist.***

Staring down, it took me several moments to comprehend that one of the handholds I gripped sat centred over her neck ridge while the other now lay lower on the left side. "I don't want to go back," I muttered. All those people, and none of them Yara. "We should get Rowin and just keep flying." I blinked away the black spots that sprayed across my vision.

Nardiri dipped into a descent. She walled off her mind, and ignored me for the rest of our flight back.

"Well?" Blue Braid shouted up at us, grinning despite the wind of Nardiri's landing buffeting his face. "You're still up there, so it works, yes?"

I nodded. "The neck strap shifted a bit, but only on more advanced manoeuvres."

"Advanced manoeuvres?" He rolled the words around in his mouth like a bad taste, before tugging at the errant strap. "All right, dragon man. Since I have never built a harness for a Guide, the first repair is free." His face broke into a good-natured grin.

"Thank you." I untangled myself from the harness and dis-mounted, flexing my stiff fingers.

"You want food? Is the boy hungry?" That was a trade offer, disguised as benevolence.

"Rowin?" I turned.

He sat with his narrow back to me, pulling apart strands of grass. At the sound of his name, he flinched and shook his head, obviously still upset at having missed out on our flight.

"My stomach hasn't quite landed yet," I said to Blue Braid.

He shrugged, laughed, and backed away from me in his characteristic exit. "I'll get more rope to strengthen the harness." He tapped his temple.

I nodded.

Nardiri and Rowin both remained silent while we waited, which suited me fine. When Blue Braid returned with a fresh coil of rope, he mumbled to himself and examined the dragon from every angle. She complied with all the requests I passed on from the absorbed ani, but didn't answer me.

"There." The rope maker announced when he was done, hand pressed against Nardiri's neck and eyes shining as he stared up at her. "I added two straps, here and here." He pointed to the additions, seamlessly woven into the existing harness. "That should stop the twisting, dragon man."

"Thank you." I smiled dismissively.

"I have something else for you." He reached into his belt and held out a smooth crescent strip of wood. Two horizontal slits had been carved into it and lengths of sinew cord looped around either end. "Snow guard." Blue Braid grinned. "Not built for flying, but it should cut the wind a bit."

He wouldn't put his hand down, so I took the polished piece, flipped it over and ran a thumb over the hollow that had been grooved for the bridge of the nose, before holding it out. "I cannot accept it, Ani. I've nothing else to trade. My dragon has no more scales to shed, and I've no more stories to tell."

But he pressed it back toward me, shaking his head. "Not a trade. A gift."

"A *gift?*" I scoffed.

He nodded. "Please."

"I didn't think aeni believed in giving gifts."

Blue Braid flashed his winning smile. "I didn't believe in Speakers riding dragons, either." He held his hands up to Nardiri before nodding at me. "The world is changing, yes?"

"Thank you," I murmured.

"Nasheira's peace with you." He bowed his head.

"May her Guides mark your skies." I answered.

We left after that.

Without Nardiri's comfort filling my head, there was nothing to distract me. My mind frayed into destructive thoughts, and my skull ached. Rowin leaned as far away from me as he could in the harness and, when we landed for the night, the daeson turned his back to me and curled into the moody dragon's forearms. I clamped my jaw and started a fire, determined not to be the first one to break the silence.

I wasn't. Rowin was. The boy had barely closed his eyes before he started kicking in his sleep. The tendons in his neck bulged and a keening noise threaded past his lips far too similar to the wails that had torn through me on sacrifice night.

"Rowin." Gooseflesh prickled on my arms. "Wake up. You're dreaming."

I remembered my boyhood nightmares; how cruelly they'd intensified the closer the moons came to eclipsing. After Tanar escaped, I'd been a solitary prisoner with a death sentence, and my only comfort had been Iva and Fraesh's company through a set of wooden bars.

Rowin bolted upright, back rigid. His eyes opened wide, but I recognized the distant and unfocused look of a dreamer captured in the cobwebs between asleep and awake.

"Rowin," I repeated. "I'm here. It's all right."

He clamped his hands over his ears. The whites of his eyes flashed and he whispered in a clear, high voice, "Behind you."

Fingers of ice plucked down my back. I turned, but saw nothing. Nardiri's senses rippled away, scouring our surroundings.

She shifted uncomfortably. *There's nothing out here except us.*

"He's dreaming," I murmured, rising from my squat as the boy scrambled to his feet and ambled toward the fire. Guiding him away from the flames, I walked with him as he paced, panting and scratching his arms, gaze searching but listless. Then he stopped mid-step. His sharp eyes focused on me and he staggered several steps back, shoulder thumping into the nearest tree.

"Easy." I held out my palms. "You were walking in your sleep."

Clutching his shoulder, Rowin stood, blinking, like someone waiting for their sight to adjust in the pitch black.

"Bad dream?"

He hugged himself and nodded.

"Do you know how to play tavi?"

He shook his head.

I gulped against the tightness in my throat and spoke with all the brightness I could muster. "My aunt, Iva, played it with me whenever I couldn't sleep. Let's carve some pieces, and I can teach you."

We found four pieces of wood that were small enough to conceal in a closed hand, then carved two pieces with a vague dragon shape and the other two with squiggles that represented wurms. I handed Rowin one of each. "The object of the game is to guess which hand I'm holding the Guide in. If you guess correctly, you win a piece of my treasure." I held out both of my fists and smiled down at the sad pile of pine cones between my feet. "You keep guessing until you are wrong. When you're wrong, I get a piece from your pile and it's my turn to guess. We play until the loser has nothing left to wager."

Nardiri watched us with casual interest, but kept her thoughts to herself. Rowin refused to sleep until he won two tavi matches in a row. He was smart. Once I'd shown him how to watch for tells, he quickly picked up on mine and beat me soundly for the next few rounds. By the time he settled and his breaths evened out, it was well past midnight.

The world hushed around us. I pulled the ox horn hair comb from my belt pouch and ran my thumbnail down its slender teeth. When I couldn't stand the silence anymore, I reached for the dragon. "I'm sorry I pushed you away."

Her tail twitched, spikes raking through dead grass. It was the only indication that she'd heard me.

"I shouldn't have been cold this morning. I just—" I shoved the comb back into my belt pouch, stood, and found my feet following the same frantic path Rowin had earlier. "I'm broken when I think of her. I can't—" my throat closed around the words.

I didn't feel the wall crumble, only Nardiri's quiet return to my mind.

You can't what?

I can't care for a child. Guides, it's all I can do just to breathe sometimes. Tears pricked my eyes. *She was my whole world, Nardiri.*

Tell me about her. Her soft thought wisped through the ruins of my brain. *She's woven into every fold of your mind, but I know nothing of her.*

"I can't," I said. "It hurts to remember her."

It would be worse to forget her, I expect.

Something sour and biting rose up my throat, but before I could lash out, Nardiri added: *Just share one thing about her. Please.*

My throat worked. Something airy and aching rose in me like morning mist. A frail smile cracked my dry lips. "She loved honey," I said. "The rest of us, when we found a wild hive, we'd pass the combs around and stuff our cheeks even as the bees still stung us. Not Yara," I shook my head. "She would tuck hers away and unwrap it hours later around the evening fire when the taste of sweetness was just a wistful memory for the rest of us. She'd break the comb into tiny pieces and hold each one on her tongue, letting it melt, just so she could draw out the enjoyment. And she was good at it—not just honey. She was good at wringing every moment of joy out of life. Any small thing that brought her happiness, she kept. Some days she'd empty out her gathering sack and it looked like a squirrel's nest." I snorted. "Bright feathers and lacy bits of moss all poking out from her haul for the day. And rocks. There were always rocks."

Why?

"She said she liked the weight of them in her palm. She'd scour riverbanks when we fished together, and you'd think she was an ani trader the way she turned a prospective pebble in her hand. I think she liked fishing for stones more than anything we could catch in a net." A long sigh wrung out my lungs before I could speak again.

"The vaiyas were absolutely taken with her. Vax was a lovesick fool."

Your vaiyas?

My throat worked and I nodded, but could not speak.

You are allowed to hold onto little bits of joy too, you know. Without her. Smiling, dreaming, enjoying a sunrise flight—would she want you to punish yourself for those things?

I leaned against her snout and wrapped my arms around her cheeks, pressing my forehead against hers.

You loved her. Deeply. Nardiri spoke carefully. *But Yara is not your whole world anymore. You need to find another reason to live.*

I contemplated her words, but didn't know what to say. After a moment, Nardiri asked, *What's next?*

"I don't know," I croaked. "I can't think that far."

What is it you want?

Shaking my head to clear it, I stared up at the thin column of smoke rising from our fire. Arsu's face burned in my mind like a brand.

I want to kill her.

You want murder to be your purpose?

I didn't answer, but my heart quavered at the thought.

There are more boys like Rowin out there. Like you. Ones that haven't been cut yet. We could save them.

How, Nardiri? What are we supposed to do, kidnap every dae-son we come across? Anxiety pulled at my ribs. *Even if we could collect them, I don't know the first thing about caring for children.*

We've managed with Rowin just fine.

A tired laugh burst past my lips. *Even if that were true, it will not be so simple with a group of them.*

I am meant to mark people and you are meant to lead them; neither of us are made to abandon those who need help. I will lay eggs and you will pair strong Speakers with my young. We cannot hide from what we are.

Her words, firm and certain, struck a fear in me so deep and vast that I could barely keep from being overwhelmed by it. I wanted nothing more than to fly Rowin and Nardiri some-where so isolated that the rest of the world could never touch us. But if we left, daeson would still be dying. Dragons and wurms too. There was nowhere we could go to escape the guilt of leaving them all to be slaughtered. Yara would have tried to save them all without hesitation. She'd been utterly fearless in her compassion. How could I even think of doing something like this without her? I'd never been strong enough, or brave enough, on my own.

You aren't alone.

Not Alone

—YARA—

I sat on the bedroll, my cheeks tight from dried tears and my head still swimming with Vax's death cry and Akrist's agonized screams. The bitter aftertaste of the sedative tincture burned my throat. I remembered Fraesh asked me to lie down... and then nothing until I woke to Baline lowering me into a travois. We slipped away from camp amidst muffled thunder and snow sifting through skeletal branches.

Now, I wove drunkenly between trees with scraped knees and cold-numbed fingers, my heart thrashing like a bird between my ribs. Vomit crusted the front of my tunic. I barely remembered stealing the bag of food slung over my back. It had seemed like a dream, the air too thick and my limbs too heavy to move. But I'd somehow crept away from Fraesh and his family as they slept, and I'd been running ever since. Back to Akrist. Only I had no idea where he was. I had no idea where *I* was.

The wind wiped out any trace of footprints we'd left, and my memory of our travel so far was hazy. I spent the night stumbling along blindly, sobbing, gagging, and stopping to massage my cramped legs.

It was my own funeral pyre that saved me from a frozen death.

When dawn bleached the horizon and the storm evaporated, a column of black smoke smeared the grey sky to the west. I froze when I saw it, mouth dry as autumn leaves. Oh Guides, if I were discovered, my "death" would all be for nothing. Arsu would delight in torturing me, and she'd find a way to kill my baby. I clutched my stomach.

"Don't be stupid," I murmured to myself. "There's no one there."

Tradition dictated that camps travelled the morning after the sacrifice, because Nasheira desired a fresh start after the moons eclipsed—that's what I'd been taught as a girl. Now, I knew the reality of it. Camps left their daeson behind so that, even if the boys survived being castrated and exposed to the elements for two days, they wouldn't find their families again, so that heretic mothers had little chance of acting on regret and attempting to save the children they'd mutilated, and everyone a daeson ever knew could forget them a little more with each mile that stretched between them.

Akrist, Jule, Fey, Gideous and Henri were somewhere nearby. Butchered, bleeding and alone—if they hadn't already died of exposure from the previous night's snowstorm. The thought sliced through me, sharp enough to take my breath away.

Akrist couldn't be dead. Considering the idea opened up a dangerous, dark void in my chest. I'd given him the medicinal pouch from Fraesh with the flint shard hidden within. My mate should have been able to cut his bonds, free the boys and stop their bleeding. The children were small, but surely with an adult among them, they could have shared enough body heat to survive the night together. They *had* to be alive.

Skirting wide around the pyre's smoke, I headed north. Every twig snapping sounded like Arsu's hunters coming to find me and each bird call seemed like the echo of a daeson crying. By the time evening fell, I'd combed through endless miles of brush, clogged leaves and melting slush. My legs were numb, my leggings soaked to the knees, and I had no supplies to build a fire. Guilt soured my stomach as I forced down a chunk of blood sausage and flat bread before settling under the shelter of an ula tree that hadn't yet shed its leaves.

Your mate is out there. He has no food, no clothing, no shelter. And yet you stop to sleep? But I couldn't get back up, couldn't even see past my own hand with the moons not out yet. Wrapping my arms around my stomach, I cried quietly in the dark. That's when it struck me, as I huddled in the moldering leaves, a fear so staggering and unexpected it felt like a spear slipped between my ribs.

I haven't felt the baby move. When had I last? I couldn't remember anything since Akrist and I embraced. My hands trembled as they smoothed the thick coat over my belly. Surely there'd been a kick or a stretch and I'd missed it as I'd tumbled through the woods today? *But your baby is most active at night, just before you sleep, and there is nothing now. You've felt nothing all day.*

Fraesh had been adamantly against the ox's bane and gifen tincture. He'd said too much could hurt my child. Squeezing my eyes closed, gulping in shallow breaths, I pressed two fingers to my forehead and prayed. *Don't do this to me, Nasheira. You are a mother too. Don't you dare.*

I didn't sleep, and I didn't feel the baby move all night or the next morning. When I crawled out from under the ula tree and stood, dizziness swept in so fast, I clung to the nearest tree to keep my feet under me. "Find some water," I gasped. "You just need water." I found a stream and filled my stomach and water bag both. Later, as I picked my way alongside one of the hunter's eastern traplines, I spotted a hare dangling from a loosed spring snare. It was dead, but still warm as I clutched it to cut it down. By midmorning, I found another—a live one still bucking and screaming as I closed in. I drew my knife and dispatched it quickly, frowning as I lashed it to my pack with the other carcass

Why are there still traps set if the camp moved on? One could have been missed, but two was no coincidence. Our hunters were diligent about filling in pit traps and gathering snares before they abandoned trails. Leaving an active line was dangerous and a waste. It also attracted wurms. No, our hunters had scoured their lines on the day before sacrifice. I'd *seen* them returning to camp with coiled nooses and bundles of stakes. Gatherers had been packing, loading vaiyas. My camp *had* been planning to leave. Besides, all of the traplines I'd crossed yesterday had been disabled. Why would the hunters leave one line live?

And then it hit me. The easterly line. This was Iva's trapline. Akrist's brother Jin had taken it over when she was murdered. If he'd set snares on the day of sacrifice, he'd been intending to return, to come north instead of going south with our camp. *He planned to come back. He intended to rescue his brother. Perhaps he already has.*

Hope bloomed in my chest. I followed the trail uphill, mind buzzing with possibilities. If Jin was with Akrist, he and the daeson were already free, clothed, with food in their bellies. Perhaps they hadn't even passed the night cold and alone. Maybe Jin had slipped away and found them right after they were cut. I was so tangled in my own hope-swelled thoughts, that I crested the hill and nearly walked right into a wall of white flesh.

Wurm. My mind blared the alarm seconds too late. I yelped and stumbled backward, drawing my knife.

Rearing taller than me, its feelers wriggled frantically, a harbinger of Pau. The pechi tree beside it bounced wildly.

My heel snagged on a root and I tumbled to the ground.

The wurm whipped toward me, teeth grinding.

Screaming, I scrambled back and smacked into a tree.

The wurm lunged and the pechi tree nearly doubled over, then shuddered as the fleshy creature recoiled.

It's trapped. My eyes focused on the taut cord anchoring the wurm to the tree. Several of its feelers bulged dark blue and flaccid below the cinched snare. *It sprung one of Jin's traps.* But the trap wasn't designed for wurms. If it struggled hard enough, could it break free?

The wurm's segmented flanks heaved. My eyes burned as the rancid smell of it overwhelmed me. I'd never seen a live one so close. I could feel it track me without eyes, feelers wafting scent toward its mouth, those endless circles of white teeth nesting in pallid grey gums. I wanted to run, but I was frozen, like a stupid hare under the scrutiny of a hawk.

The hares! You've got two bloodied, dead animals on you and it smells them. I stood with excruciating slowness as the wurm's breaths came faster and its giant body coiled. Twisting, I grasped the carcasses tied to my pack and slipped my knife under the cords holding them.

My legs ached to run spurred by my heart already bolting in my chest. I held the hares away from me.

The wurm lunged, faster than anything I'd ever seen. A sharp crack snapped through the bowed pechi tree. I hurled the carcasses toward the wall of white, spun and sprinted, wholly expecting to feel the clobber of a massive body against my back or the latch of poisoned teeth on my leg, but none of that came. As I pounded down the hill, I risked one glance backward and saw the creature at the summit, shattered treetop swinging free beneath its tentacles, both hares gripped in its mouth.

I didn't look back again, and I didn't stop running, not when my knees weakened, not when my lungs felt full of coals, not even when white spots snapped before my eyes. It was a deep cramp stabbing from my lower belly to my groin, intense enough to make me double over, that stopped me, miles from the encounter.

"Just a cramp," I wheezed. "Please, just a cramp."

And that is when the baby kicked, a quick but unmistakable jab under my ribs. "Oh Guides," I blubbered and curled around it. "Thank the Goddess." *I'm not alone. My baby lives.* Elated, exhausted laughter poured out of me until I was breathless and on my knees.

I wouldn't use the goddess's name in praise again for a very long time.

I searched for Akrist for five more days, through torrential rain and frigid nights, but I didn't find any sign of him, the daeson, or Jin. I never saw the wurm again either.

Though I stretched my rations and foraged as much as I was able, a week after the moons eclipsed, I had barely a day's food left. I could starve for the chance to rescue the man I loved—a man whose chance of survival grew dimmer with every day—or I could save the bright vigorous life that was growing and stretching against the boundaries of my belly each night.

When I turned my back on Akrist, that's what I tried to tell myself—I was doing it to save my baby. But that wasn't true. My reasons weren't noble. I didn't leave my mate for the sake of my unborn child. I just did what I'd always done when my life was threatened. I reverted to survival, like a desperate animal. Desperate animals left others behind, chewed off limbs they thought they couldn't live without. They saved themselves to live another day. No matter what the cost.

I chose to survive, no matter what the cost.
And I hated myself for it.

CHAPTER NINE

I T IS DIFFICULT TO appreciate the vastness of a world when you've spent most of your life in just a small part of it. Na-Jhalar's camp hadn't traveled often or fast, and we'd never reached a boundary in our vast landscape that we couldn't navigate around. We followed herds. Fresh territory continuously rolled out before us, only sparsely interspersed with other camps and aeni, but mornings always greeted us with the same faces, rituals, and familiarities. Seasons remained predictable. The world felt comfortingly small when you knew what to expect.

On dragonback, the absolute enormity of the land staggered me. After the second aeni group, we didn't encounter any other people for a week. We zigzagged southward, following arterial rivers, searching for aeni with daeson in tow. I had no idea how much ground a dragon could cover in a day of flying, but it felt immense. Dappled forests receded to large open plains. Sweeping, lush grasslands faltered into cracked and windswept deserts, and sand dunes rippled against the base of mountains so high, their tops still wore swathes of clean snow. In mere hours, we covered distances that would take the fastest aeni days to navigate on vaiyaback. The horizon opened towards us like an unfurling blanket, and I considered the months it would take an average camp to travel the same distances.

One afternoon, in mid flight, we heard it: the bugling call of another dragon far ahead of us.

Nardiri's wings froze into a stunned glide, and her head snapped toward the source of the call. She stretched all her senses toward the horizon. I held my breath, scrutinising the bright band of sky while Rowin clapped his hands over his ears at Nardiri's blasting return call.

Gold flashed above the horizon.

Nardiri lunged and Rowin's head smacked into my chest. The harness shifted back despite my grip on the handholds. "Careful," I gulped.

Another dragon! She pumped her wings and barked another deafening call.

The foreign dragon trilled back.

Slow down, I urged as we careened toward the newcomer. *You're carrying a child!*

Nardiri shed air as the pale gold dragon slalomed toward us.

I hadn't realised until then how much a dragon's company had skewed my memories of previous close encounters. When I'd been marked, the Guide splayed over me had looked similar to Nardiri. I recalled a mottled hide, missing teeth and pinholes scattered across swathes of her wing sail. Yet, regardless of all that, I remembered her as a magnificently deadly apparition, one that had dropped all of us to our knees.

But, as we closed on this newcomer dragon, a cold flutter pinched my stomach.

A female. Nardiri faltered at the appearance of the dragon, the strong rhythm of her wing beats wavering, dropping us momentarily in the sky as she scrambled to recover.

Up close, this dragon was not golden. Dull, flaking hide wrapped her thin frame. Emaciation had eaten at her until muscle melted into bones. Her hips jutted sharply, and strands of sinew braided her wings to her knobbed back. All of her joints looked swollen.

We shifted to a hover, close enough now to hear the poor dragon wheezing in between joyful hums.

A soft croon fluttered up Nardiri's throat, and the pale dragon craned her neck to gaze at Rowin and me. An odd, chuffing snort quivered past her nostrils.

What is she saying? Guides, she's so small.

Something is wrong with her. She only speaks in colour.

"Like a wurm." The skin between my shoulder blades crawled as I took in the dragon's sunken eyes and willow thin, wrinkled neck. "She's starving. Perhaps she hasn't learned how to hunt."

Then we will hunt for her.

Nardiri managed to communicate to the dragon a desire for her to land and wait for us. I wasn't sure if the strange dragon would listen, but she was waiting when we returned with a fat black ox in tow, as towering dark clouds swelled in the south. We skirted wide from the storm's bloating white edges, and delivered our offering.

As Nardiri nudged the ox toward her, the starving dragon froze, then struck with surprising speed, latching onto the ox's haunch with a wet crunch.

Rowin flinched and I pulled him closer.

The dragon growled and snapped at Nardiri, fanning her spindly wings, and baring her bloodied teeth.

"What's she doing?" I gaped.

She thinks the ox is her kill now, and that I mean to steal it. Nardiri's thoughts were tinged with orange confusion. She backed away and launched into the sky as the emaciated dragon stared after us, snarling. When she judged we were far enough, she gripped the ox in her jaws, hauled it into the air and, with great difficulty, winged away from us.

Are they all like that? Nardiri's aching thought trickled into my mind as she hung in the air, watching one of her own kind fleeing toward the bruised clouds. ***Hollow? Sick?***

"I don't know," I croaked.

Rowin shivered and whimpered as the wind whipped around us.

We have to go. The storm is coming. We can't follow her.

Updrafts sheered through the humid air to buffet us. Nardiri's wings righted our jagged flight with a thousand subtle, instinctive adjustments as Rowin and I clung to her, hair whipping our cheeks.

I pressed the snow guard up onto my forehead. Broad curtains of pink suctioned into the leading edge of the storm and hurtled up the central column before spilling over the mushroomed head and fading to faint purple. Cold plumes of blue from high behind the clouds rushed in to replace the ground-level pink currents. They coalesced and dove like a great school of fish, mashing into the ground amidst swathes of rain.

Hold tight. My dragon's clipped command reached my mind just as she tucked in her limbs and dove to evade a sheering blue edge laced with sleet.

My stomach scrambled into my throat. I curled over Rowin and a swarm of ice pellets blasted my back. Clawing the slotted wood visor back down over my eyes, I shielded the boy as best I could.

Nardiri shook herself, shedding tension like it was dust. Her emerald eye rolled away from the gathering storm with slow suspicion, and then her neck twitched beneath me. Faint yellow surprise spiked her next thoughts as she dipped her head, nostrils quivering. *There are people down there. Three of them.*

I straightened in the harness, squinting through the snow guard despite knowing full well that my eyes could make out nothing from this far up. *They were with the dragon?*

I don't think so. We are far from her now. They look to be hunting. They're following a gazelle herd.

We're not landing for hunters. There'll be no daeson with them. Are they aeni, or can you see a camp?

The hunters need to fly from this storm, too. It's bad. Nardiri wheeled back to the south, extending her loop to offer a broadside view of the front of the storm. Lightning fractured the flat underbelly of the clouds.

They can spot it as well as we can. If they don't know well enough to run, they are fools.

They are turning, look. Nardiri projected three green pin-points steering away from the skittish gazelle herd. They must be returning to their group. ***We could follow them back.***

They're moving right into the path of the storm. I frowned at the visceral air currents churning behind us.

If they are in the path of the storm, then so are the rest of their people. Nardiri's thoughts piqued yellow. ***What do humans do when a storm comes for them if they are not fast enough to fly from it?***

I stared back at the bloated, roiling cloud stretching its charged spine. The silent movement, the fact that not a breath of wind stirred the humid air around us made the scene wholly unsettling, like the whole world was holding its breath for the explosion of this storm. *We try to ride it out. We shelter. That's all we can do.*

In tents? Nardiri asked in alarm.

Or grass huts.

Oh, so much better. She grunted and pressed into a deep down stroke.

The storm swallowed the sun just before we overtook the three loping hunters. I watched as our wedge-shaped shadow was devoured by the billowing silhouette of mushroom clouds across the prairie. Just ahead, threading through the grassland, three tall figures with bronze skin and bare arms faltered to a trot, their faces upturned. With no shadow to betray us, and Nardiri slipping into a momentary curious glide, the hunters couldn't have seen or heard us coming, but they knew.

I shared my dragon's vision to verify it, but found, as I expected, none of the hunters' auras stood out from the rest. No one receptive here. Somehow, people could sense a dragon's proximity the way a thirsty human could sense water nearby. We had forgotten everything else about our Guides, but our bones still knew, still pulled at us when gold unfurled above us in the skies.

Nardiri trumpeted in alarm, swooped over the hunters, and sailed beyond them. She'd picked up the clumped green spread of the camp they stumbled toward on the horizon. The blackening storm stretched across the sky, its towering top clenched like a lumpy fist directly over the large settlement.

Warm wind fanned through the grass, sucked toward the storm. Nardiri struggled against the whipping gusts and dove for the centre of the camp.

They have no daeson. If they did, there'd be smaller huts to the north. I pointed and braced for landing, scanning the shocked faces below me.

We need to make them move. Nardiri punctuated her observation with a staccato bark that brought people streaming from their shelters to drop before her.

What do I tell them?

Tell them to run! The dragon's gaze rolled toward the storm.

Hair prickled on the back of my neck as I twisted in the harness to take in the bruised sky from ground level. A mottled purple base ploughed toward us, churning like water draining from an unplugged clay pot. Flares of pale green lightning spidered across the surface of the storm, spearing deep into the column. Resonant, grinding thunder rushed toward us like an avalanche. Air currents muddied and mixed, a smeared painting, pressing into my eyes like an afterimage. It looked like death. Deep, dark, and immensely unavoidable.

I grunted through clenched teeth, turning back to the camp and thrusting my finger at the storm. "You're right in its path!"

But every person who'd spilled out of their huts had toppled prostrate before Nardiri. "Put us down," I growled. Yanking at the harness slipknot, I grabbed Rowin's arm. He flinched and pulled away, but we were already sliding out of the slack ropes as Nardiri crouched down. Skidding down her arm, I pulled the boy with me and we tumbled to the ground.

I gripped a slender forearm and yanked a wide-eyed woman to her feet. "Get up! Go." I bellowed in her ear. Dragging Rowin past her, I grabbed a broad-shouldered man by the front of his tunic. When he shied away from me, I shouted, "You need to run."

The man blinked at me like I was headless. Several others surrounding him peered past their clasped hands with white-rimmed eyes full of fear and awe.

Jerking at the collar of my shirt, I exposed my scar, slapped at it with an open hand, and advanced on two women, an elder, and a youth. "A Speaker tells you to run! Run!" The two cowered at my feet, screaming prayers into the wind. Several others farther out tottered to their feet and stood swaying like paralysed vaiyas. Rowin shuddered and wailed in my grip. I drew a breath in frustration. Of course... why would they pay attention to a Speaker when a Guide was standing before them?

Nardiri growled, pressing up to her full height. Screams burst out of the camp's terrified supplicants as she lifted her foot to step over them before flanking the immobile group and flaring her wings wide. Then she blasted them with an ear-splitting, outraged roar.

They scattered before her like leaves. After that, it felt strikingly similar to herding prey. I hoisted Rowin under my arm and headed off the stragglers that broke from the group to duck back into huts while Nardiri drove the main group scrambling away from the storm. We'd just hauled a man clutching a stack of clay pots out of his doorway when I saw something from out of the corner of my eye. Curls. A dark-robed, slender figure with coiled hair haloing her face darted between two huts.

I froze.

Rowin bit my hand and wormed out of my grip, eyes wild with fear.

I grabbed for him, but he darted away. He'd go to Nardiri; he felt safest with her. Turning, I sprinted for the woman, mouth dry and gaze fixed to her back as she streaked past huts with door flaps streaming open like flags. Closing in on her, I gripped her shoulder, throwing her off balance. I caught her as she reeled.

The woman clawing to escape my frozen grip had red hair, an oval face, and watery blue eyes. *Not Yara*. Lightning washed out my vision as she jerked away from me.

Akrist! Nardiri's call boomed in my head.

A fat raindrop slapped my cheek. Another icy drop pattered my shoulder. I blinked, staggered, and recovered, legs sluggish, bones icy. I caught sight of the cyclone, fully formed and boring into the grasslands, shedding coils of dust and clumps of dirt like a snake shrugging out of its old skin.

Akrist!

I couldn't see the dragon, but I sensed her moving toward me from and stumbled to meet her. A sudden sheet of rain drove into the ground like a volley of pebbles. Nardiri's head materialised out of the dark as she loped toward me, wings pressed tight to her back.

Her foreclaw extended and I lifted my arms, coughing as she scooped me off my feet.

"Where is Rowin?" I bellowed over the descending hiss of cold rain. *Oh Guides, I left him.*

He's ahead. I herded most of them into one group. Nardiri's senses filled my mind, and I saw the green congregation, massed and milling. Two pinpoints broke from the group and weaved back toward us. Nardiri roared in frustration and unfurled her wings. *Why do they keep going back?*

They think the huts are safe. I scrubbed rain out of my eyes and spotted two people as they skidded to a shocked stop, walled in by Nardiri's wings. She charged at them, teeth snapping, and they fell backwards, spearheads and lumpy packets of food tumbling from their fingers.

Is that everyone? Nardiri dumped me into the midst of the screeching crowd. Hands clutched at me as I slipped in the mud. Far above me, the dragon's great head snapped back toward the huts.

Two more, she relayed, pale flank flashing as she spun away from us in the dark. *Small. Children, I think. I'll bring them. Keep the rest together.*

Linked to the dragon's vision, I maintained a semblance of sight as peeling rain engulfed us. Screaming rose in my ears. A small green aura darted away from the group; it had to be Rowin. The press of this frantic crowd would be choking him as much as it was me. I shoved through a blockade of petrified limbs. Breaking past the edge of the group, I loped ahead. My hand raked down a slick shirt back and snagged on a small belt. Hauling back, I caught Rowin's elbow in the chest.

I held him tightly as lightning blinded us and he howled and flailed in my grip. "It's all right. I'm here, Rowin. Stay with me."

His nails scratched at my cheek. Something heavy slammed into my shoulder. I yelped, stumbled, and felt ice on my overcoat where I'd been hit. Another fist-sized projectile pelted past with a low whistle, bouncing off into the grass. "Mother of Yurri," I hissed, lunging back toward the crowd and curling over Rowin. *Nardiri! Hail! It's big!*

I'm coming.

Another low whizzing sound, followed by a sharp scream as the hailstone struck someone in the crowd.

"Hands up!" I bellowed. "Protect your heads. Close together now." I pressed back into the frenzied fray with Rowin still wailing and kicking. Smothering sobs and heavy breathing engulfed us. A pounding, rolling wave of hail cut toward us. Ethereal lightning sprayed the sky, and I caught a flash of gold—Nardiri pounding toward us with two bundles of cloth cradled in her foreclaws. Children. The crowd erupted into a communal squeal, stumbling over each other as my dragon skidded into us, the curtain of her wings raking over our heads.

"Under her!" I hollered, but the crowd needed no direction now. They clogged together, elbows jamming against soft stomachs, feet stomping on toes as they pressed against the dragon's ribs. She drew them beneath her like a mother bird fanning over her chicks.

Huge hail stones bounded into the grass surrounding us. I heard the hollow thud of them striking Nardiri's back. In the snaking flashes of lightning, the membrane of her wings shuddered under the barrage.

Rowin went slack in my arms, still panting but spent. My hand clutched at the dragon's ankle as a wash of blue flooded my mind, and her strangled grunts reverberated through me.

Are you hurt?

It stings. She shuddered and dropped lower.

Fingers pressed against foreheads. Palms pushed up against Nardiri's wings. Everywhere, the stifling press of wet bodies and harsh exhalations. All around me, the whites of eyes flashing behind ribbons of plastered hair. The howling chorus of screams crescendoed until I realised that the sound wasn't coming from the people anymore, but the wind screeching around us, trying to pluck us out of the dragon's embrace.

I screwed my eyes shut as Nardiri transmitted her vision of the storm. A muddied, massive cyclone of colour coalesced in my mind. The funnel carved toward us, shredding everything in its path.

Oh Guides. "It's coming right at us!"

The screech of the cyclone intensified.

It will turn, she shot back.

Despite my closed eyes, I saw the dense base of the cyclone swallowing the camp's huts, chewing toward us like a massive wurm.

Nardiri! I clutched at her leg, fingernails digging into hide.

It will turn! She roared.

And then it did. Halfway through devouring the huts, the cyclone shied away and swung to the left, raining down clods of grass, shredded panelling and hunks of wood in its wake.

Nardiri's claws ploughed deep into the dirt, her wings shivering over us. I didn't realise the cyclone had dissolved until my ears popped, and the distraught keening of my dragon reached me.

There were three, she wailed. ***Three I didn't get to in time.***

CHAPTER TEN

W E COULDN'T FIND THE hunters. From the air, the fish-hooked shape of the cyclone's path looked like a flayed wound. Raw soil opened up to a world of debris and scattered heaps of storm-harvested grass. With no trees to obscure our sight, I had assured Nardiri we'd be able to find them, if even just to return their bodies to their shocked families. We'd seen them, after all, not far from their camp before the storm struck.

I had wanted to leave Rowin behind to spare him from what we might find. But he screamed when the clouds cleared and I tried to mount the dragon without him. He sat ahead of me now, flinching every time my leg brushed his, hugging Nardiri's neck like he could become a part of her if he squeezed tightly enough.

*I should have picked them up when we first saw them.
I could have carried them,* Nardiri lamented, shuddering as
we crossed the bared lip of the cyclone's corridor yet again.

I patted her twitching neck and Rowin imitated me. *You
couldn't have known—*

I did know! I knew the storm was bad. She shook her head
hard, and I ducked as her crest cut the air above us.

You saved twenty-eight people, Nardiri.

A long exhale bled out of her and silence settled like cold grey
sludge between us.

How did you know the storm would be so bad?

*I felt it. And I knew the cyclone would turn before it
happened. I saw it in the wind and when I did, every
fibre in me screamed to rescue those people. It was a need,
Akrist, just as strong as the urge I felt to mark your
receptive brother.*

What does it mean?

*Your father told you that dragons used to guide your
people away from storms. I think I'm meant to do that
just as much as I'm meant to mark Speakers.*

She leaned into a slow loop and craned her neck to the east. *I
see the camp's vaiyas. We should bring them back, at least,
if I cannot bring them their hunters.*

Rowin hummed and picked at the harness ropes with distracted fingers.

By the time we'd ushered the agitated vaiyas back to their
half-crushed camp, the horizon had swallowed the sun. Dark-

ness spread over the prairie like an ink spill, compelling us to spend the night. Rowin clung to Nardiri and fell asleep in the crook of her arm. Guides, I wished I could do the same, but my restless body longed for motion. I helped scavenge through wreckage by torchlight, making hasty repairs to the remaining huts so that we could house the group's exhausted children. When we were finished, the rest of us tucked under Nardiri's wings to stare into a single, roaring hearth fire.

The elders in the group called Nardiri "Mother," stroked her extended wings, and uncapped precious pots of scented junab to dab onto areas where the hail had bruised her. The dragon was a living, breathing Speaker's hut in the centre of the camp, a golden refuge shifting against the glow of the fire.

The camp's storyteller, the red-haired woman I'd mistaken for Yara, at last asked the questions itching everyone's minds. "Who are you? How did you come to find us?" Her tired, pale blue eyes scrutinised my face. Her voice sounded like crumbling leaves.

I turned a chunk of blood sausage in my fingers. The dusty bite in my mouth wouldn't moisten no matter how much I chewed, but this camp—these people sifting through the waste of their homes—had offered it and I would finish every bite. Swallowing with difficulty, I answered, "Your hunters saved you. The dragon saw that they were in the path of the storm, and we followed them back, overtaking them in our haste to warn you. Please believe me, we meant to save them too."

Had we? I'd been so focused on my own interests, I'd pushed Nardiri right past the three hunters.

"Of course." The woman's face froze as she digested my words, saw my furtive glance at Nardiri, and comprehended. She leaned past me to press a palm to the dragon's shaking forearm, and offered a heartening smile through fresh tears. "Of course you meant to save them, Mother. They would be honoured to know they led our saviours to us."

I am not her Mother. Tell her I have no ties to your goddess.

I swallowed, but didn't have the heart to relay her words.

"And you..." The red-haired woman pointed to my chest, and then my cheek. "You are a man with many marks, Speaker. The stories they must hold! Tell me about yourself, if you would."

"My name is Na-daeson Akrist." I enunciated my titles slowly. They felt like water and oil together.

Her cheeks puffed with a short, barking laugh. She leaned back with raised eyebrows. "That is not something you hear at every hearth! Go on."

"Nardiri found me at the last eclipse and recognised my mark." I ran a thumb over the pocked edges of the scar where it flared past my collarbone. "Our bond saved me." I turned to Rowin. Relaxed in sleep, he looked like a regular child, not a haggard survivor of sacrifice. "Most daeson are not so fortunate."

The woman nodded slowly "That I should live to see this..." Trailing off, she craned her neck to take in the vast wing of Nardiri above us. "I thought the stories of bonded Speakers and dragons were only elders' tales."

I allowed a small smile to touch my lips. "We'll make a fine tale, won't we, storyteller?"

"Call me Ana." She tugged at the beads in her hair. "May the Guides mark your skies, Ana."

Ana

"Nasheira's peace with you, Na-daeson Akrist, and Mother Nardiri." She pressed two fingers to her forehead. "Are there other pairs such as yourselves?"

"Not as far as I know. But we are seeking out Speakers who can be matched with dragons of their own, both those already marked and those yet undiscovered."

"Perhaps we could help you with your search. Are any among us worthy enough to mark?"

I sagged at the hope in her voice. There was no one receptive here. "All of you are worthy, but it is not for me to decide. Nardiri says—" I cleared my throat, breaking eye contact with the storyteller and choosing my next words carefully. "She says you are all strong, but she doesn't think any here are able to bear the mark yet."

She nodded, then slapped her knee. "That is a disappointment, but still, it is good to see a sign of hope in this wretched world. We will share your story. And we summer with camps led by Speakers already marked. Shall we send them to you?"

The proposition terrified me. I didn't want our story shared. I wanted to quietly steal daeson and bring them to safety. I wanted to control who Nardiri marked next so that the world was not overrun by broken leaders like Na-Jhalar. The idea of other Speakers flocking to us, strangers who had presided over the sacrificial ceremonies of their own daeson a mere half a year ago, made my skin crawl. "We'd appreciate an audience with any Speaker who wishes to seek us," I answered, "But while we are on the move, I don't know how they'd find us. We fly too fast."

"I understand, but surely you realise how quickly followers will amass. Your dragon is the closest thing to Nasheira most of us will ever see. You'll be drowning in worshipers soon." She clicked her beads against her teeth, watching me with unsettlingly shrewd eyes. Something about the subtle upturn of her lips irritated me.

I scratched the back of my neck. "I sense you have a solution for me, wise Ana."

"I do." Her smile quickened, her pale eyes bright. "But like all good things, it involves a story."

I swallowed the sharp ache in my throat as the sudden jovial image of my aunt Iva flooded my mind. Mother of Yurrii, I missed her. Settling further on my haunches, I crossed my arms over my knees. "I'm all ears."

Ana leaned toward me. "You may not believe it, but I once had a secret lover, a lovely ani with blond hair and eyes like coals." She waited for me to respond, but when I only stuffed the last of the sausage in my mouth, she chuckled quietly and carried on. "We rode different winds, like two seeds. How were two young drifters on separate paths to ever find each other?"

"I have no idea," I spoke around the crumbling meat in my mouth.

The storyteller rocked forward on her toes. "It's simple, Na-daeson Akrist. Nasheira has already given you time keepers. Use them."

I frowned. Nardiri's gaze turned toward us, curiously appraising our quiet conversation. "I'm not sure I understand."

She dropped her beaded hair and pointed a bony finger straight up. "The moons. My bronzed boy and I would arrange to meet when Yurrii was full. We'd pick a landmark and agree to meet there the next time the small moon hung full-faced in the sky. It worked until that son of a wurm left me standing like a fool under the moons two months in a row." She shrugged, a small, self-deprecating smile pressed to her lips. "I can't see why it wouldn't work the same for a Speaker with a devoted following. You pick the landmark. We'll spread your story."

It is a good plan. Nardiri brightened.

Other than my nagging fear, I could think of no reason to object to the idea, so I sighed and gave in. "You're brilliant, Ana."

She grinned before sobering and glancing at Rowin. "Will you take him with you on your travels? He looks as wind-burned and scrawny as a mountain tree. Has he been eating?"

"He eats as often as I do." I bristled.

Ana looked me up and down. "Not nearly enough then. That boy needs parenting."

"He's a daeson," I said bitterly.

"I should think daeson would need love most of all." Ana's voice was unexpectedly sincere.

"An odd thing to say for a camp who isn't sheltering any daeson at all." Nobody cared about what the spawn of Pau needed. "What are you playing at, Ana?"

Her eyes shone. "We haven't sheltered *daeson* for a long time. We've plenty of eldest sons though." Rolling up her sleeve, she showed me the mark on the inside of her wrist, a circular tattoo around a raised bump of skin. Ana's tattoo was thick and faded with age, but the colour was unmistakable. Only healers knew the recipe for the brilliant blue ink, and they guarded it fiercely; only women who'd sacrificed their daeson to Nasheira were allowed to wear it. My neck prickled.

"I was very young when they took him from me," Ana rasped with tears in her eyes. "I tried to hang on to him, but they took him anyway. He was so sweet and small. He looked nothing like the evil sons of Pau I'd been warned about. He was just a baby. I swore I'd make it right." She let her sleeve fall back over the tattoo and beckoned to a girl with long, loose brown hair who couldn't have been more than sixteen years of age. "Come here, Serin. Show him your wrist."

I flushed at the odd request and the girl balked. Women often showed men their daeson tattoos when they wanted to bed them. It was supposed to be alluring, the opportunity to share each other without the worry of conceiving an unwanted daeson. "That won't be necessary," I choked.

"Don't be daft." Ana wrinkled her nose. "Serin, show him."

The girl tentatively held out her wrist. A bright, fresh daeson tattoo stood out on her dark skin.

"Have you borne an eldest son?" Ana asked her, and when the girl's eyes widened and her gaze flicked to me, the storyteller nodded. "Go on, you can tell him the truth."

"No. I haven't borne any children, Speaker." She dipped her head in a quick bow.

"My mother was a healer." Ana waved the girl off and turned back to me. "I was meant to be one too. She taught me how to make the ink before she died, but I found healing didn't suit me." Ana sniffed. "When our camp's Speaker died, we never sought out another, and I have been giving the mark to any woman old enough to bear a child ever since. Any woman who wants it."

"Most people would consider that to be a high sin, Ana." I spoke in a low voice, brushing a finger over my scarred cheek. "If another camp catches word of what you are doing here, they'll overrun this place, brand you all and take all your sons."

She pinned me with an intense gaze. "Then they mustn't catch word of it."

"You just told *me*, a stranger you've only just met."

"And you shared your past, Na-daeson Akrist. You have a dilemma. You'll be collecting Speakers and daeson both—"

"I never said I was collecting daeson."

She pursed her lips. "Of course you are. What else would a man with your history and your means do? Now, I don't imagine the first group will appreciate the second. Perhaps it would be best to keep them separate for now. Have your followers congregate at your landmark and bring your daeson to me."

"Why would you do this?"

"Nasheira has owed me a son for a long time." Ana smiled slowly. "Now she will repay me in multiples. Your eldest boys are welcome here. Just find me a landmark before you fly, Na-daeson Akrist."

Sweet Nasheira, what had I just set in motion?

—YARA—

Fraesh once told me that watching a birthing was like witnessing a storm from the edge of the water, waves scouring the shore over and over again, exposing raw soil, drawing everything into its depths. In the end, for all its electric power—the storm unearthed something so fresh, fragile, and new, something the pliant banks had cradled for so long, that those lucky enough to see it crowning felt privileged just to witness it. He'd called childbirthing "beautiful."

But he was a liar.

There was nothing beautiful about this. It was all screams, sweat, and blood, and when you were experiencing it yourself, alone in the woods, it felt more like dying than delivering life.

The first contractions woke me in the middle of the night, as Pau rose half full on the horizon ahead of Yurri. It was easy to be calm then, despite knowing what was coming, because I had prepared as best as I could. I had collected enough herbs for Fraesh in the past to know which medicinal plants were valuable. So I had gathered enough before winter to trade with the first aeni I'd met for a blanket, a flint fire starter, and a decent supply of food. But the food was long gone, and I was alone now.

Shelter in an aeni tent cost more than I was willing to pay, and, with my naked wrists, I refused to risk my child in a camp. If I bore a son, the healer would take my child from me as soon as the cord was cut. No respectable camp would let a mother raise her own daeson. So, I'd prepared to give birth alone.

I slept as much as I could that first night, noting the position of the moons every time a twinge in my stomach woke me, trying to guess the time between contractions. In the morning, I walked. I gathered bundles of firewood to keep the wurms away and enough water to last me well into the next day. I stoked my fire through the afternoon, paced, cleaned my knife and set it beside my water bag, clean rags, and a cord to tie off the umbilical cord. The contractions came like Fraesh said they would, in waves, small ones that seemed manageable until lack of sleep intervened.

Twenty two hours later, those waves had worn me to the bone. I'd misjudged how much firewood I would need and, while the blaze had lasted through the night, my fire crumbled by mid-morning. I squatted beside its smokey ruins, legs too weak from cramps to walk, hair slicked to my face, and sweat dripping from my nose despite the crusted snow surrounding me. My legs trembled. My lips were chapped and bleeding from biting them. Every contraction felt like someone setting hooks deep into the raw nerves braiding my spine and tearing them out through my lower back. But I was too terrified to cry out.

There were wurms in the area. I'd seen their tracks yesterday and knew how hungry the horrid things grew during the scant winter season. With my fire dead, there was nothing to keep them off me if they found me, and if I screamed, they were sure to congregate along with any other monstrous soul attracted by the howls of a vulnerable woman. Guides, how I longed to release the tension of those spasms ripping through me. How I ached to feel Akrist's strong hand gripping mine, his lips kissing my forehead, his calloused fingers sweeping my curls from it. I wanted to hear him tell me everything was going to be all right, that this was not going to last forever. The pain would end. I needed to fall against his broad chest and believe him. Believe he wasn't dead. I squeezed my eyes closed and fell into that fantasy.

He's right here protecting me, and it will all be done soon.

It was the only thing that carried me through the agony.

When it came time to push, the pain receded and relief swept in to take its place. My body bore down like it had done this a thousand times before. I reached between my legs and felt the baby crowning and then slipping back up into the canal, cradled in the waves of my own muscles, every push nudging them closer to birth, every relaxation holding them in. I grunted past the burning tension as the head emerged, wadded my skirts beneath me and reached down to help my baby into the world. One contraction later, their shoulders twisted and they slipped out, all gushing wetness and waving limbs.

Sinking onto my backside, I pulled the quivering infant over my arm and cleared their mouth as I'd seen Fraesh do. I massaged their back. One wet cough and then a tiny indignant cry shredded across the brisk afternoon air. Tears filled my eyes. Bright reflections winked off the crusted snow around us, a million tiny suns. Winter birds chirruped in the trees. I blinked and refocused on the umbilical cord pulsating between us. Then I took a deep breath and turned my baby over to look between their feebly kicking legs.

And I cried.

PART TWO

"SPEAKER"

CHAPTER ELEVEN

I SQUATTED DOWN TO Rowin's level, but the boy turned his head to avoid my gaze. "There are other children in this camp. And Ana has promised me she'll feed you far better than I have."

His nostrils flared. He shook his head and blinked rapidly.

"Nardiri and I will be back soon. Other boys need us to bring them here so they can have a home too. "

He could come. He's light. Nardiri crooned from behind me.

We are not bringing him near those who would murder him.

The daeson darted toward Nardiri. I caught him by the wrist and he crumpled, wailed, and landed hard on his rear end.

That's when I noticed the bruises. Mottled bands of blue ringing his arm where I'd held him yesterday and dragged him through the storm. Mother of Yurrii, had I gripped him so hard? "Rowin. I'm sorry," I gulped, pointing at the bruises.

He snorted and pulled his sleeve down as Nardiri stepped forward to let him pat her nose. We wallowed in awkward silence, avoiding eye contact.

"Could you look after these for me?" I finally said, reaching into my bag and pulling out the tavi set we'd carved on the night he couldn't sleep. "I don't want to lose them. I'd like a rematch when I get back." I held the pieces out and waited. Nardiri nudged him forward as he stood and took them. He backed away again, like a wild animal snatching food.

"Thank you," I said and he hurled the game pieces at my face as hard as he could.

One of the wooden tokens sailed past my ear, another struck my cheek hard. Rowin tried to dart past me, but I hooked an arm around his waist before he could escape. He howled, twisted, and raked his nails down my face hard enough to draw blood. "Stop it," I said.

Pounding both hands against my chest, Rowin broke from me and tumbled backward. Breath sawed out of him, and his eyes narrowed to slits as he snarled. He stabbed a finger toward my chest before drawing an s-shape down his flushed cheek and thumping his chest. He did it twice more before I finally grasped what he was saying.

"I have *not* cast you out!" I dabbed at my stinging lip and frowned at the blood on my fingers. "These are good people."

He bent, spat on the ground between us, and turned from me and stomped away. That was our goodbye.

We had flown for less than an hour when we saw it, half-buried, jutting proudly from the flat grasslands as though Nasheira had dropped it there for our purpose. I peered past a wing tip as Nardiri banked towards the massive, erratic boulder. No, boulder was an inappropriate term. This was a slab of some far away mountain, all sharp, flat planes and cream-coloured layers ribboned in rust. It was long, three or four times as long as Nardiri, and wedge-shaped, collapsed toward a fractured, crumbling centre. It looked like some petrified fallen sentinel, broken-backed but resolute, granite-willed against the wear of wind and rain.

"It's enormous," I murmured as Nardiri landed, and the formation's shadow swallowed us. I slid out of my harness and approached it with the wonder of a toddler. Pressing a palm to its cool surface, I ran my fingers down a vein of grainy, glossy pink. *I wonder where it came from?*

Nardiri sniffed the stone.

A pale mark on her chest caught my eye. "Are you hurt?" Stepping past her neck, I ran a hand along a pair of parallel channels marring her golden hide.

The dragon lifted a wing and twisted her head. ***No. It itches. My belly and legs itch too.*** She lifted a forearm to expose more ragged grooves blanketing the round of her belly.

"Stretch marks." I ran a finger down a thin-skinned tear. *They mean you are growing. Fast. Stand up a moment.*

Nardiri complied. I ducked between her forearms and looked up at her chest. It was several heads higher than I remembered, but I didn't have a clear marker of her original height. *Guides,* I shook my head. *You grow so fast, sweet bird. Five weeks out of the cocoon?*

Striding to her back leg, I squinted and noted several bands of thin hide on her mid thigh. "I should have been oiling you. Your poor hide needs something to help it stretch and keep it soft."

The salve they put on my wings. It smelled awful, but it felt good.

Junab. I gripped the harness ropes and hoisted myself onto Nardiri's shoulders. *It is expensive, but I will bathe you in junab if that's what you'd like.*

This is a good landmark. She tipped her head back to the reclining formation as she gained height to wing back toward the broken camp.

"It's perfect."

We stopped long enough to give Ana directions to the meeting place and its description.

She nodded once, her face streaked with dirt after scavenging through the cyclone-torn remnants of her camp. "Yurrii's full moon is only five nights away and we both have a fair bit to work on." She winked. "I'll tell your admirers you intend to meet them the full moon after next."

"Where's the boy?" I scanned over Ana's shoulder for Rowin.

"He ran," she shrugged.

"He *what*?"

Nardiri stiffened beneath me.

"Don't look at me like that, Speaker," she chuckled softly. "Did you expect him to do otherwise? I've a hunter on vaiyaback following him; we'll bring the boy home when he gets tired. Sometimes there's nothing better for anger than exhausting oneself."

Nardiri's senses peeled away from us, revealing two humans and one vaiya aura not far from camp. *He seems safe. Tell her what I told you.*

"Nardiri says there'll be storms that follow the same path as the first. She says to relocate further north, beyond the bend in the river. The big storms will divert before the river valley."

"Thank you, Mother." Ana bobbed her head and pressed two fingers to her forehead. "Nasheira's Peace with you."

I re-checked the knots on my harness and smiled down at the gaunt storyteller. "May the Guides mark your skies, Ana. Thank you for looking after him." Her red hair was the last thing I saw as the half-hollowed camp dropped away beneath us.

At dusk on the eve of Yurrii's full moon, we came across our first wurms.

Nardiri announced their presence in a reverent voice pricked with curiosity. *There are five of them.* She cocked her head and crabbed sideways to shed elevation. I swallowed against a heaving protest from my stomach. The queasy sensation gripped me long after the dragon's descent curved into a glide.

They feel different from other animals, Nardiri observed. Her great head tracked toward a tangle of thick brambles. The snarled wood looked like jetsam floating on a lake of silver seed-head grass.

I pursed my lips as the oily smell slithered past my nostrils and tumbled into cold coils in my stomach. *Don't fly so low.*

I would never hurt a hatchling.

I leaned low over her neck, squinting to catch the first glimpse of pallid white even as the stench made my eyes water. *It's not the hatchlings' health I'm concerned about. Are they hungry?*

Yes, she replied. Through a gap in the brambles flashed the pale yellow coils of a wurm's back. Nardiri drew up into a silent hover so quickly, my shoulder slammed into her neck. I grunted at the impact, then refocused my gaze on the bulbous, white flesh below. It was a slight wurm, smaller than Nardiri had been when she'd found me. Cold repulsion twisted beneath my ribs. I bit my tongue, both in surprise and in a bid to withhold the unflattering response from the dragon's attention.

Did I stink like this?

I clapped a hand over my mouth and nose as Nardiri manoeuvred to get a better view. *Not to me.*

White tentacles burst upward like froth, sending shards of wood careening toward us. A large wurm stretched skyward, feelers grasping spasmodically, jawless mouth quivering. I clutched at the harness, and Nardiri winged backwards with a strangled grunt. Three more faceless heads whipped up at the sound. Black, oily liquid clotted their feelers as they poised to strike, rearing their thick, segmented bodies.

They know we are here now. My neck prickled.

I looked like that? Nardiri snorted. The wurms jerked at the noise and the largest one bunched and surged toward us with impossible speed, slamming sideways into the sharp hold of the crunching brambles. Black serrations opened like angry mouths on its side where the thorns had slashed it.

The wurms fastened onto the side of their fallen comrade. Seconds passed as their feelers dabbed at its wounds and scrambled over its blood-smeared skin. Then they devoured it. I was disgusted, but also curious. The wurms had examined the body of their prey before eating it, looking for something. A scar, perhaps? Did that mean Speakers were safe from consumption?

Nardiri's shock swam through me. For long seconds, we hovered in air thick with the stench of wurm blood and the sounds of tearing, grinding, and slurping.

The dragon shuddered deeply and turned away from the roiling scene of black smudged on white.

"You weren't like that," I said. "You were warm, comforting. You saved me."

I attacked my own kind.

"To protect me."

A long exhale bled out of her as she set her shoulders and settled into a glide away from the disturbing scene. Just below my feet, a grainy layer of clouds rushed by and my Guide's flickering shadow skimmed over it like a wraith.

I understand now.

Understand what?

You said you only bonded with me because someone tied you to a tree and you couldn't escape. If you'd had a choice, you would have killed me instead.

"Nardiri." I deflated as the word pressed past my teeth. "I didn't know."

They're repulsive.

I blinked.

A shiver rippled through the dragon's shoulders. *I cannot fathom the idea that I will lay eggs, and my hatchlings will look—will act—like that. I understand now, why your people kill them. Even if I lay my mark on a hundred Speakers, what in the wide sky would convince them to stand and accept the bond of my appalling offspring?*

Shaking my hands out of the handholds, I hugged Nardiri's neck. One of the bony ridges along her spine jabbed me in the chest. I ignored it and pressed further into the embrace. "*We* will." I gulped. "We'll convince them."

CHAPTER TWELVE

W E FOUND A CAMP just before dawn; my eyes were immediately drawn to the pair of diminutive daeson shelters on the settlement's northern border. I pressed my tongue to the roof of my mouth and stared unblinkingly at those huts until my eyes watered. The moons had eclipsed less than half a year ago during my sacrifice, and already it was starting again, the horrible cycle of shunning and culling children.

Red crackled through my mind, interrupting my thoughts. *Someone receptive?* My stomach dropped.

Two, Nardiri answered and her need pressed into me.

It took every fibre of control in my body to resist the impulse to dive into the sleeping circle of huts, tear through the shelters, and close the connection between us. The scar on my chest burned, and an urgent hunger pulled at my bones and crawled under my skin. Saliva filled my mouth and my heart quivered in my chest.

Sweet Nasheira, it ached like a raw nerve, like the hole a knocked-out tooth left behind, like breathing in without ever exhaling. I'd felt something similar when I'd been marked, but not to this scale. This felt like the seconds before lightning struck, electric and unavoidable. No wonder Nardiri hadn't been able to resist marking Dero.

"Hold," I grunted. *We will not tear them from their bedrolls.*

Nardiri hissed, but checked her descent. ***I will wake them, then.***

She inhaled to roar and I pinned my heels against her neck and barked, "No." *Control yourself.*

She growled.

Let me gauge these people first. Please, trust that I have our best interests at heart. I swallowed against the sickening hunger. *Wait for the sun to come up, at least. It won't be long.*

Nardiri snorted and tossed her head in frustration.

We suffered through the awful, itching anticipation for what felt like hours. As the blush of dawn rose on the horizon, I felt almost as frantic as the dragon.

The southernmost hut.

A woman with dark skin and plaited grey hair stretched in the open doorway before walking toward a tall stand of grass bordering the dwelling. Her stride was the patient mince of an elder. I turned my face as she hiked up her skirts to relieve herself.

She sees us. I can mark her now? Nardiri pleaded.

Not yet. Give her some privacy. I sighed.

Can humans not urinate without privacy?

Most prefer it.

She's finished.

To her credit, the woman didn't cry out at the sight of us. She dropped her gathered skirts and pressed two fingers to her forehead. For a moment she just stood there, wide-stanced, face upturned and squinting. Then she beckoned us with a lazy wave.

Nardiri landed with hardly a rustle of grass. I pinned her with a firm thought. *Do not make a move without me, understand?* She stiffened, tail twitching, mind swimming in red, but she crouched obediently. I undid my harness straps, slid down her side, and strode toward the lone elder.

"Nasheira's peace with you," she croaked, still staring past me.

"Can I speak with your leader or your council?" I asked.

The woman pursed her lips, and they caved in over empty gums. "Always wanted to see a Guide up close. Not quite how I imagined the encounter in my head, though."

I repeated my words slowly, in case the woman was hard of hearing. "Your *council*, can you take me to them?"

She hobbled closer, brushed the end of her thick braid against her chin, and gazed back at me with unreadable eyes. "I expect they're still asleep." She matched my exaggerated articulation. "All got bigger bladders than mine."

You are sure she is receptive?

Yes, Nardiri snapped and impatiently shared her sight. A virulent green aura haloed the woman.

She is so old.

Why does that matter?

I looked back at her over my shoulder. *You said you want strong pairs for your hatchlings, and this one looks like the next brisk wind could take her to Nasheira.*

"You're speaking with her, aren't you?" The old woman's voice lowered to a reedy whisper. "What's she saying?"

"She wants to mark you," I replied evenly.

"Me?" she blurted.

"Yes."

Her cheek twitched. "Your dragon wants to mark me. As a Speaker?"

"She does."

The elder held my stare for an uncomfortably long time and then, without warning, she threw her head back and guffawed loudly. Spit flew past her lips. Her cackling laughter cut through the quiet air, and I stepped back as I heard complaints from several huts.

"Me!" she gasped between peals of laughter, "Your dragon wants to mark me? And you wait until this morning, when I'm midway through watering the grass, to land as pretty as you please and tell me that I'm to be a Speaker. Ah!" She doubled over, gulping for air. "Where've you been all my life?"

Half-clothed people spilled out of huts. A few of them screamed when they spotted Nardiri, most fell to the dewy ground in prayer. The thin elder before me continued to whoop with laughter the entire time, hands fiddling with her thick braid at the base of her neck.

"Is there a leader among you?" I called to the gathering crowd.

"There is now!" she shouted and slapped her knee.

Nardiri shifted behind me. The old woman's laughter muted as the dragon's shadow fell over her.

The other receptive one is in that hut.

Clearing my throat, I addressed our audience. "Nasheira's peace with you. We didn't mean to shock you with our arrival, but this Guide has detected Speakers among you, and she wishes permission to mark them as such."

"Who are you?"

My eyes focused on a man with sagging eyes and thin lips.

"I am Na-Akrist." I pointed over my shoulder. "This Guide and I are bonded, and she wants to mark this woman…" I turned to the still smiling elder.

"Venda. Name's Venda."

Venda

"Venda." I pointed at the hut Nardiri had indicated. "And whoever is in that hut. My Guide wishes to mark them both."

A round-faced woman sat up, her hand slipping from her forehead. "My son! You're going to mark my son?" Her chin quivered.

"Only if he chooses it. If he desires, we will mark him as a Speaker. If he doesn't..." I shrugged. "The choice is his."

The choice is not his. I need to mark them. Red clobbered my mind and I stifled a flinch and fired back, *you can do this, Nardiri. Hold!*

The urgent cry of a baby peeled through the morning air. It came from one of the two tiny huts beyond the northern boundary, white roots emblazoned above their crooked entrances. No one moved to comfort the unseen infant. I couldn't help but think of Sivi, Arsu's eldest son. His jagged cries had filled our camp for days until I gathered every last shred of courage in my fifteen-year-old body and went to comfort him. Arsu caught me in her daeson's hut, dragged me outside, and kicked me so hard she broke my ribs.

I am not a broken boy anymore.

"In exchange, I want your daeson. All of them. Bring them to me."

A flurry of exclamations rattled like leaves through the crowd. Nardiri growled.

"Your Speakers," I projected to the back of the camp. "will have the option of pairing with a dragon."

Venda's wobbling mouth dropped open. Her fingers pressed to her forehead again as she stared at Nardiri. "Mother of Yurrii," she rasped. "Can't be true."

"It is true." I nodded. "And I'm proof. All those who this dragon marks will have the opportunity to meet her hatchlings when she lays, and perhaps be chosen to bond with one of them. And if you decide not to pursue a dragon, you'll still bear the honourable mark of Nasheira's chosen, and you'll have unburdened your camp of their daeson. I would think it an easy choice."

"What do we have to do?" A small voice piped from behind the round-faced woman. A tanned boy, all long limbs and white-blond hair peered over his mother's shoulder. "If we want to be marked."

The daeson baby wailed again, a high, forlorn cry. I clenched my teeth. "Someone bring me those boys. After that, simply bare your chest. I recommend you gather a fair supply of junab and cold compresses first. The mark stings like nothing you've ever felt."

"I birthed nine children, Speaker," Venda said.

"When will we get a dragon?" The receptive boy's question held the undiluted yearning of a child who spent his nights dreaming of gold in the skies.

"There is a giant rock formation in the middle of the plains south-west of here. Do you know it?"

The boy shook his head, but his mother murmured, "Nasheira's Heart."

"I'm sorry?" I frowned.

"It turned to stone the day Yurrii died and she cast it out. It's been sitting in the grasslands ever since. She won't take it back."

"Nasheira's Heart. That's the place." I cleared my throat. "We will be there on the eve of Yurrii's full moon every month. Come to us there, and I'll teach you everything you need to know about raising a hatchling."

The young boy squirmed and glanced at his mother. The crowd around him broke into babbling chatter, ignoring the shrill cries from the daeson hut.

"If someone does not bring me those daeson, right now," I bellowed. "My dragon will hunt down their fathers and eat them."

I will not! Nardiri reared back and roared.

The crowd screamed at her sudden outburst. Those who were kneeling dropped flat to the ground, breathing in ragged puffs.

They brought me their daeson.

The white-haired, receptive boy was named Amar. Venda giggled and pinched his elbow as Nardiri closed on them while their camp stood by with stinking pots of junab salve. "I'll go first, boy. Soften up that tongue for you, eh?" Unashamed, she shrugged her narrow shoulders out of her shift and exposed a sagging chest with a pale, faded burn scar across the sternum.

Why do you all mutilate yourselves like that? Nardiri's thoughts were coloured with pink distaste.

I smiled faintly. Guides, I had wanted a chest scar so badly as a boy, but daeson were not allowed to wear them. It's a rite of passage into adulthood. *They should flatter you—they're meant to be a tribute to the mark you give.*

They're ridiculous.

Venda sat, skirts flaring around her, and then settled onto her back, her arms draped wide, and her thick braid flicked over her head. As Nardiri approached her, the woman frowned and held up a knobby hand. "Wait." she said.

I leaned forward to hear her.

"You tell your Guide to miss my jugs if she can." Venda patted her dark, deflated bosom with both hands. "They were really nice once."

Nardiri snorted and splayed one foreclaw over the elder, using the other to keep her balance.

Be gentle, I warned. I remembered the moment of my own choosing—the unknown dragon's jaws dropping open to reveal its huge teeth. Its eye, that emerald, sentient eye, had been the size of my head. I remembered screaming when that barbed tongue snagged on the smooth skin of my young, unmarked chest.

Venda didn't scream. Amar did, but only a little, and after a few short, adrenaline-soaked moments, both elder and child were being slathered with junab while their camp closed in to inspect the raw, revered wounds.

I left with two howling daeson babies wrapped against my chest, feeling as though the world had changed forever.

CHAPTER THIRTEEN

T HAT MONTH, I FOUND three more daeson, all of them older boys who'd survived sacrifice before becoming aeni slaves. Scratches riddled my arms and face from transporting the children to their new home. Two of them fought each other constantly. I never saw them without bite marks on their arms and puffy, blackened eyes. The third refused to leave his hut. Any time Ana brought him outside, he screamed like the sun was scorching him and beat his head with his fists. None of the daeson slept well at night. We all had that much in common.

Rowin refused to acknowledge me the first time I came back, but he warmed on my second return and we spent many nights playing tavi together. When I wasn't out with Nardiri searching for receptive souls and daeson, I hunted. Ana had lost three of her best hunters, after all, and the daeson ate like each meal was the last they'd ever see, so Nardiri and I were often occupied keeping the camp well stocked. Before I knew it, Yurrii's full moon was nearly upon me and a group of people twice the size of Ana's camp had set up tents under the shadow of Nasheira's Heart.

On the night before the full moon, I sat awake long after the daeson and the dragon had dozed off. Ana joined me at my lone hearth fire.

"What troubles you, Na-daeson Akrist?" She crouched beside me.

A coal flicked out of the hearth, and I pressed it out under my boot. "Tomorrow night. Half of them will be here just to see a Guide up close."

"Of course." Ana looked at me with eyebrows raised.

"How do I convince them of what I'm about to do when I haven't even convinced myself?"

"Pshhhht." The storyteller flapped her lips. "You convinced yourself the moment you started marking Speakers and claiming daeson. But if you'd like advice on getting others to listen..." She leaned toward me and pointed a finger at my stomach. "Feed them. Get Mother to find us a nice fat ox tomorrow morning. We'll build a fine fire at the rock. It is remarkable how well a person listens after you've filled their belly."

I met her gaze and held it. "You are one of the few people who knows I'm not just an outcast—I'm a daeson." I shook my head. "Who will side with me, once they learn the truth?"

"Nasheira is on our side." Ana patted my knee. I did my best not to flinch. "She led us to each other. The Goddess is ready for change." The storyteller pointed toward the eastern horizon, toward Nasheira's Heart dozens of miles away. "Convince the rest that they are ready for change too."

I swallowed. Nasheira wasn't on my side. She'd abandoned me long ago.

The next night, I stood spotlighted by the same moons that had heralded my sacrifice nearly seven months before. They hung like two mottled eggs suspended from the heavens. Before me stood an eager crowd of people with sated stomachs and unsated questions.

Hope and dread filled me simultaneously as I scanned the crowd for familiar faces. If anyone from my old camp was here, they'd not be placated with hypocritical words about how the Goddess had "sent" me. Part of me wanted to bury my past and my dying faith together, and part of me wanted to tell these people the truth about who I was. How could I ask them to trust in a deity who'd abandoned me?

Just tell them you are a daeson. Tell them what wurms really are. Nardiri urged from her perch on the rock. *The sooner they know, the better.*

I shook my head. *It's too much.*

You presume what they can handle! She snapped testily.

We're doing this my way. I cleared my throat.

"If you've come here," I projected my voice over dozens of heads, and Ana nodded from the back of the crowd, "you already know who I am, and you want to know what comes next. My dragon has marked Speakers, and we will train them here. I want to head camps and aeni alike with leaders bonded to

Guides as they were meant to be. I'll need all of you to spread the word for me. This Guide caught the meal that fed all of you today. She can track animals without seeing them, sense storms before they strike. If there is drought or flood or fire, she can scout the best path to safety. She represents the past we've forgotten, and our future."

Several heads bobbed in approval. Several more simply gaped at Nardiri, who was preening herself behind me. One man with a straw-coloured beard and red cheeks bellowed, "What is the cost of this training? What do *you* get for giving us Guides?"

I paused while the whispers died down, until everyone was waiting for my response. "I want your daeson. *All* of them."

Silence. Then, a thousand questions and comments were thrown at me at once.

"Why?"

"Are you planning to sacrifice them early?"

"You think you're a god, now?"

"What do we care if he takes our daeson? Good riddance!"

"It is not Nasheira's way."

Tell them the truth!

Nardiri hissed, which silenced them all.

"I will take your daeson on behalf of Nasheira," I said, the lie rolling smoothly off my tongue. "It is her wisdom that leads me to do so."

Tell them how we bonded, what I was when you met me.

"Why should we listen to you? You are shunned." The comment came from the back of the crowd.

"I bring change," I said, and the truth of the words tasted bitter. "I am an outcast *and* a Speaker. Banished *and* chosen. You wouldn't be here if you didn't need what I have to offer. We can't continue to ignore how camps are growing smaller.

How storms overtake us too often. How we starve when trails go cold. We are slowly dying without the dragons to guide us. *I am bonded with a Guide. Bring me your firstborn sons. And in return, you will gain *everything*. The choice is yours."

I waited as voices thundered.

Why should I guide people who still mindlessly butcher hatchlings? Nardiri's thought snapped with red. ***Tell them about the wurms.***

Gritting my teeth, I said, "There's one more condition." I waited for the voices to die down. All eyes were on me—some angry, some confused, some curious. "No more killing wurms."

Faces froze. A few people mouthed, "What?" with perplexed frowns pressed onto their brows.

"It is Nasheira's will." I prayed my voice wouldn't waiver, and it came out strong and hard as flint. "Bring me your shunned sons, or defy your Goddess by keeping them and burden your camps by feeding them for the next twelve years. Send me your Speakers, or let them live half lives as hollowly-marked leaders with no dragons. Leave the wurms be, or let Nasheira's wrath fall upon. Choose as you wish. Nasheira watches."

Nardiri's anger burned into my mind. ***If you were really acting on behalf of your wretched goddess, you'd tell them the truth!*** she snarled as I retreated and the crowd dissipated under the baleful light of the moons.

I told them to give up daeson and spare the wurms. Right now that's more than any of them were ready to hear.

You are supposed to speak for me, not muzzle my words. The dragon walled off our connection, launched with a huff and left me alone amongst strangers.

A small camp of new followers set up permanent residence at Nasheira's Heart. Nardiri and I marked two more Speakers in the next month and brought home another daeson. When Yurrii was full again, my followers diligently brought me five more firstborn sons. The month after that, dozens of daeson came.

Nardiri and I threw ourselves into hunting. We supplied both Ana's hidden camp and the settlement of new Speakers at Nasheira's Heart with food. We also gave meat to the people who brought daeson—payment for time spent traveling that would have otherwise been used for hunting or gathering.

Some of the daeson I ferried back to Ana's camp were older than twelve, but confided that they had not been sacrificed. A few had escaped. Others had been hidden by those who loved them. That revelation filled me with an incongruous mix of relief and anger. It proved there were indeed good people in the world, who'd shielded their firstborn boys from a horrible fate, who wanted a better life for their damned sons. And it sorely highlighted the fact that my parents were not among those compassionate souls.

I tried to provide a better example for Rowin. I brought him flying with me when I could. On evenings when I was free, we played tavi, and the game became such a popular pastime among the daeson that their caretakers threatened to confiscate their game pieces if they shunned their chores. Those were not the boys we were concerned about.

Sadly, expectedly, some of the daeson we recovered brought considerable issues with them, and required constant care night and day to ensure they didn't hurt themselves.

While Ana's camp, hidden among the trees a half-day's walk from Nasheira's Heart, attended to our daeson, Heart camp dedicated their efforts to processing, drying and smoking the kills we brought in, stockpiling blood sausage, smoked meat, and freshly-cured hides and furs. We gathered copious amounts of Guide's leaf tea for full moon ceremonies. We stockpiled more food, wood, and herbs per month than my small child-hood camp had ever gathered for an entire winter season.

At night, I dreamed of Yara. Shedding lonely tears in the darkness, I clasped her comb in my hand until it cut into my palm, letting the emptiness in my chest swallow me until morning. And every time Yurrii waxed close to full, Nardiri and I left for days at a time, seeking daeson.

We came back in time for the eve of Yurri's full moon, made an appearance for our amassing followers, drank bitter ceremonial tea, and returned to our search as soon as we could. I lost Rowin's fragile trust every time I left, and had to win it back each time I returned.

It was a frenzied routine. I would have even dared to say it was going well. Until the night of the summer's-end full moon ceremony. That was when everything changed.

—YARA—

Joining a camp was my only chance of survival, but they were suspicious of a lone woman wandering the wilderness with a babe in arms. After receiving the free night of food and refuge, I had to offer them something that made keeping me worthwhile, and I didn't have any medicinal herbs left. I spoke with the group's healer, but she was unwilling to take on a stranger as an apprentice, so I offered what desperate women with nothing left have bartered with since the beginning of time.

I didn't receive the title of chani for my efforts, as this camp didn't have a Speaker. No extra hunting shares for me—just the scraps of whatever the men paid me. I wasn't human anymore, just a common vessel to fill, all false smiles and swallowed fear, a body to warm a bedroll, so terrified of letting her baby out of her sight that she conducted her sordid business while her child slept right beside her. Sometimes the baby didn't sleep. Sometimes, my child cried until it was over. I waited until afterwards to shed my tears, until the sobs were replaced by numbness. Sometimes, the fierce pain of missing Akrist penetrated the fog, strong enough to nearly drop me where I stood. But desperate animals didn't lay down and die. They didn't know how. They just kept going, scavenging for food, seeking protection, guarding their young. Desperate animals didn't feel shame. How could they? They didn't have the capacity for that.

CHAPTER FOURTEEN

W E LEFT NASHEIRA'S HEART late, but the full moons still provided enough light for Nardiri and me to search the heavily-wooded southern foothills. We'd been flying under partially overcast skies for hours so, when the shadow first arced over us, I presumed it was a bank of clouds swathing the moons. It was not until I straightened and a peculiar gust of wind blew my hair against my face that I realised we had company.

Nardiri faltered in the air. A short squeal squeezed from her throat as she flapped to keep us aloft. I clung to the harness. Through the slits of my visor, I glimpsed a flash of gold-scaled hide. Nardiri bobbed like a boat finding equilibrium in the aftermath of a rogue wave.

A dragon glided like a ghost at Nardiri's left wing tip. Moss green eyes studied us silently while long, mottle-patterned wings effortlessly matched Nardiri's unsteady pace.

I didn't sense him. Orange-yellow shock soured my dragon's thoughts as her big head swung in a sweeping arc to meet the dragon's gaze. *He masked himself somehow.*

I tucked my calves under her shoulders and squeezed my knees tight, unable to take my gaze off the other dragon. The tapered tip of his wing wobbled inches from Nardiri's. He was smaller than her, but bulkier.

I swallowed, noting Nardiri's gaze darting all around. *What are you looking for?*

Edging away from the dragon, her senses unravelled outward as far as she could stretch them. Her nostrils quivered. *I'm not sure. Perhaps... another dragon? His mate? I don't want to get into a fight if he is taken.*

I jammed my hands into the handholds and ducked against her neck. *Maybe he doesn't have one.* It dawned on me that Nardiri might be of fertile age.

She banked away from the dragon hard enough that I had to dig my heels in to keep my balance. The harness slid a handbreadth but held as I clung to it. Scattered layers of clouds swung up to swallow my line of sight.

Nardiri climbed and then dropped into an arcing dive that lifted me off her neck. Behind us, a deep whooshing and a subtle grunt informed us that our male company easily kept pace.

Hold tight.

I nodded, arms braced as she tucked her wings. Our free fall shifted into a pulling spiral that corkscrewed us through the cloud base while the grey forest canopy cart-wheeled below.

Pounding blood rushed to my head, and I only relaxed once we pulled out of the manoeuvre.

I don't think there's anyone else. Her thoughts pressed through the rushing sound in my head in tones of green-yellow intrigue. *It's just him.*

Stretching my cramped arms, I exhaled over my shoulder and stared up at the broad belly of the curious male. *Can he paralyze me?*

I would stop him if he tried.

His barbed tail dragged through the clouds like a fishing lure. He chuffed and stretched his foreclaws toward me.

I flattened against Nardiri. *He's going to pull me off.*

He won't. He's not interested in you, only me. She crooned.

I gulped several lungfuls of damp night air. Nardiri turned to take in her admirer.

He's small, but well built.

Biting down a nervous laugh, I twisted further in the harness to take in the compact dragon above us. *That pleases you, does it?*

Shouldn't it? A playful trill fluttered up her throat.

The male's jaw dropped and he answered with a lusty bugle that pounded through my chest.

He's not like the driftling we met before. He's not speaking, but his colours are brighter. He sends me green and red, but the red is different from normal hunger.

My entire field of vision was consumed by dappled wings. It wasn't just the moonlight. While Nardiri's hide glowed with tones of sunrise and cream, her suitor's colouring was cold gold ribbed with silver, and his turquoise dipped wings held more of a green undertone. He stretched into a proud glide to display their richly patterned edges. *What do you think he hungers for?* I prodded, a nervous smile twitching my lips.

Me. Nardiri's tail flicked lazily. **Driftlings this size are probably ready to mate.**

And you are not?

The male extended his legs toward Nardiri and she quickly ducked away from his grasp.

My stomach clenched. *You don't think we should leave?*

She nipped playfully at the male, dodging away from his attempted entanglement, wingtips slapping him smartly on the ribs.

Perhaps... She slid her wingtip under the male's and trilled. Flat chest scales flashed in the moonlight as he puffed up and answered in a powerful bugle that sounded, to my ears, more than a little frustrated. **But he is lovely to look at. I'll be even happier to meet him when I'm older. I wonder how he masked his presence. I would like to learn how to do that.**

I wondered how long it would be before she matured enough to take a mate, and the jealousy that stabbed my chest surprised me.

The male flew with us for the next half hour. His advances turned more curious than arduous. I relaxed enough to notice a fresh scar on his haunch that appeared to be gouge marks from another dragon. He also had a missing claw on his right hind leg.

When he finally looped away from us, banking toward the brother moons with a last bugle, I breathed a sigh of relief.

We were alone in the sky when the screaming started.

A man's wail for help cut through the canopy ahead of us. Then a wordless, gulping shriek.

My neck prickled as Nardiri's senses pinpointed the source. Her head snapped to the right and she leaned into a turn.

Three people, and there are wurms too! A trio of green forms clumped together with two wurms closing in from afar with frightening speed.

"Find somewhere to land." I scanned for a break in the trees. *Wurms do not congregate with such speed unless they smell blood.*

"Help. Please!" a man's howl pierced the night.

There is nowhere! The trees are too thick.

"Can you paralyze the wurms?" I fumbled to untie my spear from the harness as Nardiri dove. The frustrated pink aura that filled my mind answered the question.

"No... Please, NO!" the voice rambled below us, wet and shaking. *He can smell them coming now.* The smell of death. The stink of wurms.

The canopy is too thick. Nardiri's thoughts flared orange as she skimmed the treetops.

"Hover over one of the trees." My hands fumbled with the harness knots.

What are you doing? Her words yellowed in sharp terror. *Set down over top of them, and I'll climb down.*

You'll fall!

Something rustled deep in the undergrowth. The squealing voice cut off, falling into breathless silence.

"Nardiri. NOW!" I bellowed. I tore at the harness. The cross straps slackened over my thighs. *Low as you can.* Checking that my knife was firmly sheathed in my belt, I slung my spear on its strap over my back.

I kicked out of the ropes and slid down her neck, clinging to the harness. My crippled hand slipped. *Oh Guides,* the numb thought struck me hard. *You idiot. What have you done?* My legs dangled meters above the closest tree and my fingers burned as they skidded down the neck strap.

Nardiri grunted and twisted to grab me, but I hung out of her reach. Her hind legs extended. Branches crunched and leaves clotted around us as she latched onto a tree and pumped her wings to stay in the air. ***I cannot land!***

"You don't need to," I puffed. "Lower me through the canopy."

We sank into the shuddering tree. Branches raked me and snagged at my limbs. Twigs lashed my cheeks. My hip crashed into a bough and I let go of the harness to fold over it.

Akrist! Nardiri's wings pummelling me with debris.

"I'm all right." I gasped. Swallowed by darkness, I shimmied down the bough blind. *Share your sight. I cannot see.*

Green flared to life below and to my left. Rough bark cut into my hands, and my boots skidded down the thick trunk to find purchase. As I climbed lower, the gut-wrenching, sour smell of wurm enveloped me.

They are coming fast. Nardiri roared and pumped her wings. ***I will try to distract them.*** Trees bucked and groaned. Branches rained down, clattering as she dragged her tail through the foliage above.

The glowing silhouettes of wurms slowed, reared, and turned toward the commotion. Columns of moonlight filtered through the canopy as Nardiri tore into it. I twisted through a maze of branches. When I spotted the ground below me, I dropped, landing hard enough to send pangs of shock up my ankles.

Groping through the moss, I stumbled toward the silhouette of a man slumped against a tree. He yelped and shrank from me when my hand closed on his shoulder. "We need to move." My voice cracked.

I could barely see the whites of his eyes as they flashed toward me. "Y-you're not him," he said in a high voice.

"Get up!" I hissed. Shrugging my spear from my back, I drew my knife as the wurms swung back towards us.

"I can't," the man said. A thin band of moonlight illuminated his lower half. Dark smears of blood painted his bare, twitching legs. He was lashed to the tree with a thick rope.

Guides. I cast aside my spear and dove behind him, sawing at his bonds, skinning my knuckles against the tree that restrained him. *This can't be happening again.* My eyes watered and my nostrils burned as the horrible stench of wurms congealed around us. Something thicker clotted in my chest, clutching at my hammering heart. Images of the gully pounded through me like well-aimed spears. Henri screaming and kicking at his mother as she bent over him with a sickle-bladed knife. Gideous's terrified, wobbling voice as he regained consciousness in the dark. The utter silence of the toddlers, Jule and Fey.

"Hurry!" the bound man said.

Nardiri trumpeted overhead. ***Akrist. They are coming!***

Ropes slithered away from the tree. The man stood and cried out, doubling over, air hissing out of him. Mottled moonlight highlighted the curve of his pale back and the blood between his legs. A pale green aura clung to him like floating seaweed. "To your right," he rasped.

I turned and faced two babies laying side by side, both wrapped in bloodied blankets crusted in leaves. One of them had a green aura, the other had none. *No.* Breath drained out of me. There had been three auras before we had landed. Now there were two. My knife slipped from my fingers and thudded to the ground. I crashed to my knees and scooped up both children. One squirmed feebly in my grip before curling into my warmth, but the other flopped limp and listless in my arms. I couldn't rise. I couldn't see anything other than Jule and Fey's delicate faces, their waxy skin and dark lips, the frost crusting their eyelashes. *You let them freeze. All of them. Your fault.*

Akrist, run! Nardiri commanded.

"Get up!" the man said.

But the roar of blood between my ears drowned me. White flashes thumped behind my eyes, in time with my pounding pulse. A deep, leaden ache pulled my sternum toward my spine.

The man, so thin I could see his ribs poking out from his naked chest, found my spear, grabbed it and limped toward me, wheezing. Behind him, the yellow silhouettes of the wurms crashed towards us, visible between the trees.

A hand gripped my arm. The man leaned close enough that his rotten breath overpowered the scent of wurms. *He has a brand on his cheek.* As I processed this, he snatched the living child from my arms.

"No," I barked, scrambling to my feet.

"Pick up your knife!" he bellowed, tucking the baby into the crook of his arm and lunging away.

Akrist, RUN! Nardiri's screech exploded in my head.

I flinched, clutched the lifeless baby tight against my chest, and snatched up my blade. Low-hanging branches shattered and trees trembled, but I did not look to see how close the wurms were. I turned and fled.

Moonlight ribboned over our retreat. The man stumbled, dropping my spear.

I shifted the baby onto my hip, shoved my knife into my sheath and caught him by the elbow, pressing him onward. When I glanced back, white tentacles gripped a nearby tree. A thick, quivering wurm jerked toward us.

"Nardiri!" I hollered.

I'm here. Something massive crashed down from overhead. Pale gold hung directly in our path. A diamond fluke. Spikes longer than my arm.

Grab on, Nardiri roared.

"Hold on!" I steered the man into the dragon's tail and hooked my leg over the lowest spike. No sooner had we clasped onto the thick, ridged barbs than Nardiri hoisted us skyward. White blurred below us. The canopy crashed by. Nardiri's foreclaws extended down to snatch us from our precarious perch and tuck us against her chest. Through the hole in the canopy below, two large wurms thrashed and curled around my abandoned spear.

The dragon's heart thudded against my back. Wide wings walled us in as she heaved into a deep downstroke. The forest dropped away. I clung to the cold, tiny body in my arms and gaped at the terrified man curled in the crook of Nardiri's opposite elbow.

He was panting. Tendons stood out on his neck as he pressed the baby so tightly to his chest that the child squawked. Moonlight limned his red, disheveled hair as the wind whipped it around his branded cheek.

Red hair.

Son of Pau.

"Tanar?" I blurted out.

He turned to me, pain hollowing his features, and teeth bared in a cold, humourless grin. "Akrist."

An hour later, I held back the tent flap to Ana's hut and peered in. The light from the stone lamps flickered from the breeze, and the storyteller straightened, blood on her fingers and a needle in her hand.

Tanar didn't even flinch. He lay with one arm draped over his face and the other clenched at his side. His narrow chest, damp with sweat, rose and fell with shallow breaths. A cloth over his groin was his only modesty. Several more red-smeared rags lay crumpled between his legs. The smell of blood, mixed with the sharp tang of junab ointment, reminded me of every wound Fraesh had ever stitched for me.

"Speaker! Can this not wait?" Ana snapped, pinning me with a disgruntled gaze.

"It cannot."

"For Nasheira's sake," she grumbled and tossed a hand toward the entry. "Close the flap at least. The wind is ruining my light."

I stepped inside, jamming the pegs into place, and crouched near Tanar's head with my hand gripping my sheathed blade's handle. The lamplight stabilized, and Ana pursed her lips and shook her head, refocusing on the delicate task of stitching Tanar's wound. She'd already done the same for the surviving baby.

The child was currently full of warm vaiya milk and sleeping in the stout arms of one of the surrogate mothers. The other baby was beyond our help. We could offer him nothing except a pyre when this was all done.

"I assure you, he's no danger right now." Ana glanced pointedly at my knife. "Boy's got enough gifen running through his veins to drop a bull ox. It's astounding he's even awake."

"Tanar." Guides, I couldn't even say his name without picturing the madman pinning me with my blade, licking my blood from his fingers. "What did you do?"

He jerked up, his green eyes flaring in anger.

Ana pushed him back down, hissing, "Be still!"

His arm slid from his face and he turned and blinked at me, his gaze turning dull and unfocused. "What did *I* do?" His words slurred together. He giggled. "Walled off the hunger. Didn't matter, though. Evil still found us."

My mouth went dry. "What happened to you?"

Tanar barely reacted as Ana continued stitching. He licked his cracked lips and said, "I thought you were him, at first. Come back to finish us."

"Who?"

"You look just like him, you know." His green gaze fluttered over me. "Black hair. Speaker's scars, and dragons between your knees. I quit yelling when I heard your Guide call. Thought you were him."

Ana and I glanced at each other. "He's sedated, Speaker," she spoke in low tones. "You expect to get anything out of him other than nonsense?"

Tanar snorted. "I know what I saw." He reached out and clasped my wrist, the one that held the knife. I cringed but his grip was shockingly strong.

"You were insane when we last met," I gulped, running my fingers over the thin scar on my throat.

He frowned and let me go, his hand brushing over a purple, ropey scar on his right thigh. "That was the hunger. Not mine.

The wurms." He shook his head, eyes glittering in the lamplight. "I can control it now."

I closed my eyes, took my hand from my blade, and pressed my thumb and finger against my aching sockets. He was still insane.

"Are they well?" he glanced at me urgently. "The babies?"

I frowned. "One did not make it."

Tanar bared his teeth, clutching the bedroll beneath him. His nose whistled as he exhaled—and I remembered how Na-Jhalar had broken it when we were young. "Pau damn it," he hissed.

We sat in aching silence while Ana finished stitching. I don't know what compelled me to stay, perhaps some childhood allegiance to be there for Tanar whenever he'd been hurt on my behalf. Ana applied a layer of junab, wiped her hands, and left us.

Tanar suddenly sat up, startling me by grabbing the front of my shirt and pulling me close. My heart spiked in response, and I clenched my fists at my side against the compulsion to strike him and back away.

"The Children of Yurrii are coming," he whispered, his breath sour in my face.

As I met his crazed eyes, hatred and fear drained away, displaced by pity.

He was still mumbling when I left him.

CHAPTER
FIFTEEN

—TANAR—

I HAD THOUGHT I was escaping the day I slipped out of camp with a stolen cache of food on my back and Xen strapped to my front. I'd even convinced myself that I wasn't deserting my only friend. We hadn't really been friends to begin with. We'd been using each other, and Akrist didn't have the stones to act. No matter how much he prepared, he couldn't leave his stupid vaiyas. *I* was the one who acted, and I'd be the one who saved Xen and gave him a normal life.

Except I didn't escape.

I walked out of that camp and right into the jaws of evil.

One thing people don't tell you about evil. It's not dark, like they say in stories. It's all sorts of colours in your head. But mostly, evil is red and hot. And always hungry. It fills your skull and stabs your guts until nothing else matters but filling the holes it made.

The hunger had wriggled in my brain from the time I could stand on my own two feet. I figured every daeson felt the same thing. That itch deep in your skull. The chasm yawning in your chest no matter how full your belly was. I thought that was why the whole world called us Sons of Pau, because he planted wurms in our heads.

But I'd learned otherwise when I met Akrist. He didn't feel it. It didn't warp his mind and burn his insides to ashes. He wasn't like me, and nothing makes you feel more evil than keeping company with someone who's good.

So, I left.

That winter, Xen died. Not by my hand. I wasn't a murderer then. He just got sick and died like babies sometimes do. No warning. No fixing it. Just gone. And what was left of my heart gone with him.

The hunger swallowed me whole after that.

It left no room for grief, compassion or sanity. It just slipped my body on like I was a coat and took over. I don't remember the first person I hunted down. Guides, I don't remember most of them, I don't even know who captured me and branded me for murder. The hunger filled my life with larger and larger holes, but I do recall when the dragons started pulling at me.

They'd wing in from beyond the horizon and I could feel them coming, burning like miniature golden suns, claws hooked deep into my chest even though they were still miles away. I figured the growing evil in me threw a bad enough scent to attract the attention of Nasheira's Guides. They meant to kill me, I was sure of it. That was their job, wasn't it? Lead people toward good and devour evil. My father had told me that often enough "Guides have big mouths and sharp teeth to swallow evil whole." And I was overflowing with the stuff. He'd told me that, too.

So, I spent a lot of time cowering in woods too thick for the Guides to reach me. At some point, I learned to hide from them right out in the open. If I thought of curling in a burrow deep in the earth, or diving under water until my lungs burst, if I pictured walls around me, the pressure in my chest eased and the dragons lost interest and banked away. That's how I survived, hiding and bowing to the waves of red hunger when they came. Until that's all I was. Until Tanar was scoured away completely.

One night, I clawed my way to the surface of my mind and found myself standing at the mouth of a cavern, kneeling on top of a man and pressing a knife to his throat. He said Xen's name and I recognized him, even though he was a gaunt, haunted version of my boyhood friend. Things got fuzzy after that. That feeling of invisible claws hooked into my chest. A dragon, right there in the cave with us. She skewered my leg with her wing talon and I screamed. Then I ran. I didn't know if Akrist lived or died. I hoped he lived.

Days later, my leg burned with infection. It throbbed with the same intensity of the hunger in my head. The pain was so strong that, when I first came upon the scene, I thought I was hallucinating.

A gazelle hung from the crotch of a tree, head locked between the branches, tongue black and lolling. It hadn't been dead for long. Steam still rose from its opened belly where two wurms gorged. As I stood there, terror-stricken, one raised its head and a curl of green curiosity bloomed in my mind before being snuffed out by a familiar red. The hunger rose sharply enough to take my breath away.

My feet shuffled toward the scavengers, even as a whimper escaped my lips. I didn't want to approach them, but I wasn't in control. Visceral need drove me to stumble toward the wurms, even as I gagged at the smell of them. I longed to crouch between them, dig my hands into the warm hollows of the gazelle's belly and stuff my mouth—never mind that the harbingers of Pau would kill me. Hunger flooded me so fast, I drowned in it.

That's when the tension broke in my mind. This moment of incongruent quiet.

A staggering revelation.

It's not mine. The hunger. Never was. What I felt was coming from the wurms. They were broadcasting it. The closer I got, the more suffocating it became. Somehow, I stopped, scuffed to a standstill in the wreath of bloodied snow around the gazelle.

The wurms regarded me silently, stringy gore dangling from their jawless mouths. I don't know why they didn't eat me. I'm not sure what saved me, but one instant their attention was honed on me and the next, they'd turned and latched back onto the fat carcass between them. The red in my mind loosened its hold enough for me to back away. The further I got from the wurms, the weaker the hunger grew.

This whole time, I'd been driven mad by a hunger that wasn't even my own. I'd been sensing wurms all along. My father was right, I was full of evil. The Harbingers of Pau sensed enough of it running through my veins to consider me as one of their own.

"What are your needs?" the ani asked.

"Junab," I spoke through my teeth, both hands gripping my swollen thigh.

"And what do you offer?"

"Pau damn it, you know I've only one thing left!"

The ani's impassive gaze flicked down to my putrid wound then back to my cheek. "You're branded. I shouldn't be trading with you."

I puffed out cheeks flushed with fever. "Then why speak with me at all?"

"I'm generous. A man's past is his own business. I'm interested in your future. Your life. I'll accept your service in return for healing your leg."

"Agreed." I had no other choice.

"Swear it to Nasheira, on your soul. One life saved. One life owed."

"I swear it." I gulped.

The aeni group healed my leg and kept me as well fed as their vaiyas. As much as I hated to admit it, the life of a servant wasn't so bad. Wurms were reluctant to approach a group bristling with weapons and vaiyas, so the hunger in my head faded like it had when I was a young daeson taken in by Akrist's camp. Now that I knew the feeling came from outside of myself, I built walls to keep it out. I blocked dragons and wurms alike, and pieces of myself came back, like jetsam pushed back to the shore after a long storm. Perhaps I might have known happiness as an aeni servant. Certainly, I found a measure of contentment. But as it turns out, I didn't serve the ani who healed my leg for very long.

If there was one thing aeni liked better than slaves, it was trading them, and they'd barter anything for enough dragon scales.

Three weeks before the full moons, a Guide came rocketing out of the sky.

The aeni screamed. Their vaiyas scattered. All of us dropped to our knees. And then we spotted the man perched on the dragon's neck. Straight-backed. Black hair streaming in the wind. Speaker's scar on his chest. A face I'd known since childhood.

He recognized me. "Tanar," he said, focusing on my red hair.

"Dero." I croaked.

Akrist's little brother bought me. He paid with a thick stack of dragon scales. When his dragon snatched me up, I was certain it would swallow me whole, but no. The Guide carried me back to the very camp I'd run from when I was a boy.

The group was nothing like I remembered.

The camp reeked of wurms. I covered my nose as we landed, catching a glimpse of the circle of pikes surrounding the huts. Each one brandished a severed wurm head, flaccid and grey, leaking black blood like tar.

I soon discovered that Na-Jhalar, the camp's Speaker, was dead. Half the people I'd known were gone. The woman who hated Akrist led now, and everyone, including Dero, bowed and simpered to her.

They caged me and kept me fed for days. At first, I couldn't work out what need they'd have for a branded slave. What worth had Dero seen in me that made him pay so many dragon scales?

As the days went on, snippets of conversation passed between the bars of my cage. These people called themselves the Children of Yurrii. They were paying aeni handsomely to bring them dead wurms and live daeson. We were a rarity though, it seemed. Dero only found two babies—ones who cried like the world was ending and flinched when I tried to hold them, just like Xen had at first.

I knew what the Children of Yurrii were keeping us for then. Gathering us stragglers from far and wide. Feeding us up for the full moons in two weeks time. Sacrificing all of the daeson who'd missed the eclipse. And damned if I didn't deserve it, but these babies didn't. There was no evil in them at all. Me, on the other hand... I was about to get what I deserved.

Tanar

—AKRIST—

I dream of Yara again. She presses against me like before, all soft skin and hungry mouth. This time her belly is swollen with pregnancy. It ripples with movement, but the motion looks nothing like a baby kicking—more like wurms beneath her skin. She asks me to touch her stomach, but I can't. I can't hold her at all. My hands are tied.

I lurched out of my hut, rubbing my wrists, still so tangled in the dream that I nearly tripped over Rowin.

"Guides," I said, blinking down at the tightly-curled form at my feet. The boy shared the hut next to mine with two of the other daeson, but he rarely used it. He used to sleep next to Nardiri when a bad dream woke him, but more and more often, he'd taken to curling up outside my doorway. He refused to set foot inside.

At my exclamation, his head popped up in the dark, grass matting his brown hair and hazel eyes meeting mine. That happened sometimes now—an occasional direct glance.

Pau's waning face hung low on the horizon. "Where is your blanket?" I asked.

He gaped at my bare chest and I shivered. It had been more than a decade, and I still hated it when people stared at my Speaker's mark. *That's all you are to people. One scar or the other. Speaker or outcast.* Sweat cooled on my skin and Rowin didn't answer so I ducked back inside and scooped up my tunic and blanket.

Tossing the hide to him, I shrugged into my shirt, and we both sat in my doorway and stared out at the night. The air was sweet with the scent of dew and incense. I inhaled deeply to clear my dream from my head. Habitually, I reached for Nardiri's mind. She was sleeping at the edge of camp with the vaiyas. I found it simultaneously endearing and unsettling how little fear Ana's flock had for the dragon.

"Tavi?" I asked, and Rowin reached into his belt pouch to pull out the four wooden game pieces. Then he carefully unfolded a cloth and set it between us, lining up its contents into neat rows. I leaned closer to study his wager pile in the weak moonlight.

A cracked wooden spoon. Two awls. An assortment of flint shards, and five iridescent bird feathers.

"Impressive." I nodded seriously and reached back through my doorway to retrieve my own wrapped pouch. "I have something to add to your pile before we start." Flipping the pouch open, I revealed a set of round tavi pieces, each one a rich translucent blue and polished to the sheen of water droplets. "I got these from an ani from the east. Sea glass, he called them. Said he gathered them from a beach so long, he could not find the ends of it. Go on. Take them. You're a seasoned player now. You deserve a proper set."

Rowin took two of the tavi pieces hesitantly, held one of the glossy stones up and ran his finger over the wurm pattern carved into it. A slow smile brightened his face and it thawed the last of the ice from my chest.

"Now for my wager." I revealed a pile of dried haskap berries, one of the only fruits that clung to the branch all winter and into early spring. I popped one into my mouth before palming my tavi tokens. "Shall we play?" I held out my fists.

Rowin beat me soundly. When the sun rose, I asked him if he wished to come hunting with Nardiri and me, and he nodded vehemently, lips stained blue with berries.

The sun climbed between the basin of two mountains. A small, clear lake glinted like polished flint in the valley. Rowin and I stood on its mossy shore and watched sun-splintered waves melt into stillness as the wind of Nardiri's ascent faded. She'd spotted a herd of harek and wanted to track them alone. It was a chance for her to stretch her wings and hone her skills without me. I'd told her to take her time as I'd packed two practice spears for the occasion.

When Rowin saw them, his eyes lit up.

I smiled. "You are young yet, but it's not too early for you to learn. Here," I handed him the shorter staff. "Find the balance point and grip it there, with your thumb along the bottom."

His tongue pressed into his cheek as he fumbled with his hand placement.

"Good." I nodded. "Let's aim for that stump at the edge of the bank. Do you see it, the rotten one?"

Rowin nodded.

I broke down the steps of throwing the spear, demonstrated them slowly, and then buried my spear in the spongy centre of the crumbling stump. "Your turn."

The boy braced, took a short step, and threw wide to the right. He flinched when his spear sailed past the target and rattled to a stop in the grass beyond.

"It's all right. It's practice." I smiled. "Follow through. Turn your whole body. Your throwing arm should be pointing where you want to aim, understand? Now go fetch them and let's try again."

We practiced for nearly an hour, and then we sat at the water's edge and shared a packed lunch of roasted hare and onion tallow cakes while Rowin tossed rocks into the water.

I couldn't avoid my rippling reflection in the lake. A gaunt man with hawk-like, gray-blue eyes, a dark scar bunching one cheek, and a mane of unkempt black hair glowered back at me. Guides, no wonder the daeson were terrified of me. I looked as unhinged as Tanar. Would he be whole now and Xen alive if I'd escaped with them back when we were boys? Exhaling, I looked away, and massaged my aching hand.

Rowin heaved a rock into the lake and then—out of nowhere—grabbed my hand and turned it over in his, running his small, cold fingers over my knuckles.

My breath hung in my throat. Although every fibre in me wanted to jerk my arm away, I held perfectly still while the boy frowned and tried to straighten the last two fingers on my right hand.

"They don't work anymore." I croaked. "They've healed wrong. But I can still throw a spear, because I practice."

Rowin looked up. The wind blew his wild hair into his face and he tossed his head and fixed me with a questioning gaze. When I didn't answer him, he tapped my fingers and shrugged.

"What happened?" I cleared my throat. "I broke my hand on someone's face. I don't recommend it."

He grinned.

My throat worked as he picked up another pebble and tossed it into the water.

He hummed tunelessly and kept his small hand tucked into mine until Nardiri returned.

I would have stayed at the quiet lake forever. I longed to throw the weight of my responsibilities into the rippling water with the same careless abandon of Rowin tossing stones. When was the last time Nardiri, Rowin, and I had shared a quiet day alone like this? When had I last had the chance to breathe? But there wasn't time. The Speakers camp needed more meat and wood for drying racks. Daeson needed to be fed. Others needed to be saved. I had to court and win over the groups that made the pilgrimage to Heart Camp and convince them I was worth following.

So we dropped Rowin off at home and fell into our never-ending work. I clung on as an exhausted spectator while Nardiri hunted, pushed over trees, stripped logs for firewood and carried it all back toward the rock.

Make this quick. I cannot take their questions today.

Nardiri tensed beneath me. Faint anger curled like crimson smoke around her thoughts. ***You marked a camp full of Speakers, promised them all dragons, and delivered nothing, yet you expect no questions?***

"*I* didn't mark them." I spoke through my teeth, but the excuse felt like dirt in my mouth.

Segregated groups of vaiyas called out a harmony of greeting calls as we approached the camp borders. As we passed over, people waved from behind carcass hanging stands, hide-stretching frames, and drying racks. I recognized Venda, the Speaker, standing just outside of the camp border, gripping a stout man by the elbow. Behind him, two tall girls with blonde hair stood swaying like willowy sentinels. A child stood between them.

Something familiar about them sparked joy in me before I completely recognized them. As Nardiri circled to land, the man beside Venda ran his hands through his short pale hair before crossing his arms over his chest.

Oh Guides.

"Fraesh." My breath spooled out of me like an unravelling thread. *It cannot be.* I blinked and focused on his broad shoulders, the deep, upturned crows feet around his eyes, and his solid stance. *It's him. Oh Guides, It's Fraesh and his daughters. Celi, Baline, and her son, Galeed.*

What is it? Nardiri hovered, feet tucked as she grazed the ground.

Land and let me down. I yarded at the slipknot at my waist, gripped Nardiri's dorsal ridge and swung my leg over her neck. My feet hit the grass at the same time as Nardiri's, and my knees wrenched as I smacked the ground, but I ignored them and trotted toward the knotted group.

Halfway to them, with my uncle still solidifying in my mind as the jovial, durable fatherhood figure of my childhood, I noticed the hollows under his cheeks and how his tunic hung slack off his shoulders. My legs jellied and I stumbled to a stop, my breath slowing like sap. "Fraesh," I choked.

My uncle, my old camp's healer, the one who had raised me like his own, pursed his lips, pressed his hand over his mouth and studied me with bright, glossy eyes before charging through the grass. He grabbed both my cheeks and held me like that, staring.

Guides, he looks so old.

"Fraesh, I'm so—"

"Look at you!" he burst out and tears rolled over his tanned cheeks. "Just look at you." The crease between his eyebrows deepened as his thumb brushed over the ugly brand on my cheek. He blinked rapidly and his gaze flitted up to Nardiri. "We came for the full moons, but we were late. We missed you..." His words choked off and his throat worked before he spoke again. "Iva would be so proud."

My throat filled with fire. "Fraesh, I didn't..." but I couldn't finish. *I didn't murder your mate. I didn't kill the woman who championed me when I was nothing, who treated me like her son.*

He clenched his thick jaw, shook my face and rasped. "Of course you didn't. I knew it was Arsu."

"I let Arsu lead," I babbled. "I trapped Iva." *And I haven't done any better since. I've marked Dero.*

Behind us, Nardiri growled, and we both jumped. ***The snake set the trap, not you.***

"Akrist." Fraesh shook me again, blue eyes as hard as flint. "I'm only going to say this once. You did not make Arsu a murderer, and you didn't make Na-Jhalar a weapon. Never apologize to me again. You were just a fallible boy." His face crumpled and he sagged against me, warm hands pressing my hair back from my face. "If anyone's to ask for forgiveness, it should be me. I didn't save you."

I pulled Fraesh to me and clutched his broad back. When I buried my face against him, he smelled of junab and smoke. Though my next words were muffled against his neck, I knew my uncle heard them by the drop of his shoulders and his snuffling inhale. "You did save me, Fraesh. I wouldn't have lived without you."

"I need to tell you something." His rough whisper blew against my ear. "About Yara. Akrist, she—"

"You do not need to say it." I gulped. "Jin told me. I know... I know how she died."

He gripped my arms, pulled back and shook his head. "No, Akrist. She's alive."

CHAPTER
SIXTEEN

I DID NOT HAVE my own dwelling at the Speaker's camp, but Venda and Amar were good enough to lend me their tent so that I could recover from the shock and speak to Fraesh privately.

Bolstered by several cups of strong black tea and Nardiri crooning outside the tent loudly enough to smooth all my frayed edges, I set my cup down and raked my hands through my hair. "I don't understand. Jin said Yara died. Even the vaiyas knew it."

Fraesh's blue eyes found mine, aching and apologetic. "I had to make it convincing, Akrist. If the flock called out a death, Arsu would have no reason to doubt Yara's demise. No one would. Besides, I needed a body to burn on the pyre in Yara's place."

"A-a body?" I stuttered.

"Vell was the vaiya closest to Yara in size."

Nausea bloomed in my stomach. Nausea, confusion, and a bud of hope.

"I led him away from the flock and I cut his throat."

"Guides, Fraesh," I gulped.

"While the vaiyas called his passing, my daughters wrapped his body so that it would pass for Yara's on the pyre."

"What happened next," I rasped.

"Everyone was convinced. Arsu, Dero, Na-Jhalar... even Enna." Tears rolled down Fraesh's cheeks. "I had no idea she would take her own life in response. Pau take me, I will rot with the wurms for that."

I could only stare at Fraesh, waiting breathlessly for what came next.

"We fled into the night. Yara was still drugged. She slept in the travois. She'd said she would stay with me and the girls, but..."

"But what?"

"We stopped to rest. I swear, I only nodded off for a short time, but when I woke—" Fraesh's voice wobbled. "Yara was gone. And a bag of food had disappeared as well. We think she went back to find you. We searched, but..." He shook his head. "We had hoped she'd heard word of you and come to the rock too."

"She hasn't." My hands shook.

Maybe she was alive. Or maybe she had died trying to save me, stumbling through the woods alone, heavy with child. I couldn't decide if this was better or worse... not knowing.

And that was when my uncle reached into his belt pouch, leaned toward me and pressed something into my cold hand. I gaped down at it. A wretched sob tore out of me.

It was a black ox hair comb with carved flowers on its spine. The matching pair to the one I kept.

"Where did you get this?" I rasped.

"In the spring, we met an aeni group that had traded with a camp who'd taken in a pregnant woman. That girl is a survivor, boy. She's out there somewhere."

Venda intercepted me as I strode out of her tent. "A word, Na-Akrist."

"Not now, Venda."

"Never now, eh Speaker? I shall be meeting the Goddess before we speak, I think." The old woman grabbed my elbow with gnarled fingers as I tried to pass.

"Something urgent has come up," I said.

"We have some matters of urgency to discuss too. Two vaiya patriarchs killed each other sparring yesterday and one of the hunters was gored trying to stop them. We need wood for taller corrals, more junab, or better yet, a healer's touch. I know there's a healer in that secret camp of yours."

"There is junab in the woods south of here. Send a gathering party on vaiyas and they will reach it within a day or two."

"The woman's wound will be well-infected by then, I'm sure, and the vaiya flocks scattered. Do you not care at all for us, Speaker? Are we just bodies for your dragon to mark and leave in her wake?"

"Venda!" I pulled away from her. "We will speak when I return. I promise."

"Full of promises." She shook her head, thick braid wobbling and eyes as black as coal staring right through me. "And all of them hollow, it seems."

I bit down an angry response and broke from her, striding toward Nardiri. Yara flooded my thoughts. *Yara.*

The boy, Amar, met me with a bright smile on his face that withered when he saw the expression on mine. He ducked his head and backed away from my dragon as I hoisted myself aboard and cinched my harness ropes.

Where are we going? Nardiri asked in flat tones.

West. That was where Fraesh had met the aeni.

Right now? You told Rowin we'd be right back. Perhaps he could come?

"We'll fly faster without him."

At least let us say goodbye before we go. It will only take a moment, she pressed.

"Are you my keeper, Nardiri?" I snapped. "Tell me, at this moment, what could be more important than finding Yara?"

She snapped her jaw closed. Great green eyes narrowed as she turned to pin me with a long stare. ***To you? Nothing, it seems.***

"Do we fly, or am I walking?"

My dragon huffed, walled off her mind and crouched to take off.

We soared westward for two days and nights. The vast grasslands creased into rippling hills strewn with low brush. From the air, the landscape looked like bodies swathed in the folds of a heavy blanket. Gentle curves spoke of limbs curled in repose, and sharper, more abrupt ridges reminded me of bones covered in moss, hollow corpses twisted and softened by time. Over it all, the wind roared as loudly as a dragon, bending and sculpting everything it touched into wild shapes.

Rain fell—an icy mist that felt like sand on my cheeks. It hung in the air, crept between the seams of clothing, and swept into my lungs with every breath. It was the kind of wet that made me forget what it had ever felt like to be dry. In the brief hours we rested, I huddled under Nardiri's wing, my fingers and toes white, water-logged and wrinkled no matter how often I wrung out my gloves and boots.

Under Wing

None of it mattered. My mind reeled with raw memories of my mate. I blinked away exhaustion and surveyed landscapes with burning eyes. Nothing would keep me from finding her. She was alive. My Yara.

Gaps of time peppered the days. Often, I fell asleep while we were aloft, realizing it only when I pressed away from my dragon's neck, groggy, legs prickling and the imprint of Nardiri's neck ridges stamped into my cheek.

We found another aeni tribe—the third since we'd started searching. By the time we landed and pressed through the arduous routine of calming our screaming hosts, pulling them off their knees and explaining who we were, I was exhausted and barely had the breath left to ask after Yara. They did not know her and looked at me with white-rimmed eyes when I dissolved into wet, gagging coughs. They did not invite us to share their meal.

Sickness scuttled its way deep into my chest and nested there like a bird on an egg. When not in the grip of a hacking fit, I dreaded triggering the next one, winced at the preliminary pain of it cracking through my ribs and twisting up my spine. Despite a pale sunrise warming my back, my lungs felt stiff and full of syrup. I slumped like a slack water bag against Nardiri's back and recognised the morning passing only by the shortening shadows on the lee side of steaming, humid hills. When we stopped for the afternoon, my bundle of kindling had dried enough to make building a fire feasible, but I had no energy to tackle the task, and no hunger for the thin gazelle Nardiri had hunted. I suggested she eat it all, and she did.

We didn't find Yara that day, or the next.

Countless days passed with little sleep and less food. Nardiri insisted we return to Ana's camp to rest and resupply. I told her she was welcome to go back alone. Perhaps she would have done so if my illness hadn't worsened.

My lungs burned and my cough stabbed through my ribs, making my head throb so loudly I didn't hear Nardiri when she announced our landing. I blinked at the ground rising to meet us, clearing my throat weakly. *We've only been up for an hour.*

We've been up for three. You fell asleep again. Her wings pivoted, pressing me further into her neck as she extended her legs to land in front of a ridge with an undercut that gave shelter from wind and rain. I slid off her back and stumbled to the ground.

I pushed my visor up, brushed dripping hair away from my eyes and pressed my damp palms against my eyes. I scanned the vaguely familiar foggy terrain around us. My hands fell from my face. **Did you turn around?**

She was silent in response, and I had my answer. I pounded a fist into my thigh. *You betray me while I sleep?*

Angry arcs of red met my thoughts. **I have done nothing but obey you, when you have only kept the barest of promises to me and everyone else following you! There is no way Yara is further west than we have already flown. Your mind is addled with illness, and you refuse to listen!**

She roared, her body trembling.

Filled with rage, I couldn't respond. My vision swam—with anger or fever, I couldn't tell.

If you want to find your mate, we need to search closer to our camps.

"Because you are desperate to return to our camps!" I spat out.

How are you not? How are you so selfish? They are depending on you. You gathered them all and, now that they

are ready to follow you off a cliff, you cannot stand their company, neither the daeson nor the Speakers! You do not deserve them. You do not deserve me. And you certainly do not deserve Yara if she is half as compassionate as you say she—

"Don't you speak of her!" I roared.

A wall of ice severed our mental connection, leaving me gasping. Nardiri snatched me up like a vaiya grabbing a chick by the scruff of its neck, hauling me to the undercut by my tunic and dropping me onto the dry ground.

I collapsed.

She took off.

I wanted to yell after her, but I could barely breathe. My cheeks burned, my pulse flared and my heart screamed to get up and continue looking for Yara on foot, but my limbs were saturated, swollen things that wouldn't listen. My eyes closed without my permission. The fever consumed me.

She had left me. Nardiri was gone. Yara was gone. And I was alone, feeble and helpless as a child among wurms.

Hot and cold washed over me in opposing currents. I grabbed at scraps of alertness, but they disintegrated like dry leaves in a fire. Occasionally, I was aware of the scratch of roots against my cheeks, the chill of the damp ground leaching into me and the counterpoint of steady warmth, something large and breathing against my back. A crooning hum fluttered through my chest, easing the tightness that bound it. Soft green filled my frantic mind as fresh as the first buds of spring. When the fever broke, I woke with my hair plastered to my face and my overcoat twisted around me. I felt Nardiri's warm hide against my back. She had returned.

Of course, she huffed, but orange worry cracked over my mind like a broken egg.

"I was sick." I croaked, blinking up at the underside of her wing.

And stupid.

"How long have I slept?" I sat up carefully, dizziness sluicing through me.

Mother Hen

Not long enough. You are still unwell. I brought brush for you to burn. I dug a pit for water. There are hares. You need to eat and drink. She withdrew her wing and blinked down at me, eyes filled with concern and something sharper too. Hurt. My memory was a cloud. I'd hurt her, hadn't I? Called her a betrayer.

My fingers fumbled with the kindling and flint. I mumbled a quiet thank you as Nardiri moved to block the wind so that I could start a fire. Neither of us relaxed until hungry flames crackled high over a lucent coal bed.

As the hares roasted, nausea swept through me, hot and horrible. I'd driven Nardiri away. I'd purposely done it. If she hadn't returned, if she hadn't saved me, if I'd died out here alone, what would have happened to her and the camps, the daeson, and Rowin? Could she bond with another Speaker, or would she just drift away like the hollow dragon we'd met?

Sweet Nasheira, I'd been so wrapped up in my desire to see Yara, I hadn't even considered what I stood to lose on this mad search for her. Without Nardiri, everything else came toppling down. Ana's camp would starve, Heart Camp would crumble. People would stop bringing daeson.

"I'm sorry," I croaked. "You were right. I don't deserve you. I don't deserve Yara. I don't deserve to be a Speaker."

Nardiri sighed softly. *It does not matter what we deserve. It matters what we do. People need you, Akrist. I need you. I can't do any of this alone. You are my Speaker.*

"I have not been." I shook my head, voice wavering. "I've been small-minded. I've thought about nothing but my own short-sighted wants."

Listen to me. She shifted toward me, warm, sweet breath washing over my cheeks. ***I'm still here because I choose to be. You need to be here too. In the present, not in your past.***

Smoke stung my eyes and scalded my throat. *I cannot bear to know that she lives and I am not with her. That I may be a father and my child does not know me.*

There is a whole world that needs us. And if she lives... Nardiri snorted. ***If she is half as stubborn as you are, she will find you.***

Something drained out of me at those words, something raw and desperate and dense, but its absence did not leave me hollow. Instead, a calm resolve settled over me and I swallowed and nodded my head slowly. "Let's go back," I rasped.

Camp. The single word lit my mind like a warm candle. We were at least four days West of Nasheira's Heart, but we must have drifted. There'd been no sign of this settlement on our initial search.

Below us, swathes of grass glowed in the setting sun. Unfamiliar stout roofs of dozens of huts rose out of the green like giant mushrooms. Hearth fires winked. Numerous, well-worn trails spider-webbed away from the camp. I squinted, but couldn't see any daeson huts on the north end. Several small forms already stood frozen with faces upturned toward us on the southern edge of the settlement.

She could be here. A tiny flare of hope rose in me at the dragon's words. ***I'm landing.***

Nardiri set down quietly, but the crowd squealed and dropped to their knees anyway. Their sounds of alarm drew out more members from their huts, and I watched them kneel in succession. One woman held a wooden spoon in her hand that dripped soup down her hairline as she pressed her fingers to her forehead.

I sucked in a jagged inhale before addressing them from high up on my dragon's back. "I'm looking for a woman," I said.

Nobody answered. Bowed backs and furtive glances were my only response.

Perhaps they didn't hear you. My dragon crouched and tipped a shoulder.

I realised she wished me to dismount, but the idea of it stirred sluggish fear in my stomach. How long would it take for the babbling to quiet enough that I could speak over it? How many questions about who I was, and why I was here would I have to field before these people would hear my questions about Yara? How long would I have to wait, just to be disappointed again? As the camp's last stragglers trotted out of their doorways and sagged to their knees, I scanned for honey-brown curls amongst them and saw no one who looked like Yara.

Can we just go? I swallowed.

No. You have not even heard their answers, and you could use a break by a fire and a cup of tea. You're still recovering.

Over the heads of my stricken audience, my gaze fixed on the camp's cooking hearth, well-stoked and ringed with several fat clay pots filled with steaming contents. Suddenly, nothing seemed more important than warm feet and a mug of hot broth in my hands. I fumbled with the slip knot and slithered down Nardiri's side. For a single, excruciating moment, as my feet hit the ground, I thought I might collapse, but I found my balance, stretched, and straightened.

Bracing for the cough that was sure to come, I announced again, "I'm looking for a woman."

A few people in the front row tipped up at my cracking voice, but I didn't have the volume to project my words further. Already, the cough clawed at my throat. "She has brown, curly—"

"Akrist?" My name burst from the back of the crowd.

CHAPTER SEVENTEEN

I STAGGERED FORWARD, AND my eyes found movement in the crowd. I spotted the boy who had spoken. He had close-cropped, dark hair and wore an enormous tunic, while his thin legs swam in oversized trousers. Wide eyes locked onto mine as he stumbled through the knot of stunned people, one hand hitching up the waistband of his pants. My insides dropped into a jellied mess and my throat ached intensely enough to cloud my vision. *I thought it was her.*

His aura's changing! Nardiri said.

Blinking, I leaned ahead to stare at the boy lurching toward me. *Not a boy.* My mind trembled as my gaze snagged on small details. A soft curl of hair at the nape of her neck, a round face tapering to a delicate chin, the soft spray of freckles across her nose. Eyes deep brown and doe-like. I watched, astounded, as the figure I'd mistaken for a boy shed her bland disguise and coalesced into my brilliant angel. *Yara.*

How did she do that? Nardiri shared her sight. Veins of pale olive fell from around Yara's shoulders while vibrant sheaves of fresh green uncurled beneath.

"Is it really you?" Yara stopped before me, feverish eyes drinking me in and coming to rest on the ugly brand on my right cheek. A frown creased her brow, and her small hand twitched upward as if she'd intended to touch the scar, but then changed her mind. She sobbed.

Nardiri crooned in excitement, the thrum weaving through my chest, but I barely heard it over the rushing in my ears. *Say it. Say it quietly, so quietly. If you speak too loud, if you even move, it'll unwind into nothing.* "Yara?"

And she didn't vanish. She stood there, flesh and blood. The huge tunic's neckline slumped to reveal the curve of a collarbone kissed by a beauty mark. "I tried to find you," she gulped. "After... I tried..."

I reached out, hesitantly. Part of me recoiled, terrified that this mirage would ripple into nothing at my touch, but my need to know if she was real overrode all fear. My thumb and forefinger closed on a dark, close-shorn lock. It slipped through my fingers, downy and soft. "Your hair," I blurted.

A frantic giggle broke past her lips. "That's all you have to say?"

She's real, Nardiri? A cavernous numbness yawned in my chest. Messy emotion sloshed in to fill the hollow in my rib cage before draining away. The roaring thrashed through my skull so loudly now that I couldn't tell if Nardiri answered me or not.

And I didn't care that there was a crowd of strangers watching us with confusion on their faces.

Yara's arm slid past my ribs. One hand pressed against my back, while the other flattened over the scar on my chest. My cheek wedged into the warmth of her neck. I felt her pulse and breathed in her earthy scent, wrapping my arms around her.

"You're here," she gulped in my ear.

I couldn't see. I couldn't breathe. The only thing my senses took in was her.

Yara ushered me into her hut while Nardiri paced outside. I sat, dazed, on her bedroll while she lit a lamp, filling the space between us with the scent of burning moss and hot lard. A lump rose in my throat as I surveyed her slender form, much thinner than it used to be. Dark circles under her eyes lent her an air of wildness, like she'd been backed into too many corners and fought her way out of all of them. "The baby" I asked hoarsely.

"She's here." She peeled open the folded neck of her oversized tunic to reveal a sling riding high on her torso. Over the edge poked a small head. Jet black wisps of hair swirled in a pattern that reminded me of a fingerprint. One pale round cheek was all I saw of the face that nuzzled into the hollow of Yara's chest.

"A-a girl," I said in surprise.

Yara pursed her lips. "She's small for her age. She's nearly—"

"Seven months old," I interrupted, my eyes drinking in the crescent curve of our baby's spine and the perfect way her legs folded in repose. It was all I could see through the fabric wrap. Frowning, I found Yara's eyes for confirmation.

"Yes," she breathed. "How..."

"I have counted every day," I said, my voice breaking. "Every hour. Every minute that I've been away from you. A daughter ..." I swallowed. "Have you named her?"

"Enna." Yara blurted and I couldn't help but flinch at the name, cringing at the memory of Yara's skeletal mother. She had hated me.

"She is beautiful," I whispered reverently.

How many times had I rehearsed our reunion in my head? How many times had I stood before Yara in my mind with well-polished words falling from my lips like round stones rippling into water? And in my imaginings, she smiled that radiant smile, the one reserved only for me. My lips parted, but only breath left them, threading in and out like sinew through brittle hide. Yara wasn't smiling. She looked like she was trying to swallow something painful.

I hesitantly opened my arms, and she fell into them. We clutched each other, crying wordlessly.

Reunion

Between us, our baby squirmed once and then settled back into sleep. Our silent crying turned into agonized sobbing. Nardiri crooned, threading tones of comforting blue and green through my head, but it was a long time before I could draw enough breath to speak.

With tears drying on my cheeks, I cradled Yara's head in the hollow of my shoulder while she inhaled in sniffs, fingers tracing the outline of the scar over my collarbone. "Do you want to hold her?" she asked.

I don't think the child is female.

"What?" I flinched.

"Would you like to hold her, Akrist?" Yara repeated.

What are you talking about? How can you tell?

Nardiri's foot scuffed outside. ***I don't know for sure, but Yara's aura changes whenever she speaks of the child. It mutes. I've never seen an aura like this.***

My eyebrows knotted as Yara stared at me expectantly. "I can't." I shuffled back on my knees. As if on cue, a wet cough clawed up my throat, and I turned from her. "I'm sick. I don't want to make her sick." *Show me.* But somehow, even before Nardiri shared her sight, I knew the dragon was right. Of course I would have a daeson.

"Sick?" Yara bent toward me with concern. Green flashed around her. "More than a cough?"

"What's his name?" I croaked.

Yara's head snapped up and the green around her muddied and faded.

"Our son's name. What is it?"

She tucked her chin to her chest, wiped the back of one hand across her nose and gulped. "If you could tell within minutes of being here, then I have been too obvious. *Guides!*" She pounded a small fist against her thigh before whispering. "I thought I was being so careful. He's rarely been away from my chest. No one else has held him, touched him. I told them he was—she was—too colicky." Fresh tears rolled down Yara's cheeks. "I'm a fool to think I could hide him."

"No, you did well." I gripped her shoulder. "Nardiri—the dragon—told me."

Yara squinted. "She—she told you? She speaks?" The sling at Yara's chest shifted as our baby stretched. Elbows and feet pressed outward.

"What's his name?" I murmured.

Yara's lips pinched. "Sun," she replied, smiling. "On the day I birthed him, the sun shone so brightly, the way it glittered off the snow... I wanted him to be that, the total opposite of the moons."

"Sun." I tested the name on my tongue. "It's wonderful."

Yara's face lightened into an instant smile. Ducking her head out of the large tunic, she slid an arm under our baby's back and shrugged her shoulder out of the sling. Fabric fell away and I saw him.

I saw my Sun.

Downy eyebrows pressed into a permanent frown even as his eyelids drooped with sleep. Wet, black eyes blinked and searched for Yara. I'd never seen anything so pink and smooth and new, the way his dimpled hands clasped each other before spreading wide to grasp his mother's chin. All of it undid me.

I didn't realise I was crying again until my son blurred from view. Yara shifted toward me, and I inhaled sharply. "*Guides,* he's perfect, Yara. He's beautiful"

I couldn't stop staring, the way the round of his cheeks bunched into a drool-creased smile when Yara cooed at him, how his wrinkled fingers found her hair and clamped on with vigour.

"Every time." Yara beamed, even as she sighed, cocked her head and gently un-threaded Sun's fist. "Never pulls on his own, just mine. That's why I cut it."

"I thought you were..." I swallowed. "I didn't recognise you."

Yara's gaze settled on the brand on my cheek. "I didn't recognise you either, at first," she whispered.

I couldn't imagine how I looked. I hadn't braided my hair away from my face or shaved in weeks. Cold rain had been my last bath. Clearing my throat, I focused on Yara's dark hair. "Did you colour it?"

"What?"

"Your hair. It's almost as dark as his."

She laughed. "The opposite. I stopped lightening it after Sun was born. I didn't have time, and besides, cinnamon and honey are worth more than I could trade for."

"Cinnamon and honey?"

"You make a paste out of it, to lighten hair. I've done it since I was a child. My brother had blonde hair, and I always wished I did, too." Sun fussed and nuzzled into Yara's chest. Without looking down, she shrugged out of the last fold of her wrap and offered him her breast.

I stared at the soft curve of her shoulder, the way she held our son like she'd done so since the beginning of time, how he tucked into her like a nestling under wing.

I wondered what else I didn't know about her. Yara had always been maddeningly elusive and straightforward at the same time. Guides, I ached to know every side of her.

"Come back to my camp with me," I murmured. "I Speak for a camp now. Well... two, actually. Come with me."

She diverted her gaze to our nursing son.

Something cold and hard settled in my throat, like a jagged rock tearing at soft tissues as it sank to my stomach. *Mother of Yurrii, she doesn't want to come.* I swallowed, but the rock remained.

"I thought you were dead," she said quietly. It took me a moment to interpret the look in her eyes when she met my gaze. I finally realized it was guilt.

A horrible, crushing thought bore down on me and I sagged beneath it. Of course our reunion was too good to be true. Of course things were complicated. I forced the words from my lips. "I understand if there's another..."

"Another what?"

Guides, don't make me say it. "You have another mate, don't you?"

—YARA—

Another mate. The words knifed into me. Akrist didn't understand. Just like he hadn't understood the night I was announced as Na-Jhalar's chani. I'd seen his eyes before I ducked into the Speaker's hut—the shock, the naked fear, and, simmering beneath it all, disgust. Akrist had been so repulsed by a choice I'd been cornered into that he hadn't spoken to me for months afterward. That same fear swam in his eyes now. It was only a matter of time until disgust followed.

Heat churned in my stomach. "No," I said, voice quavering. "No other mate." My mouth clamped shut. *When he finds out what you've done, it will break him, and he already looks so broken.* I swallowed. "I've been alone here." My voice cracked. Liar. *Not alone. You shared your bed with anyone willing to trade. You sold yourself. Tell him now. Wipe that loving look off his face and tell him what you really are, Yara. Someone undeserving of love. More animal than human, not the girl he promised himself to.*

"I've done things..." Air swept out of me. I balled my fists and tried again. "I've done things I'm not proud of to protect Sun, but none of them were my mates, Akrist. None of them held my heart."

He'd leave now. I steeled myself for it. Guides, I'd just found him again and now I'd lose him.

But instead of leaving, his eyes softened.

"I'm so sorry." Akrist's voice broke. "This is my fault. If we'd left camp together... if we'd taken the daeson away earlier..."

Tears stung my eyes and every emotion in me boiled over. "None of this is your fault. *They* took you! They treated you like an animal. I heard you screaming when they branded you. I heard Vax—" A weak sob wrung the rest of my air out of me. *I didn't do anything. I didn't save the man I loved.* "I heard Vax die, and then you were gone. They just took you. And I... I left to save myself."

Akrist pulled me against his chest and I let him. I breathed in the smell of him as Sun squirmed between us, still nursing, oblivious. "Listen to me." He breathed into my hair. "I love you, Yara, and no-one will ever take me from you again. Please, let me bring you somewhere where you don't have to hide Sun. We're going to change the world, and I can't do it without you."

Change the world. Mother of Yurrii. He sounded like an insurgent, full of charged words and fresh fire. It would have thrilled the old me, but now, with our fragile child cradled between us, Akrist's words terrified me. But I would go with him. If he wanted me, nothing would stop me from being by his side.

CHAPTER
EIGHTEEN

Introduction

*Y*OU ARE CARRYING EVERYTHING *dear to me right now,* I told Nardiri. Yara perched before me, legs wrapped so tightly around the dragon's neck that her heels dented Nardiri's soft hide. She grasped the harness with one hand and clung to Sun, nestled into the sling at her chest, with the other.

Nardiri stretched, rolled her shoulders and pumped her wings. Bits of dry grass swirled around us. ***I haven't dropped anyone yet, but you're both welcome to walk back to our camp instead if you're so concerned.***

"Ready?" My lips brushed Yara's ear. She nodded, eyes wide.

I braced for takeoff, but Nardiri's launch was the gentlest I'd ever felt. Her great wings reached and filled, surrounding us with the deep whoosh of displaced air. Yara's camp dropped away below us. I licked my lips. *No rolls. Under no circumstances—*

You think I would turn upside down with your hatchling on board?

Sorry. I'm... nervous and overthinking.

Don't think. Just fly. She hummed. ***It is a beautiful morning.***

Every time a soft current buffeted us and Nardiri smoothly course corrected, Yara gasped. I soaked in the sensation of her back against my chest while the mid-morning sun warmed us, and vibrant grasslands scrolled by far below.

We did not speak until we landed for the night. Nardiri captured four harek and left half of one of them for us. She even went so far as to delicately peel off the larger panels of armour with her teeth. I started a fire and we passed a bowl of steaming mint tea between us and leaned back against the warmth of the sleeping dragon's ribs while large slabs of harek sizzled over the coals.

"Your camps..." Yara's face flickered orange from the flames. Sun nursed quietly at her breast. "Sun will be safe there?"

I swallowed a large gulp of tea, passed her the bowl and sighed as I pressed back into Nardiri's bulk. The sky swam with stars tonight, a dark dome with enough quiet depth to humble anyone who stared for too long. *Sweet Nasheira, where do I even start?* I puffed out my cheeks and sighed. "I have so much to tell you."

I started at the beginning, from the moment we parted. Yara's tears had been still wet on my cheeks from our goodbye, before I was sent to be sacrificed and she escaped. I told her how Nardiri had bonded with me as a wurm. How she'd taken care of me. The deaths of the daeson. Tanar's return. Nardiri's transformation. How the two camps came to be, and how we'd been marking Speakers, promising them dragons. How I'd been too terrified to tell anyone the truth about wurms.

It all spilled out of me.

But when I came to my reunion with Fraesh, my words dried on my tongue..

Yara raised her eyebrows. "What is it?"

"Your... your mother, Yara."

"What about her?"

"She died."

I didn't think we had more tears left in us.

We burned the harek meat, but it did not matter, we were not hungry anyway. Afterward, I salvaged and wrapped what I could and then Yara and I lay by the fire, numb in each other's arms.

Two days later, as I slathered junab over my dragon's stretched hide, I realised that the foul-smelling salve that usually aggravated my cough had not done so today. Relief swamped me, and raw excitement tingled my spine.

"I think my cough is gone," I whispered to Yara at the fire that night as she bounced a giggling Sun on her knee. Unconsciously, I reached a finger out as his hand flailed at the air between us. He clamped on with a surprisingly strong grip, and I laughed. His head bobbed back, gummy smile dissolving into a concentrated frown as his large, liquid eyes studied me.

"Oh Akrist, you should hold him if you're well!" Yara gripped him under the armpits, and despite the look of consternation on both of our faces, pressed him toward me.

"No," I gulped. "What if I'm still sick? And my hand doesn't grip well."

"You'll be fine." Yara eased her hands out from under mine. "Just watch his head."

"I don't know how to hold a baby." I stiffened. A lie. I'd transported countless daeson babies these past months. All of them had despised being held. All of them had fought me. This was utterly different.

Sun hung from my outstretched arms, hands bunched against his cheeks, elbows jutting and legs feebly kicking. Small, even breaths whistled out of him as he fixed me with a look of deep concern. "H-how do I..."

"Not like that," Yara giggled and pressed a hand against my elbow. "Bring him in against your shoulder like this, and then wrap an arm around him, so his head rests in the crook of your elbow. There, now relax." She sat back, satisfied.

Sweet Nasheira, he was so light, so small and so utterly packed with life. I couldn't help but smile as I gazed down at the black hair pasted across his furrowed forehead. Bright eyes, black as coals, tracked across my face. He pressed his lips together so tightly his chin wrinkled, and just as my smile faltered, just as I was certain that my son was about to cry for his mother's warm arms instead of my inept ones, Sun broke into a beaming, dimpled grin, all wrinkled nose and wet gums. "Look at you." I breathed incredulously, blinking rapidly and beaming down at my perfect son.

I dreamed that night. It was the same aching imagining I'd had about Yara on the night the blue-braided ani made the rope harness for us. Her leg draped languidly over mine, her body pressed against my back, hands sliding around my ribcage. I sat up, horrified.

"Yara?" I whispered. *Oh Guides, what if all of it was an illusion? What if I hadn't actually found her?*

She sat up beside me in the dark. We lay under Nardiri's extended wing. The dim light of the almost full moons filtered through my dragon's wing and Yara's dark gaze flashed toward mine. "Dream?"

"You..." I swallowed, half-asleep and confused. "You wanted to share yourself with me. You just appeared, out of nowhere, and it was so real. Please, Yara, don't go."

"I'm not going anywhere." Her cool hand found mine in the dark.

"Where is Sun?"

"He's here," she assured. "He just finished nursing. See?"

I blinked down at the pale bundle topped with rounded cheeks and brilliant black hair. I listened to his rapid breathing in the dark. "I thought you were a dream." Cold relief washed through me.

Her dark gaze held mine. Slowly, she rose to her knees, pressed both hands to my chest and straddled me. Clouded moonlight cut past her shoulders and shadowed her face as she tipped her chin up and brushed her lips against mine. "Do I feel like a dream, Akrist?"

"We don't have to do this," I said. "If you are not ready—"

"I am." She leaned in.

"You've been hurt. I don't want to..."

"I do, please. Just a kiss."

I inhaled her, the sweet, sleepy scent of her, I lost myself in it. When her dry lips pressed to mine, I sucked on the salty taste of her, and when her tongue parted my lips, I let her. My hands found the back of her neck and buried into the thick softness of her hair before following the sleek line of her spine down to the small of her back. "Tell me to stop and I will."

"Don't stop." She pressed against me.

"*Guides,* I've missed you."

Yara plucked at the drawstring of my shirt, exposed my chest and fanned her hands over the ropy bumps of my scar. She turned her head and pressed her ear against the centre of my chest, and I knew it then, without any doubt. This was real. This was her. The Yara I remembered. Playfully listening to my pounding heart.

Leaning back, Yara smiled. She tugged the corner of the sling from its fold under her arm and began unwrapping herself. Gauzy layers fell away from her like flower petals and, when she was laid bare, I ached at the sight of her. Her breasts were larger and deeper than before, but still standing proud, milk dripping from their tips like dew drops.

My hands slid from her hips to the round of her stomach. Yara grabbed my palms and pulled them up over a trail of soft stretch marks, over the firm ridges of her ribcage to cup her breasts. A low groan escaped me at the softness. I lost track of her hands as she leaned into me to suck on my ear and nibble the side of my neck. The pleasant heat lapping from my core, the perfection of her collarbone against my lips, the warmth, I gave myself to it.

But when her hand tucked into my breech cloth, I froze. "Don't," I gulped, gripping her wrist. "I can't."

My mate leaned back. "You want me to stop?"

"It's not that. I can't... *do* anything for you." I croaked.

She pressed back into me, breath hot in my ear. "You're doing something for me right now."

"You know what I mean," I gasped. "I don't think I can fill you. I'm not whole."

"You're more than the sum of your pieces." Yara kissed my cheek, stroked my crooked fingers and lifted her leg off me. Her small hand slid out of my grip as she knelt beside me. She hooked her thumbs into the waistband of her pants. I swallowed as the swell of her hips, and then the dark dip and cleft of her womanhood slipped into view. Then she sat, eased her long legs out of her pants one at a time and laid beside me skin to skin. Her cold hand slipped into mine. "I don't care what they've done," she said. "You are whole to me," And we lay like that, utterly exposed, side by side, breathing in the dark. We fell asleep like that. And it was enough. More than enough. It was everything I'd ever needed.

CHAPTER NINETEEN

A LOW BANK OF clouds ripened into brilliant orange under the touch of the sunrise. Nardiri's wings stretched on either side of us, shoulders locked into an easy glide and mind humming with the innate processes of reading the air around her. Yara leaned against me, the back of her head rolling against my collarbone as she slept. She was so small that I was worried she'd slip out of my arms.

I think she's finally over her fear of flying.

Nardiri snorted gently, tipped her head and eased into an updraft. **It only took the entire trip to gain her trust. You should lay naked with her more often.**

I pursed my lips and shifted in my seat. My exhale hitched into a short laugh that blew Yara's hair away from my cheek. *You are shameless, Nardiri.*

Her bright green gaze rolled toward me, and my dragon's teeth clicked, neatly punctuating her next thoughts. ***I am. You think about shame far too often, but when you were laying beside her, your mind was clear, and your heart was happy. If I must feign sleep for that to happen, so be it.***

We landed only once, when Yara woke, to stretch our legs and pad a knot in the harness that Nardiri complained was chafing. That evening, Nasheira's Heart rolled over the horizon, curling out of the ground like the jagged spine of a buried beast, rust stains rippling down its flanks to where the grasslands lapped like pale green water. Where the Speaker's camp had nestled at its base, there was nothing.

I straightened in the harness and scanned the trampled, abandoned tract of grass.

Where are they?

My mouth dried out as Nardiri landed in a cloud of red dust.

I swung my leg over her neck and vaulted down. White ashes swirled in abandoned hearths. Frayed bits of rope, broken pottery and vaiya droppings peppered the trampled grass. No drying racks left behind. No tent spars. Even the corrals had been disassembled and the stout logs dragged away. "They packed and left," I said.

The grooves, vaiya tracks, and boot prints all led in one direction.

Toward Ana's camp.

A chill walked up my spine. "Let's go," I said, hoisting myself back onto Nardiri.

By the time we reached the daeson camp—and confirmed that it had doubled in size as we approached—my fear and frustration had bled into Nardiri enough that she trumpeted sharply as we landed.

Yara went rigid in my arms. Below us, children squealed and poured out of huts, adults cocked their heads from their crackling evening fires, and Ana pressed to her feet and waved tiredly, red curls streaming behind her in the backwash of our wind.

Nardiri pressed her wings tight against her ribs and crouched for us to dismount. I kept my back to Ana as she approached, taking extra time to help Yara step down onto Nardiri's forearm and exhaling several hot breaths in an effort to temper my anger before turning to the storyteller.

The ivory beads in her hair clicked as she shook her head and took in my mate with weary, blue eyes. "Speaker." Her gravelly voice sounded washed out. "I believe an introduction is an order?"

"What have you done?" I blurted, waving to the clump of new tents sprawling off the flank of our camp. "Why are they here? They've left a trail big enough for a stampeding herd to follow!"

Ana eyed the growing daeson crowd milling around us and the stony-faced adults beyond them, hunched around their fires. No one but the children had risen to greet me.

I felt unsettled, the way a hunter sometimes does when they've judged the weather wrong and the air heralds an unwelcome storm.

"We have much to talk about, Na-daeson Akrist." Turning from me, as if I were dismissed, Ana shifted to an open-mouthed, wide-eyed Yara, and ambushed her, wrapping her bandy arms around my mate as if she were a long-lost daughter. "Look at you," she exclaimed, holding Yara at arm's length, pale eyes shifting. "No wonder he flew halfway to the moons and back to find you." Then her gaze settled on the bump in her sling. "And the baby! Come. Warm yourself by my fire."

And just like that, the storyteller was steering my family away from me, leaving me and Nardiri sputtering in her wake. I stumbled after them, shouldering past the clotting crowd of daeson. "Why are the Speakers here, Ana?" I spoke to the back of her head. "We agreed to keep them separate, to keep the daeson safe. Now, with the full moon only days away, anyone who gathers there will find their way here. You've practically drawn them a map!"

The storyteller stopped so quickly, I nearly collided with her. Letting go of Yara's elbow, she spun back to me, teeth flashing and pale eyes as hard as flint. "*Days* away! Guides, has your brain been addled?"

I opened my mouth to reply in anger, but she continued.

"Yurrii's full moon was *last* week, Speaker," Ana snapped with a mock bow. "So you needn't worry about anyone gathering at Nasheira's Heart. They were all there waiting for you, and you never came, because finding *her* was more important to you than any of us." Before I could fully absorb her words, she turned back to Yara and pressed her toward her hearth. "Not your fault, love." She tucked her head close to my mate's but her words carried well enough. "He's dug this fine hole all on his own."

My thoughts were sludge. That couldn't be. How could I have missed it? I had only left the camp a few days ago. It had been a *week*, at most.

You were consumed with need for many days, and sick for many more, Nardiri confirmed. **You would not listen to reason. You would not return.**

As if walking out of my memories, my uncle rushed toward us.

"Yara," he said, pulling her into a long hug. "Thank the goddess above. We have been searching for you since the day you left."

"I've missed you." Yara gulped and pulled away as Sun squawked.

"Akrist." He pulled me into a quick embrace next. "It is good that you're back."

Guilt hollowed my stomach as I settled across the fire from Ana and Fraesh. Yara sat by my side, rocking Sun.

"What happened?" I asked, drained of all my venom.

Ana pinned me with a shrewd gaze. "Exactly what Venda told you would happen. After the two vaiya patriarchs killed each other, the old silverback remaining took their hens under his wing, but he had no tolerance for more competition, and all the young male stragglers grew too flighty and aggressive to pen in. Rather than risk them scattering to the wilds, several of your less devoted Speakers took the opportunity to seize a pack animal and haul away as much food and goods as they could carry."

Thieves. Heat stirred in my chest. *How had I let this happen?* My shame coiled like a snake about to strike. I asked, "How many left?"

"Eight birds. Ten people. Heart Camp felt the loss of the vaiyas and the food more than the deserters. As you know, there's no water supply close to the rock and your sizable following had been relying on daily vaiya trains to the nearest water source to stay sated." Ana shrugged. "We felt the pinch fairly quickly with you gone and all these boys to feed. It didn't take me long to make the journey to the rock, meet your fine uncle, and recruit some hunters to meet our needs."

Fraesh coughed and reddened.

Ana carried on. "Your remaining Speakers came after the full moon. Weren't enough vaiyas left to haul water *and* hunt with." She smacked her lips and leaned back. "The physical hunger and thirst, they could have pushed past that, I am sure, but when you didn't show up, and caravans bringing daeson did, demanding meat—demanding you, your Speakers made the only move they felt they could."

I wanted to apologize, to purge the guilt solidifying in my stomach, but, now that I was here, I had to think of our immediate safety first. "How many of them stayed, after they settled here?" My gaze flicked between my boots, unable to face Fraesh or Ana. "Did any of them leave?"

"Three or four have left, I think," Fraesh answered, looking to Ana for confirmation.

She nodded.

I scrubbed my jaw and swallowed the panic burning up my throat. "They could spread news about us, about a camp full of daeson who have not been sacrificed." I glanced at Yara and Sun bundled against her chest. *Mother of Yurrii, I'd promised her to bring him somewhere safe.*

"We couldn't have remained hidden forever, Speaker." Ana said. "Your lapse only hurried along the inevitable."

Maybe it wouldn't matter. Most camps were so concerned with their own survival, they wouldn't bother coming here to enforce Nasheira's will and ensure the sacrifice of the daeson, would they? Besides, we had a dragon for a guardian. What camp would confront us?

CHAPTER TWENTY

THAT NIGHT, WHILE YARA and Sun slept in my small hut, I nursed a miserable smoky fire outside, unable to sleep. To keep my hands busy, I inspected Nardiri's harness, testing knots and oiling lengths of rope. It did nothing to soothe my swamped mind.

I'd promised my daeson safety and my Speakers dragons. Then, at the very first opportunity to prove myself, I let my selfishness nearly destroy them all. I was just as bad as Arsu.

Footsteps scuffed beyond my fire, rousing me from my thoughts. I had expected a daeson's company, but not the one who stood across from me now.

Instead of Rowin's tangled brown hair and hunched shoulders, red hair and hard green eyes greeted me as Tanar stepped out of the darkness.

I sighed. "You're still here?"

He smirked and squatted across from me. "Surprised that I'm more faithful to your camp than you are?"

The barb stung. "I'm surprised that you haven't stolen a vaiya and left already."

"Why would I leave?" He frowned, digging dirt from under his fingernails. "These people keep me fed and, more importantly, they aren't trying to kill me."

I didn't know what to say in response to that, so I stayed silent.

In the fire's glow, I saw that his cheeks had more colour and his gauntness was filling out. His eyes were clear of fever and madness, though I still smelled gifen on his breath, even from across the fire.

He noticed my wrinkled nose. "Fraesh is trying to wean me off of it. It's... difficult," he said.

After a moment of quiet, he asked, "What's your plan, anyway? What do you expect all these Speakers to do for you?"

"Not endangering my daeson would be a start," I said.

"*Your* daeson." Tanar nodded slowly. "So you're the voice of the banished? You saved us and we belong to you now?"

"That's not what I said. Would you rather I had left you to die?"

"I'd rather you consider us before you let your cock lead you elsewhere."

I sneered, covering my guilt with anger. "I'm to be taking lessons on virtue from you? You *betrayed* me! You left me to die!

And then you came back and tried to finish the job! Nasheira knows what you did to earn your brand."

He flinched and brushed a finger over the wurm-shaped brand on his right cheek. "I acted, Akrist. That is something you've always had problems with. You never act. You *wait* until you are backed into a corner, and you only fight when it's too late."

I pulled the rope through my hand so hard, it burned. "I'd rather do nothing than have murder on my hands."

Tanar faltered. His throat worked and his eyes scanned the coals rapidly as if he saw something there that he didn't like. "I was not myself then. I am better now."

"Because *I* brought you here. And for what? The next opportunity for you to betray me again? I should just have Nardiri tear you limb from limb and be done with you."

The grin Tanar usually wore like a mask faded, replaced with fear. I saw his hands tremble. Shame threatened to engulf me, but I pushed it away.

"I didn't come to defend myself," he said. "I came to warn you about the Children of Yurrii."

I glared at him suspiciously, recalling the words from his gifen-enhanced raving.

"Arsu and Dero are leading them," he continued. "Your brother is the one who tied me to that tree and left me. I thought you were him before you rescued us. Who would have guessed there were two of you riding around on dragons?"

I couldn't process his words. They were impossible.

He read the denial on my face. "They're paying people to bring them daeson. And to kill wurms. They know about you, and they're spreading the word that you're doing Pau's work, and anyone who follows you is an enemy of Nasheira. They've got their own Guide to back their words."

"No," I croaked.

He didn't reply, staring into the embers as I processed his words. It couldn't be true. It couldn't.

It could. My own thoughts betrayed me. *Nardiri marked Dero*.

"It might help if we had more Guides to fight him with," Tanar said quietly. "It might help if you kept your promises and bonded your Speakers to dragons."

"You have no idea!" I snapped. "None of you. Bonding with a dragon is nothing like what you all think it is. Half of my Speakers will brand me as a heretic if I tell them how it's done!"

He leaned forward, his eyes piercing me through the smoke. "But half of them will stay."

I shook my head. "I wouldn't have believed it if I didn't live through it. They'll think I'm insane."

Tanar's grin returned, not reaching his eyes. "Tell me your big secret, Na-daeson Akrist, and it will not shake me. How did you win your dragon?"

I was exhausted, raw, and sick of Tanar prodding at all my soft spots like a vaiya toying with a mouse. Who would he tell anyway? No one would believe him. "I won her tied to a tree just as you were."

Tanar's exhale whistled through his nose. "What?"

"The wurms came for us just like they did with you. One of them found the scar on my chest and it imprinted. They're built to *feel* for the mark. Wurms become dragons. That night when you woke me with my knife to my throat, Nardiri was emerging from a cocoon." I shook my head. "If I tell my Speakers that, it will send them to Arsu faster than if I hand delivered them myself. I need them here. I need them protecting the daeson."

Tanar giggled and I winced at the high-pitched manic tone of it. "Wurms? Dragons are wurms?"

"They are."

"That is how you win a dragon. Win a wurm first? Then what?"

"Feed it."

"The hunger," he murmured.

"They eat as much as a small camp."

"Feed a wurm. Done." Tanar's eyes flashed. "My turn."

I frowned. "Your turn for what?"

"I've a secret to share too," he said, craning his neck past my hut to squint at where the vaiya flock rested. "Is your dragon awake?"

At the shake of my head, he said, "We'll need her for this. Come on." Standing, he started toward Nardiri.

More curious than I would admit to myself and too tired to argue, I woke Nardiri. As we stood before the groggy dragon with the vaiyas chirping anxiously around us, Tanar stood up straighter.

Shadows shifted across his face and something hungrier and more feral than fire lit his eyes. He *changed*. I couldn't even pin down the differences, but it reminded me of water rolling off a fish as it arced high out of the water. Straightening with his teeth still bared, he laughed as I shrank away from him.

He's receptive! Nardiri trilled. *He wasn't before, but now he is.*

"She feels it? You do too, don't you?"

"H-how..." My mouth gaped.

The redhead rolled his neck until it cracked and pulled his energy back in. Air rippled around him and Tanar stared back at me with that maddening grin, the space around him unnaturally still, thick and impenetrable. "I thought Nasheira was sending them to kill me because I left you. Because I wasn't supposed to live." His face twitched like he was exerting himself, holding boulders in his hands that I couldn't see. "She can't see it now, can she?"

Nardiri?

He's masking himself. Like the male dragon we saw. Yellow tinged my dragon's thoughts.

"I didn't understand what it meant—the way Guides and wurms came for me—until I chatted with your Speakers these past few days. They all felt the same pull before you marked them. And now you've confirmed it." Tanar rubbed his sternum.

I felt Nardiri's urge to mark him, even as she resisted it.

"Why are you telling me this?" I asked, suspicion flooding my instincts.

He shrugged. "You need Speakers and Guides. I'm not afraid to bond with a wurm. Mark me."

"Why should I trust you?"

"Because you want to believe we can both change."

We stared at each other—both marked, both banished, both daeson.

"What happened to Xen?" I asked. Guides, why in the wide sky did I need to know now? *Because he picked Xen over you once, and now he wants to choose you.*

"He got sick." Tanar breath rattled as it came out, like it was air he could never pull back in. "He wouldn't eat. He just…" His mouth opened like a fish. A string of saliva quivered between his lips. "He fell asleep and didn't wake up."

"I'm sorry," I said.

We sat in silence for a long while.

I like him.

I snorted.

"What?" Tanar asked.

"Nothing."

He has a strong pull. He could call any dragon to mark him, now that he knows he's receptive. But he wants us to do it.

As though he could hear Nardiri's voice, Tanar said, "You saved me. I'd like it to be you."

I sighed. "We'll do it."

And so we did. Nardiri marked Tanar with dawn a faint promise on the horizon, with no audience other than the vaiyas. He didn't even scream when her barbed tongue ran across his chest.

There was no way I could sleep after he left.

How could Dero have figured out how to bond with a dragon? I said after I'd shared everything Tanar had told me, leaning into Nardiri's thigh.

Before she could answer, it struck me like an unexpected punch to the stomach. Cold nausea swept over me as I realized how stupid I'd been.

What is it? Nardiri growled at my swing in emotion and the vaiyas around us blared an alarm.

"I told Jin," I rasped. When we'd met in the woods after Nardiri marked Dero, I'd spilled my story. Jin had betrayed me, or he'd been forced to talk. I'd given Arsu and my little brother all the tools they needed to win a dragon and hunt us down.

Tanar was gone in the morning. So was a sizable portion of our dried meat.

Why would he leave? Nardiri wondered nervously.

"Tanar runs," I sighed, head aching. "He always runs."

CHAPTER TWENTY-ONE

T HE SPEAKERS AMBUSHED ME before I finished my morning cup of tea. Venda led them, as she always did. They were smaller than the group I'd left, less than twenty people now, and they crowded around my hearth.

A growing headache pounded behind my eyes while I gulped down the last tepid dredges of liquid and shook the crumbled leaves from the bottom of my clay cup. I stood to kiss Yara on the forehead and stroke Sun's wispy black hair before leading the restless group away from them.

Keep them in your sight, please. These people are upset. I won't have my mate and child pulled into it.

I'll keep them safe. The dragon answered from her spot in the morning sun.

The Speakers followed me wordlessly until we'd threaded through camp and reached the edge of a prairie already blushing with the early colours of autumn. Venda stood with one gnarled hand gripping Amar's while the rest of the crowd fanned out around us.

"Speaker." She offered the briefest nod.

"Venda." My gaze scanned the cold faces around me. Eyes filled with impatience. Feet shifting and ready to leave. Swallowing, I held out my palms. "I owe all of you an apology—and much more. I promised each of you the chance at a dragon, the opportunity to become bonded Speakers, and I've not fulfilled it."

"You've not even had the decency to show up," said a young man with close-cropped hair and piercing, dark eyes. I cast deep for his name. Nardiri had marked him in the foothills south of here. *Oric.*

"I have no excuse for that, Oric. I did not intend to miss the full moon ceremony, and it wasn't fair to leave you all to deal with the aftermath."

"Are we Speakers to you, or are we slaves to feed your daeson? When were you planning to tell us about them, eh, Speaker? When were you planning to tell us we've been working so hard to feed firstborn sons?"

"Peace, Oric." Venda waved him off like a fly, and he clenched his jaw, crossed his arms and shook his head. She turned back to me. "We need to talk about the full moon you missed before we speak of anything else. There were dissenters among the crowd that came to Nasheira's Heart. They called themselves the Children of Yurrii."

Ice gripped my spine, creeping toward my lungs. "They said you were a son of Pau!" a blonde woman piped up. "That's why you didn't want us killing wurms. That's why you're saving the daeson."

I was quiet for a moment, waiting for all eyes to turn to me. It was time. Guides help me, I might lose them all. But it was time.

"I *am* a son of Pau," I said. "I am Na-*daeson* Akrist."

Venda stared at me like she'd never seen me before. Amar pulled away. Oric murmured, "Impossible."

"This camp. These boys." I jabbed a hand toward the closest huts. "They are not cursed. They are my wards, and if you believe their lives do not matter, you are free to go. I won't force anyone to be here."

No one moved. They were still staring at me for answers. And it was time I gave them.

"I haven't been a good leader," I said. "I haven't told you the whole truth, because I am afraid. I told you it was time for the world to change, but I didn't want to be the one to change it. I didn't want to carry that weight."

But maybe I didn't have to carry it alone. I looked around at the faces surrounding me—people who had stayed where others had left. Out of what? Hope? Despair? The fact that they had nowhere else to go? Whatever the case, they deserved the truth.

So I gave it to them. I told them my story, how a wurm had bonded with me and turned into Nardiri, how daeson were not the reason we weren't bonded with Guides anymore, how Arsu was likely assembling an army to attack us. How we were in danger.

"I will help any Speaker who stays to bond with a wurm, but know that your life is threatened by staying with me. Anyone who wants to leave, do so now."

Oric crossed his arms tighter over his chest, but did not budge. Three Speakers turned and shouldered past their numb comrades.

Only three. I had expected them all to abandon me.

When the deserters were out of earshot, I turned to the rest and said, "Get ready to move camp in an hour."

Ana's exhale whistled through her teeth. "This is not a small camp, Speaker."

"We will pack light. Carry only what we absolutely need. I can fly back later and fetch more supplies as needed. The herds are moving south from here toward the caldera for the winter. We'll follow them."

"You make it sound so easy." Ana snorted. "Do you have any idea the condition some of these daeson are in? They're barely adjusting to their new life here. A move like this when they've just settled, another change when we've just established a routine... it will shake them."

"If we don't move, they will die, Ana. I told you, they have a dragon."

I strode back to my hut. Far ahead of me, in the space between two huts, a boy stood and stared at me, thin-shouldered, wisps of wild brown hair glowing in the rising sun.

Rowin. I waved hesitantly.

He walked away.

Our caravan tracked southeast, away from Nasheira's Heart and toward the caldera the herds funneled toward. Nardiri tracked above us, flying low so she didn't obviously mark our position. She kept an eye out for Dero's dragon, circling diligently above us from sunrise to sunset.

Two days into our journey, I woke in the middle of the night to a keening wail carving through the darkness. The vaiyas' mourning cry. Whipping my blanket aside with my heart grappling my throat, I checked that Sun was breathing beside Yara.

"Oh Guides," my mate gulped. "Who is it?"

I stumbled in the dark, yanking on my leggings, cramming my feet into boots and snatching up my skinning knife before tumbling out of the tiny travel tent.

What if Arsu and Dero had found us in the night, cutting my people down in their tents as they slept? I shuddered.

Nardiri?

From the rise where she'd bedded, my dragon's senses unspooled, fissuring the night with uncertain energy.

Green silhouettes stirred in shuddering tents around me, splashing out into the night. I strode toward the flock. The vaiyas would circle if one of their own died of natural causes. They were curious birds. Yet, when I reached them, they'd already settled into silence, crests erect and trembling, exhalations wreathing their heads as they stood scattered, but staring back toward the settlement. "Not them," I sighed. "One of us then." Someone had died... or been killed.

I charged back toward the tents, gripping my knife in its sheath. Every structure I scanned had green life within, or was empty when I flipped open the door flap to check. Other roused searchers joined me, opening tent flaps to poke their heads within.

I was two rows in when I heard a woman's cry, long and low, from the northern end of camp where most of our daeson congregated out of habit. Dodging between tent pegs and ropes, I was almost upon the shelter when the thought struck me:

Rowin sleeps here.

The woman's desperate wail gutted me again.

I tore open the tent flap. Wide eyes flashed in the dim confines. The woman—a surrogate mother—had her stout arms wrapped around a tiny body. His feet were bare and the bedroll rumpled and twisted from where he'd kicked out. His arms were roped with jagged scars.

"Guides," I hissed, crashing to my knees beside the woman and sawing at the taut rope strung over the tent's central pole. It held him up by his neck. When it snapped, his head lolled back over the woman's arm and dark brown, bloodshot eyes gazed up past both of us, empty.

It wasn't Rowin. Sick relief coursed through me even as I lay my palm over a small chest that I knew was not breathing. *Mother of Yurrii.*

"He was happy today," the woman sobbed, rocking the small body back and forth. "He let me hold his hand."

I staggered out of the hut and nearly crashed into Ana. She was carrying a large blanket, but dropped it to steady me. I flinched when she grabbed my arm. Ana's pale eyes studied my numb face before she rasped, "Another's dead? Hanged himself?"

I gaped at her, unable to answer and she let go of my arm to pat my shoulder. "Not our first one, Speaker. Go. We will take care of him and light a pyre tomorrow."

The scars on his arms. I realized as I drifted back toward my tent. *He cut himself. This was not the first time he tried to die.*

Why would he take his life? Nardiri's frail thought braided with mine. ***He was fed and loved. The woman, she aches for him.***

I didn't have an answer.

Yara stood in front of our tent. At her chest, Sun slept with one plump leg dangling from his sling. A shirtless boy was facing them, all sharp quivering fists and jutting shoulders. Tangled hair trailed down his neck.

"Rowin," I whispered. Guides, how I wanted to stride across the distance between us, crush him against my chest and hold him there, but he was all edges, like a harek trying to decide between fleeing or burying its tusks deep into an adversary's thigh. His ribcage rose and fell in short bursts. "Rowin," I said, louder.

This time he turned. His gaze knifed toward me and he sank lower into his stance, cheeks mottled red and nostrils flared. Fat tears clumped his eyelashes. With jerking movements, he stabbed a finger toward me, and then at Yara before cramming his hands together, fingers interlaced.

You and her together?

I nodded slowly. "Yes. We're together. Rowin, this is my family, Yara and my boy, Sun."

His whole body twitched, his breathing quickening.

I licked my lips and signed back to him as I spoke, "But you and I. We are together too. We are family. Yara, I'd like you to meet Rowin."

The daeson barked, a short, feral howl that made Sun jolt in his sleep. Rowin glanced at him and then shook his head violently. *No. You and I. Apart,* he signed, hands jerking away from each other, fingers splayed wide. He jabbed at me again and then mashed his thumbs together and flapped his hands, mimicking flying. *You flew away.*

I nodded. "I made a mistake. I shouldn't have left you." I stepped toward him.

He recoiled and bared his teeth. His fingers curled, ready to gouge, and he was so close to Sun's soft, perfect little leg. Yara wasn't backing away because she was already pressed against the front of the tent.

Sinking to my knees, I held out a trembling hand. He wouldn't look at me, so I dropped my gaze, stared hard at the grass stains on my leggings and held my hand higher. I spoke into the ground between us, crooked fingers cramping and twitching with the effort of holding my hand open. "I love you," I croaked. "And while I have to leave you sometimes, I will always come back. I won't abandon you. Not you, not them. You are all my family and I want us to be together. Will you forgive me?"

The daeson mother wailed in the distance.

My breath sounded too loud. Cramps twitched through my legs. Had all my time spent gaining his trust been ruined by leaving? I cursed my thoughtlessness.

I did not hear Rowin move, so when his small, hot hand slipped into mine, I flinched before gripping his fingers softly. We sat there in the dark at arms-length, side by side, crying quietly, and Yara—Nasheira bless her—slipped closer to us, tucking Sun against her, and sitting with a sigh on the far side of the wet-cheeked daeson she'd just met.

"Do you know," she said, smiling. "I've always loved the name Rowin?"

His head bobbed up.

"I swear to the Goddess, it's true." Yara held out her hand. "I think Nasheira meant for us to meet."

Rowin reached out tentatively and clasped her fingers.

And there we were, this quiet, trembling, fresh connection, wet and helpless like something newborn in the unsettled night. And I was terrified to break it, terrified to move or even breathe.

Please Nasheira, I closed my eyes and prayed for the first time in a long time. *Let me keep this. Let me keep them safe.*

CHAPTER
TWENTY-TWO

O N OUR FIFTH DAY of travelling south, we reached the edge of a ravine, where the prairies sank into a sudden valley. A muddy river wound its way through the base of a canyon, ribboned with bands of sedimentary rock. From a few miles away, the entire gorge lay invisible, like a dormant, dried-out world beneath the stark plane of the surrounding prairie. After thoroughly scanning the area around us to be sure we were alone, Nardiri and I left our ragged caravan at the edge to make a quick exploration of the valley below.

Brave succulents filled cracks in the caked grey clay. Delicate fronds of wildflowers gathered in colonies of bright blue and yellow, and a sizable herd of black ox foraged on next to nothing, corralled by formidable canyon walls.

We flew for several miles in either direction and found that there was no easy access into the ravine on foot. The animals here had been segregated for long enough that we noted differences between them and the common black oxen we were used to. They were already growing long, patchy, winter hides and had stilt-like legs that ended in wide, paddle-shaped hooves. We found the bleached bones of their dead laying as they fell.

No wurms here? I dismounted to examine a fully intact skeleton.

Nardiri tilted her head to blink at the striated rock walls around us. ***Too much stone. They cannot tunnel here.***

Further east, we found caves pockmarking the canyon walls like swallows' nests. There were hundreds of entrances, all reliably ten feet or more in diameter. They honeycombed the flank of a south-facing cliff where the ravine yawned wide and the river expanded into a low, still lake far below the plains above.

"I wonder if there's anything living in them," I said.

Nardiri gave a mental shrug. ***It is difficult for me to sense life underground.***

"Land, please." I stared hard at the clustered entrances.

Don't do anything stupid. My dragon huffed, but shed air and landed in the ravine next to the still waters of the lake.

I want to see if they're empty. Unslinging my spear, I approached the nearest cave, which sat at ground level. I didn't smell wurms or harek musk, and the chalky sand was free of footprints. I didn't have a lantern, so I waited for my eyes to adjust before pressing in further.

The interior smelled of bat droppings, but a fresh breeze of air tickled my nose, suggesting it went further back than I originally thought. My breath echoed back at me in the quiet, cold air, but nothing else moved. I pursed my lips, took a deep breath, and hollered "Can you see me?" My voice rolled through the darkness, repeating itself. A swell of bat wings rustled like brittle leaves, and brisk air buffeted my face as the cloud of disturbed sleepers scrambled toward the light.

Nardiri stuck her head inside the cave and blew a puff of warm air in my face. *Only if I do **this**.*

"Dero's dragon won't be able to find us here." I smiled.

We went back for the caravan, and Nardiri spent the rest of the day ferrying people, vaiyas, and supplies down to the canyon. We shuffled through wide entrances with wrinkled noses, ankle deep in chalky bat droppings. The throat of each cave opened into a womb-like cavern with arching ceilings. When Fraesh and I shovelled debris aside in one of them, the exposed floors felt polished under our palms. We found dull, cracked rounds of yellow scattered amongst the dust and dung, and we knew them for what they were, by the instinctive shudder that clutched us by our backbones when we brushed our fingers across their ridged surfaces.

"Dragon scales," Fraesh whispered, awed.

And suddenly, I knew what this place was. *A hive of cocoons.* Radiant heat from a low winter sun absorbing into the bare cliff face outside would have warmed developing dragons inside admirably, and the eternally trapped herd of oxen wandering the floors of the canyon likely served many a fledgling its first meal.

I brushed my finger over familiar gouges in the rough, gritty walls. *You made marks like this when you burrowed. Incredible.* If wurms had buried here once, perhaps it hadn't always been rock. How long had it taken the soft walls here to compress and solidify into sandstone? How many generations had passed since ancient Guides breached the walls of their cocoons here, emerging slick, wet and golden? Perhaps they'd even been paired with humans?

Regardless of the status of its past inhabitants, the location proved perfect for our needs. We had water—the lake was clear and cool. We could winter here alongside the trapped ox herd, and with Nardiri perched on the top of the ridge, we had enough warning to flee to the caves before any dragon flew close enough to sense us. Surely, we would be safe.

I drew a shuddering inhale, held my breath, and leaned my back against the cold sandstone ridge marking the entrance to my cave. We had been here for a week, and Rowin's nightmares rattled him every night. I'd chosen a ground-level cave, thinking of Sun—who was crawling at an alarming speed now—but it was Rowin who wandered in the night.

I stood beside him now as he shivered in the entryway and stared blankly out into a brooding darkness that smelled like rain coming. "They're on me," he said, pushing away an invisible enemy.

The sound of his voice, so small but articulate, was as disarming as the first night I'd heard it. Yara had been shocked too when she heard the mute daeson talking in his sleep, but she grew used to it quickly, sleeping right through his episodes the last two nights running.

"Rowin, I'm here," I assured in a low voice. "It's a dream." I didn't touch him—that made it worse when he had nightmares of wurms—but my voice usually drew him back until he awoke, or his breathing evened out and he returned to his bedroll.

"Help," he whimpered.

My chest ached. *Guides, how many times has he needed to ask that while awake, and been incapable of saying it?* "I'm right here. I'll help," I said. "You're not alone. Just breathe. It's a dream and it's almost over now, isn't it?"

He flapped his hands. Eventually, his body relaxed, his shredded breathing evened out, and he glanced up at me with a confused frown.

I held out my hand. "Do you want to go back to bed?" Sometimes, he could slip back under his hides and return to deep slumber with the kind of careless ease only young children seemed to possess. Otherwise, we'd play tavi for hours. This time, Thank Nasheira above, sleep triumphed.

Rowin grabbed my hand and nodded.

I led him back to the bedroll beside ours and tucked him under several layers of furs.

When I slipped into the lingering warmth of my bedroll, Sun snuffled like a little harek and squirmed between Yara and me. She sighed in her sleep, rolled toward him and offered her breast. I stared at the cave ceiling and listened to the wind outside and the muffled whistle of my son's halting breaths while he drew milk from his mother. When he stopped suckling, I rolled toward him and eased a finger into the corner of his mouth to break his latch without waking Yara. I took him outside to pee. Fat rain drops pattered around us. Once we were safely resettled under our warm hides, I tucked Sun against my bare chest. The fidgeting of his fingers, pliant nails picking at the raised edges of my scar before folding into fists, the way his small, sweating head tucked into my neck, how his wisps of hair stuck like cobwebs to the stubble on my chin... I'd never known a deeper contentment.

Later still, I woke to my mate easing Sun from my arms. Outside, it was still dark and raining in earnest, but there was a softness at the cave entrance promising dawn. Yara swaddled our sleeping son, tucked him in the warm hollow where she'd been laying and stretched out, bare-skinned, against me.

We breathed softly into the quiet between us as she tugged at my breach cloth and I ran my hands over every soft curve of her and caressed the lines of the scar between her breasts. I forgot about Nardiri, our sleeping children, and the world around me. Yara and I lost ourselves in each other's heat and, when that delicate moment came, I filled her as surely as the rain filled the cracks in the parched ground outside. It was the last time I ever grew hard enough to love her like that.

As soon as the canyon camp was settled, Nardiri, the Speakers, and I scouted for wurms to bond with. Our searches took us far from the rocky terrain into the plains above. Despite leaving spoils from Nardiri's kills in easily accessible spots for the scavengers, every one of our expeditions ended fruitlessly. We found no wurms.

If the herds moved south for winter, perhaps the wurms followed? Nardiri speculated after yet another unsuccessful search.

I'd waited too long. Just like Tanar said. Cold fear gripped me. Sweet Nasheira, we couldn't wait to bond our Speakers until Spring.

The dragon sighed. ***We may not have a choice in the matter.***

Autumn encroached our lake valley with cold nights and broad strokes of frost during the week leading up to Yurrii's full moon. Half of our hides and all of our wood had been left behind when we'd fled our camp with only essentials on our backs.

"Fuel is difficult to find here," Ana lamented. "And the caves do not hold heat like huts."

"I'll go back with Nardiri." It had taken our caravan five solid days of walking to reach the ravine, but would take the dragon little less than an hour to reach the abandoned camp. I told Ana as much. "Keep everyone in the caves while we're gone. No searching for wurms." I added. "Arsu is relentless, and Dero will be searching for daeson, especially this close to the full moon. We cannot be seen."

"Of course, Speaker." Ana relayed my orders to everyone else.

I stopped at my cave before I went. "Be careful," Yara folded into me and Sun grabbed my hair and squealed in delight.

Rowin glared at me from his bedroll.

"I'll bring you back piles of fur, and we'll have a roaring fire tonight, and perhaps a tavi tournament? I'd wager Yara's gathering bag has a collection of shiny stones the likes of which you've never seen. Are you ready to lose to her, boy?" I smiled in the face of his anger and, while his scowl didn't falter, his shoulders softened and I knew he'd forgive me when I returned. He was starting to trust that I'd come back.

Outside, I checked my harness knots one last time, vaulted onto Nardiri's neck, and secured myself. My dragon lifted off like a feather, green gaze pinned on my small family waving from below.

The camp was as we'd left it, a clump of half-dismantled huts with exposed wooden ribs and cold hearths. There was an unsettling stillness about it that made my neck prickle. It reminded me of how prey hunkered down and froze while under a predator's gaze. It felt like we were being watched. Hastily, we gathered as much as Nardiri could carry and took a long, convoluted route back to the ravine even though we neither sensed nor saw pursuers. Although we had no urge to return, even a dragon could only carry so much, and we needed enough hides and fuel to last us over the winter, so we were forced to make the trip once more that week, with no incidents. On that second visit, I swore that the camp was more picked-over than we'd left it, but Nardiri said she couldn't see any difference.

The evening of Yurri's full moon, I sipped bitter Guide's leaf tea with my hidden camp and swallowed the incredible need to fly from them to search for the daeson Arsu was surely sacrificing.

You can't save them without walking into a trap or leading your enemy back here. Nardiri placated, but an awful guilt gnawed at me all the same.

By our third and final flight to gather camp supplies, my dragon was nearly leaping out of her skin with pent-up energy, and my nerves matched hers.

What can I do for you? I asked as she took off.

I've spent an eternity circling above your slow caravan, perching on that ravine edge, and hauling supplies. The only time I don't feel trapped is when we hunt, and the

oxen are so fat and slow, it is over in an instant. I need to fly, Akrist. Really fly. I can't remember the last time I've stretched my wings.

You're right. We've been looking over our shoulders for so long, we're twisted tighter than a firebow. I yanked the slip knot at my waist tighter, tugged my visor down, and looped my wrists through the handholds. "Let's fly," I exhaled.

She stretched her wings and surged ahead with a burbling cry of release. She dipped and dived while I braced myself. She flicked her wings against her ribs and rolled like a raven. The bite of the harness snagging my thighs, the way my heels tucked into the hollow below Nardiri's shoulders, the press of her neck ridge against my lower back—all of it felt like a natural extension of myself.

Soaring

Nardiri grabbed air and peeled away from the golden prairie below, pumping skyward until the ground looked like a stretched hide, spotless, beige and flat. She crowed, tucked her limbs tight, and pulled into a tight, neat loop.

I grinned and clamped my jaw as my stomach alternately dropped and fluttered up into my throat. Her wings billowed and expanded around me as she slowed and then snapped sideways. Pale grasslands smeared by as I clung to my seat. Wind roared past my ears. She rolled again slowly, inverting and letting her head hang down as she twisted.

Clenching my neck muscles and tightening my chest, I hung in the harness until Nardiri tipped like a boat righting herself. My bottom slapped back onto her neck, and I shifted to centre myself between her ridges.

Something enormous smashed into us from behind. The distinctive crack of broken ribs thumped through my back. Wind slammed out of my lungs in a harsh exhale. The harness twanged. I felt a sharp pressure and release over my thighs. My hands scrambled for purchase as I careened forward over my dragon's neck.

Nardiri's roar pounded between my ears. My clawing hands slipped past smooth scales as I pitched out and away from her. A foot caught in a loop of the dangling harness, my head snapped back, and then the whole thing slipped loose in a tangle of flapping rope.

I fell, spinning away from my dragon.

PART THREE

"BROTHER"

CHAPTER
TWENTY-THREE

I couldn't breathe. I twisted my body to look up, arms flailing, wind pulling water from my eyes and blurring my sight. Above me, two dragons receded rapidly into the blue. I couldn't stop my awkward cartwheel through the air. Pale prairie swallowed blue over and over again on the pitching horizon. The wind screamed. My shirt snapped and rippled like fire. When I opened my mouth to scream, no sound came out.

Akrist, I'm coming! The thought hurled into my head, hysterical and black as coal.

Battered against a roaring current, corkscrewing toward the hungry, expanding plains, I felt my consciousness stretching and dribbling away. Swathes of grasslands yawned around me, framed by expanding black.

Something clamped onto my chest. Pain lanced up my rib cage in a wave of crushing white. Breath billowed out of me along with the agony as my chin cracked against my chest, and my arms snapped forward like a broken puppet.

I only realized the dragon above me wasn't my own when Nardiri shouldered her aside, dove for me, and scooped me into her grasp.

She hurt you!

It hurt to breathe. Nardiri's wings stretched above us and deceleration pulled at all of my parts. High over her shoulder, another set of gold wings, dappled with teal, wheeled in the sky.

Nardiri landed, laid me down and growled, ***Wait here.***

Dry grass lashed against my cheeks as she erupted skyward.

Black blood streaked her back. A cruel, jagged hole yawned across the main panel of her left wing. Grey, wet flaps of membrane fluttered like ribbon as she scrambled to gain altitude.

Nardiri! I tried to stand, but my head spun, and my ribs screamed in throbbing protest. Levering up to my elbows, I saw a third dragon in the sky now, hovering and watching as Nardiri arched toward the first. Its mouth opened and, after a disconcerting delay, I heard a baritone bugle. A male.

She thinks I mean to steal him! Nardiri's sharp thoughts scattered like red shrapnel in my brain. Her anger vibrated through me, quickening my pulse and making me breathe faster despite the answering agony grating through my ribs.

Are you old enough? I asked stupidly.

I am bigger than she is, she crowed as the female dropped into a dive. Nardiri levelled and banked hard.

The other dragon's wings flared. Her spiked tail curled under and her legs dropped and swung almost lazily toward Nardiri's back. Talons twitched, wide and eager. I couldn't watch. I couldn't look away.

Just as the driftling's hind claws extended to bury deep into Nardiri's spine, she dropped and flipped, kicking out with both her long legs. Her superior reach surprised her opponent, and the female shrieked as Nardiri raked her underside and hammered her tail spikes deep into thigh muscle before jerking clear and righting herself.

Hissing, the driftling tucked her injured leg and scrambled to gain altitude.

She's leaving. You've scared her. Enough.

She does not know what scared is! Nardiri boomed, throwing back her head. ***You think she won't shred my wings as soon as I turn my back?***

Sure enough, the driftling tucked her wings and hurtled back towards Nardiri.

This time Nardiri did not drop away. She spun onto her back and crashed into the other dragon. Her jaws clamped around the female's throat. With her foreclaws anchored in her attacker's chest, Nardiri's tail spiralled like a vine around the driftling's. One hind claw skidded and seated itself in the open wound on her foe's bleeding thigh, while the other leg kicked at her underside.

High, whimpering cries gurgled past my dragon's gnawing grip. The driftling beat her wings against Nardiri's ribs, but my dragon tightened her hold as they plummeted toward the ground.

"Let go!" I screeched, heedless of my pain.

Choked squeals crescendoed. The driftling's wings billowed wide, but Nardiri's claws stabbed into the membrane, tearing open great, gaping holes.

Seconds before they struck the ground, Nardiri braced her hind-legs on her opponent's belly, tossed her aside, and launched away.

The driftling toppled onto the grass.

Nardiri flipped upright and kicked at the ground as it met her, tearing up great clods of turf as she re-launched with a satisfied scream.

Scrambling in the dust, the driftling pulled her shredded wings against herself, levered to her feet, and limped away.

Far above, the male broke from his hover and started a slow circle toward us, crooning encouragingly.

Nardiri's head snapped toward him. Her blasting, frustrated cry left no room for misinterpretation. With a forlorn bugle, he banked away.

She landed heavily, lacerated wing half-extended and trailing streamers of glistening, ropey tissue. Squatting over me, she scanned the skies. ***She hurt you. I'm sorry. I didn't see her coming.***

"She hurt *you*!" I gasped. *Mother of Yurrii, look at your wing.*

Purple shame swamped my mind. Nardiri drowned me in shivering exhales, heedless of the thick black drops spattering near my feet. The drifling had torn the harness right off Nardiri. Two crescent-shaped gouges oozed blood down her back.

Adrenalin still buzzed through my limbs. I felt steady and light once I found my feet. Squinting up at the jagged tears, I exhaled. "They are long, but not deep. I should be able to stitch them, but your wing..." The sight of that gaping hole, membrane unravelling like thread, twitching and jerking and laced in wet black, it wrung the last of my strength out of me. I found myself doubling-over again and sinking to my knees.

I will fly to the ravine and get help.

"No," I gulped, panic rising at the thought of being left alone. *We go together.*

I hadn't flown tucked under Nardiri's arm since before Blue Braid had fitted our harness. I nodded when she asked if I was ready, but could not suppress the curdling wail that tore out of me when she pressed me against her chest and took off. My ribs grated with every panting breath. Spots swam in my vision, and I blinked furiously and gripped her arm as the ground dropped away from us. After a few moments of flight, I couldn't tell if it was my sweat that soaked the back of my shirt or Nardiri's blood.

Don't faint, I told myself, trying to swallow my nausea. *Don't faint. Don't faint.*

I've got you. I won't let you go. I promise. Wind whistled through the ragged hollow in Nardiri's wing, and the tearing sound of the wound opening wider terrified me. She lurched through the air, but we held our height.

We are an hour from the ravine. The black thought nearly swallowed me.

I am strong. Nardiri said, but then she flinched and faltered. *The male, he is still following.*

I wanted to tell her not to take us back to the canyon, but I couldn't hang onto the thought, couldn't finish it, couldn't even breathe as white pain muddied into grey and the world feathered out of focus.

My feet skimmed above the grasslands and all I could do was gulp shallow breaths like a drowning man. We flew like that forever, for an eternity of skewering pain and cold sweat, blood and stale, hot breath. I was in and out of consciousness. I had wanted to tell Nardiri something important. What was it?

Her abrupt landing jolted me awake. Blinking, I took in an open plain with a scattering of nearby trees. I recognized the area. We weren't far from home.

I can't fly anymore, she said. ***And the male driftling is hunting us. He's close.***

Blood-streaked wings hemmed me in. Nardiri dug her claws deep into the turf and curled low. A sonorous growl rattled through her chest, and her sight bled into mine, filling my skull with a sharp yellow silhouette of our pursuer closing in. I tried to turn and look for myself, but pain stabbed through my back and sizzled across my chest.

Nardiri cut off mid-growl as the male dragon's shadow consumed us. ***There's... a man astride him!***

Pain evaporated. The dragon sailed over us and into my view. A figure with raven hair and a compact body was perched on his neck. Even from afar, I recognized the rider.

"Dero."

Tanar hadn't lied.

The pair soared away from us, toward the ravine. My muddled brain took a second to put the pieces together. The world snapped into wretched, stinging focus. My people were hidden. There was no way he knew their location. But why wouldn't he come straight for me, injured as I was, if he didn't have another target?

My mind howled. "Nardiri, stop him," I gasped.

I felt her mentally reach for Dero.

My brother tipped over, slack in his harness. His arms dangled and his dragon squealed in shock, wings faltering, but then he surged onward and out of our range. My brother turned back to us for a moment, but he was too far away for me to read his expression.

Pain took my breath again as Nardiri pushed ahead in an awkward sprint, tucking her wings behind her back and lowering her head. The male dragon's silhouette burned bright yellow in my mind as he tipped his wings and dipped below the edge of the gorge in the distance.

As Nardiri's powerful legs ate up the distance, I heard the screams. They carried all the way up the valley.

—YARA —

There are sounds that people only make when they're dying violent deaths. Harrowing screams pitched high enough to lodge in your mind forever. Rattling, wet breaths that only broken chests can produce. The terrible thuds of soft bodies slamming into unforgiving surfaces. When I heard those sounds coming from outside of the cave, my first thought was that a rock slide had injured people. I'd wrestled with the fear of being buried alive since making our home beneath a quarter mile of solid stone. That fear pinned me now as Sun startled awake in my arms. The daeson around me scrambled to their feet, whimpering.

I couldn't see the mouth of the cave. As a precaution, whenever he left with Nardiri, Akrist insisted we all congregate within the caverns so dragons couldn't sense us. This cave's throat turned sharply enough that only the dim reflection of daylight against the damp wall indicated the opening beyond.

"Not buried," I whispered, clutching Sun against my ribs and edging toward the entrance. *Not if we can see daylight.* A deep whoosh and a fresh round of screams spilled in. I gripped Sun with one arm so I could press back a boy who'd tried to flee our stifling asylum twice already today. Daeson did not adapt well to crowded confines. "We need to stay here," I said, trying to make my voice sound calm.

Oric, the Speaker tasked with protecting us, snagged his spear from against the wall. "I'll have a look."

I nodded and turned back toward the boys. Six of them, including Rowin, stood on their toes, ready to scatter.

I herded them to the back of the cave. Forgotten tavi pieces and stones that had been arranged in careful piles scattered beneath our feet.

Oric disappeared around the corner, and a dragon's roar echoed through the cavern. At first, I thought Akrist and Nardiri had returned, but then I heard claws scrabbling and wings beating outside. Inhuman shrieks crescendoed and cut off mid-breath. A pulse of wind fluttered the lanterns around us.

"Put out the flames," I said. "Keep quiet."

We plunged into complete darkness. Sun clawed at my hair, rigid in my grip.

Something smashed into the wall outside with enough force to rain dust from the cracks in the ceiling but, thank the Goddess above, none of the daeson fled. They huddled around me in the stifling dark, all sharp shoulders and trembling breaths.

I stroked a daeson's hair. "We'll be safe here." I poured steady warmth into my words, even as my throat tightened.

But I knew the daeson didn't believe me. The chaos of death outside was too loud now. It paralyzed us with its promise. Every shadow rippling across the entryway froze our breaths in our throats. The smell of urine filled my nostrils. Clammy hands clutched at me, and Sun stiffened.

A horrible silence fell outside, interrupted only by soft wails. When I finally did hear footsteps at our cave entrance, they were calculated, careful treads. *Please be Oric.*

But somehow I knew it wasn't.

"Take him," I whispered, pressing Sun into Rowin's arms. "All of you stay back here. Not a sound." I swept my fingers over the dusty floor until I felt one of the stone lanterns. I picked it up, wincing as hot oil oozed between my fingers. It was heavy enough to use as a club.

A man's shadow advanced across the floor ahead.

I pressed against the stone wall and sidled toward him, hands tingling and mouth dry. It wasn't until he stopped to let his eyes adjust to the dark that I recognized him. And then I saw the knife in his hand, blood dripping from its wicked tip. Charging forward, I hoisted the lantern over my head and brought it down hard, aiming for his temple.

It might have been a killing blow had it struck true, but Dero saw me at the last second and shrank back. The lantern grazed his head and struck above the shoulder of his weapon arm. His knife clattered into the dirt. I swung at him again, but he clamped onto my wrist and caught me with a blow to the jaw that snapped my head sideways and sent me toppling. Pinpricks swam across my vision. I rolled and scrambled for the blade, but he kicked me aside and snatched it up first. He pinned me against the wall and put the knife to my throat.

Every nerve in my body screamed to run, but I was trapped. If Dero killed me, he would find the daeson huddling in the dark beyond us, and Nasheira knew what he would do to them.

"Don't you recognize me, Dero?" I blurted out.

He narrowed his eyes, pressing the dagger closer. I felt its sting, felt blood dripping down my neck.

His eyes slid past me toward the back of the cave, and I realized he didn't know who I was. I'd always had a way of hiding myself, of making myself unrecognizable, even to those who knew me. I didn't know how I did it. Reaching deep, I revealed my true self, despite my instincts screaming at me not to.

Recognition lit his eyes.

"You're alive," he growled.

My mind reeled, conscious of a slight scuffing sound from the back of the cave.

"And wouldn't Arsu love to know that?" I said, realizing what I had to do. "Take me to her. I'll come without struggling, if you leave now and don't hurt anyone else."

Dero's frowned, fingers flexing on his knife grip. "Hardly in a position to bargain, are you?"

And then Sun wailed.

The sound of it echoed through the cave. I wanted to move, to run to my baby, to smash Dero against the wall, but his knife kept me motionless. *No.* Out of the corner of my eye, I saw my baby crawl out of the pitch black toward me, face wrinkled and red, chubby legs smeared with dirt. Nothing else moved in the darkness behind him.

"So *this* is what you were hiding." Dero smirked. "It's *his* child, isn't it?" He threw his head back and laughed. "Oh, this is rich. Yes, chani. My answer is yes. We have a bargain."

CHAPTER TWENTY-FOUR

THE MINUTES IT TOOK us to reach the ravine felt like days. Nardiri launched over the cliff and half soared, half fell to the bottom. The tattered membrane of her wing flapped wildly.

All of my organs crowded up against my lungs.

As we collided with the sandy lakeshore, Nardiri skidded and toppled onto her shoulder, wrapping me in her wings. My vision went dark.

When I awoke, my chest hurt and I didn't know why. I couldn't breathe unless I pressed my elbow against my side. The screams were all around me. Someone stumbled across my vision—a gatherer. I knew him, but his name wouldn't come to me. The man clutched his own dismembered arm to his chest.

Nardiri lay sprawled next to me, great golden head bobbing and eyes dazed. The awful, jagged tear in her left wing gaped all the way up to the elbow joint. I wanted to speak to her, but I couldn't remember how to form words.

People pulled at me, pointing, yelling. I wrenched away from a woman who wouldn't stop screaming into my face and stumbled past a fanning, arterial spray of bright red blood that ended in a dark puddle and a scuff. Beyond, a broken body lay slumped against the cave wall.

Something plucked at my mind. Names. Yara. Rowin.

"Bandages. Get me more bandages!" a red-haired woman commanded, as she clamped her hands on the stump of a man's leg. Other bodies lay strewn beyond them, like wet hides.

The air reeked of copper and punctured bowels, like Na-Jhalar's hut when he'd gutted Iva. *The caves.* I blinked at the closest entrance and stumbled into the darkness.

White-rimmed eyes. Flashing teeth. A group of children huddled against one wall, gaping at me.

"Rowin?" I blurted again, but he wasn't among them. I told the children to stay and that I'd be back for them. Backing out into the too-bright blue, I refused to look down at crumpled bodies and their twisted limbs, because I knew I would recognize faces if I did. I cared about these people, and if I stopped to let their deaths sink in I might never get up again. I let my selfish need to know if my mate was alive drive me toward the next cave instead.

"Yara," I tried to yell, but the agony in my ribs muzzled me. Stumbling through another dark entrance, I followed the sound of shuffling feet.

Soft sobs drifted from further back. I leaned into the cold wall and let it lead me through the darkness. When I rounded a corner, lamplight guttered over another knot of daeson clumped against the back wall, all wet breaths and wriggling infants in caretakers' arms. "Sun." I reached for him in the dim, but it wasn't my boy. It was a daeson baby, and the woman holding him recognized me, meeting my gaze. I put my hand on her arm and nodded—all I could do in the moment to thank her for keeping them safe. "Stay hidden," I said. Then I turned and retraced my steps, heart thrashing.

"Akrist!" Someone shouted as I broke into the light, squinting.

I turned and stepped in something soft. A slush of sand and blood. A small pink triangle of skullcap with brown hair still attached gleamed up at me. I couldn't stop staring at it.

"Akrist!" Strong fingers gripped my arm.

Fraesh spun me to face him, clutching a wad of bandages.

Something crashed into my hip and I staggered sideways. The sudden pain of the movement pounded all the air out of me. I blinked down, straining to focus.

Rowin wrapped his arms around my waist, chin digging into the side of my stomach.

"Oh, thank Nasheira!" I wheezed, clutching both sides of the boy's head, sinking to my knees, and kissing his hair. "Are you hurt?" He shook his head, clutching harder.

My uncle swayed over me, bloodied and pale.

"Yara and Sun?" I asked, my voice wobbling.

He swallowed, eyes glistening. "Dero took them," he said. "The dragon carried them away."

We burned a dozen bodies on a pyre the next morning, using much of the wood Nardiri and I had gathered, fuel that was meant to tide us through winter.

Twelve dead, including Amar. Two missing. And many more wounded.

I learned how Dero had discovered the camp—why he had flown past me and wreaked havoc here instead. In my absence, half of the Speakers had slipped out of the caves—against my orders—to scale the ladders we'd hung on the canyon wall and search for wurms up on the plains. Frustrated by our previous failed attempts together and sick of being penned up in the caves while Nardiri and I made our supply runs, they'd left to search for the bond I'd promised them. And Amar, the youngest Speaker among us, had followed.

They had been a beacon for Dero's dragon, leading him to the ravine. The dragon had dashed every person within reach against the canyon walls while daeson hid in the caves within. The Guide dismembered and consumed people while his rider dismounted to search our dwellings on foot—for what, I was unsure. For the daeson? For Yara? For anyone he could easily kill? Dero was repelled by the remaining Speakers and their spears, but Yara had gone into hiding with Sun and some daeson in an unprotected cave, and Dero had stumbled upon them. For some reason, he had left the daeson untouched and taken only Yara and Sun. I suspected Yara had done something to protect the others, kept them hidden, sacrificed herself. My mate cared for them like she did her own.

I felt empty, all the rage drained from me. Ana and Fraesh spoke to me, and I nodded at all the right places, but it felt as if I were watching them from afar, tethered to my body only by the pain piercing my ribs every time I breathed. Every careful inhale smelled of burnt hair and kiro incense, and every exhale pulled something essential out of me with it.

Nardiri was inconsolable. She wouldn't let anyone near her wounds, and she refused to rise from where she'd fallen at the edge of the lake. When dusk came and the smoke from the pyre down the valley hung thick enough to burn our throats, I checked that Rowin was asleep, and then limped out to the dragon, leaning into the comfort of her shuddering warmth. Unable to sleep, I stared up at the smoke-filled sky, praying that somewhere, Yara and Sun lived.

CHAPTER TWENTY-FIVE

T HE MORNING AFTER THE massacre, with the funeral pyres still weaving thin strands of smoke into the icy air, Nardiri growled and swung her head up to the lip of the ravine opposite the caves. *Someone is coming. One person on a vaiya. From the direction of the old camp.*

I struggled to my feet, stiff and exhausted, and followed her stare.

They are many miles away, but they ride in a straight line. They know we're here.

My chest felt on fire, but the rest of me was leaden with cold.

I recognize the aura. Nardiri said. *The one you met in the woods after I marked your brother.*

Jin. My stupid heart lifted for a single beat before crashing back down. *Of course, Arsu would send Jin as a messenger. She knows I won't harm him. Or doesn't care if I do.*

By the time Jin's vaiya crowed from the top of the gorge, I'd ordered all of our daeson to the caves and gathered anyone healthy enough to hold a weapon.

Our patriarch vaiya bawled out a lustful challenge to Jin's lone bird before Nardiri silenced our flock.

Swallowing the ember of rage in my throat, I watched Jin dismount and stare down at us. He cupped his hands around his mouth and called out, "Akrist, come up."

I could not yell back. Instead, I leaned toward Oric and spoke through my teeth. "He can come down."

"Na-daeson Akrist says you may come down to us. There is a ladder," he bellowed. We kept the anchor points obscured with vegetation. My brother took several minutes to find the grass panels, clear them, and climb down.

"Not a move unless I tell you." I spoke under my breath to the group behind me. Fraesh shifted uncomfortably. His healer's hands looked woefully out of place holding a weapon. I gripped my spear tight enough to make my fingers ache.

Jin didn't look anything like I remembered. His face bore the sickly grey-green cast of someone whose wounds have had enough time to ripen and swell. His right cheek puffed grotesquely, pulling up the corner of his mouth. His eyelid was as purple as a summer plum, swollen and distended out of the socket. A deep slash cut across the bridge of his nose. His empty hands shook. The left one was bandaged and bleeding through its dressings at the knuckles.

Before I could speak, Jin's open eye widened. "Fraesh? Uncle!" he blurted. "It is you? Thank the Goddess above! You live! Are my cousins with you? Galeed?"

Fraesh nodded coolly. My brother faltered at the angry stares of my people.

"I'm sorry for what has happened to you," Jin said.

"So, you're Arsu's messenger now?" I asked in as even a voice as I could muster.

He looked down. "Not by choice, I assure you."

"There is always a choice," Oric hissed.

Nardiri stood and roared from the lake, a sudden, shrieking blast that made everyone around me flinch.

I waited for the echo of it to die down the valley before I spoke again. "Where are they, Jin? If you have any love for me, tell me." And to Naridiri: *Fold your wings so that he does not see your wounds. He will carry every piece of information he can back to Arsu.*

Jin rubbed his fingers and thumb together on his uninjured hand. "She wants a trade. You for them." He glanced at Nardiri. "You and your dragon for their safe return."

"Do you think us daft?" Venda barked from the back.

"Unacceptable," Ana murmured, and Fraesh shook his head.

Oric's words dripped venom as he ran a thumb over the keen edge of his spearhead. "How about we send *you* back? Piece by piece."

I held up my hand, but couldn't keep the anger out of my words. "How can you do this to me, Jin?" My voice broke. "Coming here, speaking in *her* voice, after everything she's done. Am I not a brother to you? Are we not family?"

A muscle in his jaw twitched and blood trickled down the corner of his eye like a tear. "*I* am not asking it of you, Akrist.

I have no choice here. Are you coming, or are you sending me back empty-handed? If so, you might as well kill me now." He ended his speech in a whisper.

I studied my brother in silence. I knew beyond a shadow of a doubt that Arsu would not honour such a trade. She would keep Yara and Sun, perhaps to torture in front of me. And then she'd kill me. But if I stayed, I guaranteed their deaths, as well as Jin's and anyone in Arsu's camp remotely connected to me.

I surveyed the group behind me, eyes afire, ready to defend me. How many of them would die in Arsu's pursuit of me?

No more.

"I'll come, but the dragon stays."

"What?" Fraesh barked.

No! You will not! Nardiri bellowed and charged toward us, moving for the first time since she'd landed.

"Stop." The words came out as a plea rather than a command, and she hung in place, muscles bunched, every bit the terrifying guardian.

You cannot fly out of the ravine. I need you here. I need you to protect them all.

She won't honour the trade!

I know.

Pale yellow muddled my thoughts.

You may not understand, but I need to do this. This needs to end. I can't watch Arsu destroy everything I love. I can't watch her destroy you. The daeson, this camp—they need you. This is how you honour me. Take care of them.

I turned back to Jin. "Give me a moment to say goodbye." And before anyone else could speak, I skirted my armed escort and headed toward the caves.

"Speaker, this is madness!" Ana trotted beside me.

Fraesh was not far behind. "You know Arsu won't keep her word, boy," he whispered.

"It's *me* she wants dead, Fraesh. It's always been me, and we both know she will kill as many as it takes to bring me to her." I winced and curled over the stabbing pain in my side. My uncle braced my elbow and shielded me as we walked. "I am tired of people dying on my behalf. Do you understand?"

"You are going to your death," he said.

I met his pale blue eyes and saw fear in them, the same helpless terror I'd seen in my father's eyes both times the moon's eclipsed. "Nasheira has given me chances where there were none before." I gripped his shoulder. "Pray that she does it one more time."

I had one hope that I might be able to escape Arsu's clutches, but it relied on a relationship with a brother who hated me. Still, I let that hope flicker.

Rowin caught me as I was packing. His gaze flicked from the bag up to my face and his small chest heaved as he crossed the room. I tried to hold him back, but he ducked under my arm, plunged into my carry bag and started throwing my things across the cave.

"Stop it. Rowin, stop." I puffed, holding him back. I braced for an elbow to the ribs, for his sharp nails to dig into my face and neck, but instead, he collapsed, clinging to me and crying in forlorn, hitching wails.

Holding him tucked under my chin, I waited for him to calm enough for me to speak. Digging into my belt pouch, I pulled out the sea glass tavi pieces and pressed them into Rowin's hand. "These are yours now, so you can have a full set. You can give them back to me when... if..." My voice wobbled and his face twisted in anguish.

He didn't throw the game pieces. Instead, he stared up at me with utter desperation in his hazel eyes. His mouth trembled and he signed a single word.

Stay.

Hot tears welled in my eyes. I laid a rough hand on Rowin's wet cheek and he let me. He didn't flinch away. I wanted to say I would return, but my last words to him would not be a lie. "I love you. You will always be here." I pointed at my heart. And then I shouldered my bag and stepped around him.

Ana and Fraesh had to peel him off me when we got outside.

Rowin's hoarse screams echoed up the valley as I approached my forlorn dragon. *Take care of him?* I leaned against her snout. I lost myself in the warmth of her breath and the hum radiating from her chest as she crooned. For a moment, Nardiri was all that existed.

I always do. I look after everything while you run after a girl.

I laughed. *I am not running. I'm going to end it, Nardiri.*

You go to meet your own death. Yellow and red swirled into messy orange in my dragon's mind.

I rested my forehead against hers and sighed, "I see no other path."

CHAPTER
TWENTY-SIX

L ET ME WRAP THEM for you," my brother said over the fire.

It was dark. We'd traveled northwest all day and my ribs were screaming from riding behind Jin on his vaiya. I sat leaning breathlessly against that poor bird's haunch while she whimpered sympathetically. It was Vala, one of the older females. The fact that Jin had brought her instead of Voti told me that my brother was relatively far from Arsu's camp. Patriarch vaiyas were only ever used for short trips away from their flock. Anything greater than a day trip would risk the flock scattering, or shuffling its ranks, resulting in a vicious fight for seniority once Voti returned.

"We've many days of travel before us, and you won't last if you don't let me wrap those ribs."

Many days. Jin confirmed my fears. I hadn't been able to hide my injury from him. An excruciatingly slow climb up the canyon ladder had been enough to alert anyone watching that I was wounded, and we'd been forced to stop multiple times through the day when keen Vala sensed my legs losing their grip and stopped before I tipped off her back.

"*Many* days," I mumbled. "But it took you less than a day from the time Dero kidnapped my mate and child to reach our camp."

Jin pulled his pack from behind him and started rummaging through it. "Before dawn this morning, Dero had his dragon drop Vala and me less than an hour's ride from your ravine. He pointed us in the proper direction and left."

"And little brother is not picking you back up?" I asked coldly.

"Pau's stones." He swore, shaking his head slowly. "I am not your enemy, Akrist. I am not in league with Dero, and I'm most certainly not on Arsu's side."

"You told her about our conversation when you found me in the woods, did you not?"

His face fell, and he didn't answer. We sat in a silence so cold, the flames between us didn't have a hope of warming it. Finally, Jin blurted out, "Arsu wants you to suffer a long journey back." He pulled a large roll of bandages out.

"Tell me where we are going."

"She's at the heart stone," he said. "She set up camp there so that she could poison every mind bent on seeing you before they ever reached you." I sagged against Vala at the thought of traveling the six days it would take to get there. "Now, let me bandage your wound."

There was a lot of hissing and cursing as Jin wrapped my ribs, and not all of it emanated from me. Several times, my brother's bandaged hand fumbled and he sucked air through his teeth, his bruised face twisted with pain.

"What happened to your hand?" I asked, but he just drew his lips into a hard line and ignored me. When he'd finished, the wide bandage around my chest was snug enough to restrict my breathing and—I was loath to admit—it lessened the pain. I felt steadier than I had all day. I offered to stitch the gash across his nose, and he didn't say no, just turned his face toward the fire so I could see better.

"Guides, Jin, it's right to the bone." This close, it was impossible to ignore his mottled face, the anguish and exhaustion in his good eye. "Arsu's handiwork?"

A sharp, humourless laugh puffed out of him. "No. One of *your* former Speakers."

I almost dropped the needle in surprise. Of course the Speakers who had left me would flock to Arsu.

"So they turned you into an obedient little Son of Yurrii?"

Jin flinched. He leaned away from me, glaring. When I held his gaze with a bitter one of my own, my brother shook his head and stuffed the remainder of his supplies into his pack. Without another word, he tucked the bag under his head and lay in the grass with his back to me. I resettled against his dozing vaiya, sitting up.

I must have slept because the next time I opened my eyes, the fire had crumbled to coals and the constellations were tilted above us. Jin was awake and curled over something as if he were trying to hide it, so I feigned sleep and watched him through my eyelashes.

Breathing heavily, he unwound the bloody bandage from his left hand and peeled back the pad beneath. Then he leaned toward the dying fire to examine his wound.

My stomach dropped. I straightened. "Jin." His name poured past my lips before I could stop it. "Mother of Yurrii." My voice shook.

The last two fingers on his left hand were freshly amputated and the nubs left behind, angry, raw, and weeping red.

Oh Nasheira, she's torturing him. Piece by piece.

"Don't look at me like that." He growled. Turning away, he folded a fresh wad of padding over his hand and hastily re-wrapped the bandage, using his teeth to tie it.

Silence settled between us, thick, aching, and unbearable.

"Why?" I croaked. "Why in Nasheira's name do you stay with her? You could have left a thousand times by now."

He straightened. "Are you really that stupid, brother?" he snapped. "Do you think *I* am that stupid? That I would just turn on you? That I would choose Arsu over my own family? I *asked* you to help us! I *told* you what she was doing, and you left!" His voice cracked. He dropped his head and took several shuddering breaths, cradling his mutilated hand against his chest. When he spoke again, it was in an utterly defeated whisper. "Do you think you are the only one in the whole world who loves someone? Someone who can be snatched as a hostage and used against you?" Tears rolled down his swollen face.

I felt sick. "Aaron." Jin loved his mate fiercely, loyally, and entirely.

"Anything Arsu does to me, she does to him ten times over. So while you are sleeping, I am laying here thinking of how many fingers and toes he has lost by now because I initially refused to be her messenger."

I didn't know what to say. I *was* stupid. Mother of Yurrii, my brother was a good man, and I'd doubted him. "Can she be stopped?"

Jin scoffed quietly. "It's too late now. She has Dero in her clutches, just like the rest of us. People follow her, and they'll keep following her because she's told them Nasheira is on her side, and she has *four* bloody dragons to prove it."

"Four?" I frowned. "She's bonded other Speakers?"

"No." Jin blinked. "Her followers kill every wurm they cross in Yurrii's name and she encourages it. Dero is the only one with dragons.

Clammy fingers of fear dug into my stomach. "You can't bond more than one dragon." But as the words left my mouth, I realized I had no idea if that was true. My mind went back to the female that had injured Nardiri. I had assumed she was a driftling. But she had attacked Nardiri so furiously, almost like she was being spurred on to do so.

If Dero had multiple dragons, then he was the key. I had to extract him from Arsu's influence.

Or kill him.

The journey back to Nasheira's Heart was physically excruciating, but in the evenings, Jin cooked food for us both, let me lay against the warmth of his vaiya, and answered every question I asked. I learned that Aella, our mother, had died shortly after my sacrifice. A sudden and merciless fever struck her down, leaving our father, Hasev, reeling with the loss of his beloved.

A strange hollow expanded in my chest. *Do I grieve the mother who despised me? Who my father had chosen over me?* I couldn't tell. The emptiness in my core was too vast and deep to examine its source. I missed Nardiri's cheerfulness. I hadn't realized how much I relied on her to keep my mind afloat.

The camp at Nashiera's Heart was the largest gathering of people I'd ever seen in my life. Hundreds of haphazard tents and clumps of mismatched huts sprawled far beyond the base of the erratic formation. The smell of the place wafted even farther; stewing excrement from unburied waste pits and an undertone of rotting meat. Vaiyas clumped in dozens of territorial flocks, hissing and snapping, and above it all, lounging on the great boulder, watching us approach with mild interest, were four dragons—the female who'd fought Nardiri, the male we'd thought was trying to woo her, and two other dragons, smaller, long-limbed, and pale gold. They flicked their tails and yawned as we approached.

I'd never seen so many Guides in one place. I ached for Nardiri's presence, as my heart tightened in my chest and my knees loosened with the urge to kneel. I couldn't tell if that last impulse came from me, or if Dero's dragons were toying with me. Beneath my bandages, my Speaker's scar tingled.

At the outskirts of the settlement, we dismounted and passed between two tall wooden cages with stout bases and tapering sides. Carrion birds flocked around the spears lashed above them. Impaled on each tip was a severed wurm head, flaccid, faceless, and reeking. Each cage was barely wide enough for the single captive standing within. Thick, crosshatched bars spanned the top of the enclosures braced snuggly under each prisoner's chin so that they could not draw their heads down through the space between. They balanced on a single horizontal post, set like a perch so that they were forced to stretch on the balls of their feet to avoid hanging by their necks. The skin around their throats was raw and bleeding. Bird shit caked their hair. They smelled overwhelmingly of acrid sweat and wurms. One of them called out as we passed.

"Please," he wheezed. "Please, help." I would have gone to him if Jin hadn't gripped my elbow and steered me firmly forward.

"Don't look," he murmured. When we were further past, he said "She made the cages to taunt you. Out of wood scavenged from your camp. Do not give her the reaction she craves."

I pulled back, speechless and sick at heart.

Vala yanked at her lead and wailed.

Jin tossed his head toward Dero's dragons. "He parrots everything he sees through their eyes to Arsu."

As we passed tents with sullen, sunken-faced elders propped at their hearths, a raucous crowd gathered. Heads craned. Voices hissed vitreous curses. Several people pressed two fingers to their foreheads, their eyes sharp slits of anger as they jostled closer.

Vala tossed her head, crest stiff, eyes white-rimmed and wild.

My brother let her lead slip through his fingers and she slammed into the people nearest to us, toppling two men.

They crashed to the ground and the rest of the churning crowd pressed back to avoid the vaiya's spurs as she carved a path through their midst.

I tucked my elbow against my aching side, clenched my jaw and pressed through the horde clotting around us. "Son of Pau!" they spat. "Traitor. Wurm lover!"

Arsu was unraveling everything I had fought to change. My small band of Speakers and daeson paled in comparison to this angry mob. How could my camp possibly stop a force this large?

When the first stone flew, it struck Jin in the shoulder. He grunted, stumbled, and walked on while the mob cheered. I pressed closer to him, but hot, stale breaths, sharp elbows, and clutching fingers overwhelmed me. Stones rained down on us and whistled over our shoulders, striking others in the horde. Sharp screams and frenzied shouts swirled into a mess of noise. Someone hooked a fistful of my hair and yanked back hard. A projectile hammered my bruised back, tearing breath from my lungs and dropping me where I stood. Booted feet kicked dust into my face. I choked on dirt.

"Akrist!" Jin yelled, but he sounded distant, the crowd carrying him away from me in its current.

I coughed, and the agony of it curled me into a ball. Feet stumbled over me, kicked my back, stepped on my thigh. Heat pulsed behind my eyes as I blinked to clear them. A woman curled over me, eyes glossy with rage, and spit in my face.

I wanted to scream, but couldn't draw breath. Every time I came close, someone else stepped on me or tore at my clothes like scavengers tugging at a kill. Pale spores swam across my vision, muting the sharpness of the insanity around me, the pain, and the panic. New voices bellowed over the crowd. I felt the current of it falter, like water parting around a rock.

Two men staggered into my narrowing field of sight, brandishing long flint daggers and carving indiscriminately at anyone in their way. One of them slashed at a woman, cut her cheek and sent a plume of hot blood splattering onto my neck and chest.

I gaped at him in horror, took in the Speaker's scar on his proudly bared chest and recognized him as one of my deserters.

He bent, clamped his hand around my forearm and yanked me to my feet. Pain speared through me. As his cohort flanked me and gripped my other elbow, dizziness washed away everything else.

My head sagged to my chest, feet stumbling as if they'd forgotten how to walk.

The pair of men steered me toward the base of the immense erratic rock, into its cold shadow where a line of large, long, hide-paneled huts stood. I stared into the crowd, peeking into huts as we passed, straining to catch a glimpse of Yara and Sun. I couldn't stop myself from asking, "Where is my mate?"

The first man chuckled. "Son of Pau, you will see her soon. Perhaps I will see her first. Would you like me to pass on a message? Something sweet to whisper in her ear while I take her from behind?"

Sick fury burned away the fog. I found my feet and pulled back to strike the grinning man, but his companion caught my arm. And then it was too late to do anything else. We lurched into the stale, foul darkness of a hut. They hurled me to the ground and I scrambled back to my feet to fight them, adrenalin overtaking my pain. Something heavy scraped across the dirt floor. I dove toward the sound, intent on tackling my escorts, but instead, I struck a painfully solid barrier. They laughed. A triangle of light sluiced through the darkness as they swatted aside the door flap to leave, revealing the cage they'd tossed me into.

It was far larger than the pair of torture devices Arsu had fabricated at the outskirts, tall enough for me to stand inside without striking my head. I took in dirt floors, buried wooden posts as thick as my arm, and a barred door, lashed with thick rope, before the hut plunged back into darkness.

Swaying on my feet, I panted and blinked into the dark. My hands shook and goose-bumps raised on my skin, as strength leached out of my pores and evaporated. I wanted to yell. I wanted to hit something until my knuckles bled, but my whole body pounded in time with my heart and, suddenly, it was difficult to stand. I leaned against the closest wall, tracing the rough-hewn edges of my enclosure. My toes bumped against a heavy clay pot that sloshed when I jarred it and reeked of stale urine. Swallowing the urge to gag, I backed away and sat in the opposite corner, my leg muscles shuddering. *This is it, then. This is where Arsu leaves me to die. Alone. Without Nardiri's comforting presence in my head.* I should have been panicking. I should have been testing every weak spot in the bars, but I hurt so badly, I couldn't even bring myself to stand back up. When the thunder of blood between my ears finally settled, I heard it.

Breathing. Not my own.

Freezing, I peered into the black. *Mother of Yurrii. I might have known she would never grant me the dignity of privacy.* And then another thought struck me, awful but full of hope at the same time. "Yara?" I whispered.

Something moved, scuffing the dirt floor mere paces away. Light slivered under the wall furthest from me.

I blinked. In a cage that shared a wall with mine sat a man. Our enclosures spanned the entire length of the hut. Barred panels nudged up against stretched hide walls on three sides with a space for accessing the adjoined enclosures along their broad fronts.

My fellow prisoner had reached a hand through his bars to lift up the bottom edge of the nearest hide and let in the light.

Lanky black hair curtained his features. He was unclothed. Long, puckering scars criss-crossed his slack arms and across his sunken stomach. His teeth flashed as I squinted at him open-mouthed.

"Akrist," he said. "How good of you to come."

It took several swallows before I could answer the unmistakably familiar voice. "Dero," I greeted my brother, sighing.

CHAPTER
TWENTY-SEVEN

O VER THE NEXT FEW hours, Dero spoke a lot, but almost none of his words were directed toward me. I could only make out snippets of his rambling.

"You cannot eat them because we need them... There are no more to the north. Fly south instead... Because it hurts me when she is hungry, damn it! Her wings will heal soon enough. Stop carping... You tell her there are no favourites... She lies... No. No, that hurts. Stop it... I said stop. Stop!"

Most episodes ended with my brother beating his fists against his head or raking his fingernails across the raw mark on his chest until it bled. He rocked back and forth, like some daeson did when they were overwhelmed.

I recalled how strange it had been to share my mind with Nardiri at first, how we had learned to respect each other's boundaries. What would it have been like to suddenly have *four* voices vying for attention in my mind—to be bonded with four whole beings and given no freedom to adjust? The crazed man before me suggested Nasheira had never intended the bond for such a use.

Eventually, Dero's face dropped into blankness and his fists trembled at his sides. When night came and the air cooled, he shivered and looked at me with the confusion of a man who had woken from a trance. I suspected the dragons were now sleeping, relieving their hold on his mind.

He stood, walked to the far corner of his cage, and relieved himself.

I turned my head away, listened to the sound of him watering the dirt, and wondered why I'd been granted a piss pot and he hadn't. "Is Yara all right?"

My brother snorted, his back still to me. "You're assuming two things: Firstly, that I know, and, secondly, that I'd tell a piece of wurm shit like you if I did."

I crossed to the bars dividing us and gripped them. "You can see every life form in this camp through your dragons' eyes. You know where she is."

Dero smiled. "Perhaps Arsu's already got rid of that whelp of yours."

"Don't you speak of my son!" I hissed and shook the bars. Warning pain flared in my ribs.

"Your *daeson*, you mean. Yes, right. How stupid of me. Arsu is not a breaker of tradition like you. She is devout. No doubt, she is keeping your dirty spawn safe until it can be properly offered at the full moon."

"Shut your mouth!" I choked.

Dero approached until he was standing just beyond my reach, naked, scarred, and utterly certain of his invincibility. "I am so glad you came." He giggled—a sound I'd never heard from him before. "I never got to see you suffer last time."

I wanted to kill him then, felt it rising up in me, that black, impetuous rage, the tremendous urge to reach through the bars, wrap my hands around the exposed softness of my grinning brother's throat and dig in until his eyes bulged and his breathing stopped. I'd been consumed by the same monstrous need to see the life snuffed out of Arsu's eyes as I held a knife against her neck.

I had started all this. Me.

If I'd reined in my selfish rage, I could have taken Nardiri away before she marked my little brother. It was my fault that Dero was bonded to four dragons, and I could not afford more mistakes. I couldn't let him bait me now, not if I wanted to pull him from Arsu's clutches. It took every stitch of strength I had left to peel my hands from the bars and turn my back on him while he laughed.

"Go to your corner then!" He howled. "Go and cower like the miserable wurm you are."

I didn't sleep that night, but neither did Dero. It was cold enough that I was chilled, even through my layers of clothes. Any satisfaction I felt about my little brother's suffering quickly faded as I regarded the caged, naked man curled into a ball, hands tucked into his armpits and the fog of his breath puffing out of him.

His dragons breathed above us, deep, whooshing exhales that sounded like waves lapping over the edge of the erratic rock. The emptiness in my head ached like the hole an extracted tooth left behind. I'd never been away from Nardiri this long. I missed her voice, how her colour filled me up.

Our guards brought a meal the next morning. They ignored me when I asked after Yara and slid a plate of half-eaten flat bread and a jug of water through the bars to me. Dero did not get a plate or jug. The guards bowed to him, spoke in reverent tones and called him Speaker. They passed him his food directly, let him drink from a water skin and asked him to hand it back when he was finished.

"She must care for you greatly, your idol Arsu." I spoke between mouthfuls, "She imprisons you. Your followers worship you through the bars of a cage, and none of them even trust you with a plate or a pot to piss in."

"Shut up," Dero snapped.

"Why does she strip you of everything, brother? You are not even allowed clothes or a blanket to cover yourself at night?"

"Does my manliness disturb you?" He crammed the last of the flatbread into his mouth and licked his fingers.

I blinked at the scars on his arms and frowned. Had he tried to kill himself? Was *that* why he wasn't allowed any objects in his cage—so he couldn't use them to harm himself? Was that why he was caged in the first place?

Following my gaze, he traced a finger down a long, fresh scar running the length of his inner forearm and sobered. When he spoke again, it was in a murmur more to himself than me. "Arsu doesn't understand. They let me cut myself, but not deep enough. They let me tie the noose, but paralyze my arms before I can string it up. I can break as many plates as I like, and hold the shard between my ribs, but my fingers always drop it before it can dig in. They won't even let me near water... they are so smart, and one of them is always awake. Arsu thinks she's protecting me from myself, but these bars are meaningless. I'm already caged." He swallowed and whispered hoarsely. "Did you try to kill yours, before it emerged? Or did you not know what it would become?"

Shocked, I didn't answer, but Dero had started humming to himself and didn't seem to be listening for a reply.

Arsu didn't come until the third day. She swept in, flanked by two guards, her gaze raking over every detail in our dark prison as her nose wrinkled.

I crossed my cage in two strides to face her, biting my lip to prevent myself from asking after Yara and Sun. I knew she wouldn't tell me.

She ignored me and moved to Dero's cage, examining him like an aeni sizing up a vaiya offered in trade. "Are you well, today?" Her gaze lingered on his bleeding chest scar before settling at his groin.

"Well enough," Dero smiled softly, his eyes lighting up at the sight of her. "Have you a need of me?"

"Open his door, then leave us," Arsu nodded at the guards. The two men bowed to Dero, set down the steaming clay pot, a set of folded clothes, and a brick of lye soap. They picked the knots free on the stout rope holding my brother's door shut, cursing at the cumbersome boiled leather guard that prevented us from reaching through the bars and undoing the knots ourselves. Then they left.

I couldn't keep the question in any longer. "Where is Yara?" I growled.

She ignored me, placing a hand on Dero's raw chest as he stepped out of his cage to stand before her. "Is he awake, your male?"

Dero nodded. "He rarely sleeps."

"Answer me, damn it!" I barked.

Arsu didn't turn, but she motioned to me and commanded Dero, "Drop him."

My brother turned to me and then his gaze clouded.

Halfway through drawing my next breath, my lungs froze and my muscles liquified.

I collapsed, head thudding as it hit the dirt, teeth clacking and ribs screaming at the impact. I couldn't scream. I couldn't breathe. My tongue hung slack in the back of my mouth and a wet clicking noise echoed in my throat.

Arsu studied me through the bars as I choked. Her cold eyes lit with fascination. "That's too much," she murmured. "Let him roll off his back so he can breathe."

Dero's dragon eased its hold on me and I curled onto my side, gasping in pain, every fibre in my being fighting against the paralysis pinning me to the ground.

"Better," she smiled, turning back to my brother, and brushing a hand over his jaw. "Can you let him stand and still control him?"

Dero's head cocked slightly.

Life snapped back into my limbs and I coughed and convulsed. I lay panting as my body clamoured for control, chest tight and muscles tender and prickling.

"Stand up," Arsu snapped. "If you want your mate and child to remain in good health."

What I wanted was to strike her, but my limbs were trembling and unreliable, like an animal mired in mud for too long. I used the bars to pull myself up and opened my mouth to curse her, but a cold weight hung in my throat like a stone, and I couldn't speak past it. As soon as I straightened, Dero's dragon held me there.

Sweat beaded on his forehead as he held eye contact with me and the air thickened to sand. In between breaths of pain, I wondered why it took him so much concentration. Nardiri could use her abilities without effort from me. But, then, I wasn't trying to control her or force her into submission.

Arsu pressed closer to the bars of the cage, an arm's length away, no doubt to taunt me. And yet, she only spoke to Dero. There was no fire in her eyes when she looked at me, only indifference, like I was merely a slug beneath her boot. "Do you understand what your brother has done?" she asked him. "Denied the goddess her proper sacrifices. Let his mate foul her soul by raising a daeson."

Mother of Yurrii, I will kill you! My mind roared. Air hissed through my clenched teeth. A soft grunt eased up my throat and my fingers twitched. Dero adjusted his hold and my hand fell still.

"Good!" Arsu's face broke into a genuine, delighted smile. "Very good. Keep practicing on him."

Dero's eyes drank in Arsu with a look of hunger and possession. She stroked his hair, and he closed his eyes in delight. I wished I could look away.

"Clean yourself and get dressed," she purred to him. "I need you for something else."

When they left, the guards came and cleaned our cells. One held me in the corner with a spear to my neck while the other replaced the reeking pot in the corner with a clean one. Then they re-secured the door and left me in the dark.

It wasn't until hours later that the wind of a dragon's landing buffeted the hut and the guards returned Dero to our cage like he was an egg they were afraid of breaking.

"I'm keeping the clothes," My brother snapped when they waited for him to undress.

"Y-yes Speaker," one of them said. "Of course." And they both backed out of the hut.

Dero folded into the corner, clapped his hands over his ears and whimpered for a long time before quieting.

When I was sure he could hear me, I said, "You love her? She treats you like a possession."

"There are worse things to be." He rubbed at his temples.

"You think she values you? You think she *loves* you back? " I pumped as much poison as I could into my words. I wanted a fight, something to burn off the impotency and rage that had soaked into me earlier and still soured my guts. I needed to feel the pain of my knuckles bleeding. I ached to beat the tired smile off Dero's face, so it utterly deflated me when my little brother's answer held no vitriol at all.

"I am not worthy of her love," he replied. "I am a failure. She hides me, and only brings me out for demonstrations of power when I'm strong. Otherwise, the Children of Yurrii would see this." He held out his shaking hands and laughed. "They can't know what it costs to be bonded."

"What it costs?" I repeated, confused.

"You must know more than any," he mumbled. "The tearing. The pain. The constant fight for control... The damned colours flooding my vision. If only they would *listen*. If only they would *understand*."

I gaped at him.

"Only Masa speaks to me," Dero continued, "and even he fights. He's angry that I... that Arsu..."

"What did Arsu do?" I needed to take advantage of this, Dero exhausted, his shields down and his anger bled out of him. I needed every scrap of knowledge I could pull from him.

His eyelids were beginning to droop from exhaustion. "She... was impatient... cut them out... early...

It took only moments for the meaning of his words to hit me. Arsu had cut the dragons out of their cocoons early. Who even knew what bonding four adult dragons would do to a single person—but dragons that had not matured properly? Who could only communicate with emotions? Who did not understand? My anger towards Dero melted into pity.

"Dero," I spoke his name as softly as I could, like stepping onto thin ice over deep water. "She told you to practice on me. What are you practicing for?"

My brother curled into a ball and clapped a hand over his mouth. At first, I thought he was conflicted, wanting to tell me what I needed to know, but struggling against betraying Arsu. Then he started giggling. It was that same piercing, trembling laugh that had tumbled out of Tanar when he'd pinned me down, desperate, insane, and hungry.

"You think you are wringing some big secret out of me, wurm?" Dero spat. "You think that everyone except you does not already know? I'm practicing to fight you. We will be Pau and Yurrii. The creation story in living flesh. Only this time, Arsu is going to set it right, permanently. We'll fight under the full moon with hundreds of eyes as witnesses. And I will prove to her that I am strong enough. I'll slay you as Yurrii should have slain Pau in the beginning. Your warped followers will watch you fall, and word will spread to every horizon that Nasheira made no move to save Pau incarnate. It will be a spectacle no one will ever forget."

A *spectacle*. I backed away from Dero and sat heavily. *Of course. A staged spectacle.* And Arsu had built it painstakingly so that I couldn't win. Dero was capable of paralysing me, and I was wounded. Even if, by some miracle, I killed my brother, if I broke his tenuous bond to his dragons in order to save Yara and Sun and my people, I'd become exactly what Arsu said I was. A murderer.

Pau Incarnate.

—YARA—

Arsu had torn Sun out of my arms as soon as we entered her expansive hut. I'd fought her tooth and nail, as any mother would, but her guards—her Speakers—crammed me into a wooden cage too small to stand in and tied Sun by his ankle to a stake in the middle of the hut.

We'd been here ever since, hours passing marked only by the change of our guards. I'd been surprised to find Akrist's father among their ranks.

Today, he untied Sun's ankle and let me nurse him through the bars.

For a long while, we sat in silence, Hasev staring down at his hands while I smelled Sun's hair and stroked his back. Finally, I whispered, "Why does she trust you enough to leave you here with me alone?"

He shrugged. His tired eyes met mine and they were so like Akrist's, my heart ached. "Perhaps she knows I am broken. I did nothing to stop the sacrifice of my own son. Both times. I did *nothing*. I've proven to her that I'm not a man to fear." Tears brimmed in his eyes.

"It's not too late to do something now, Hasev." I caught his gaze. "Akrist is here, is he not?" I had heard the shouts of scorn that had heralded his arrival, and I had known. If the situation was reversed, I'd have come for him. Of course he was here.

Hasev flinched and nodded.

"It's not too late to help us."

CHAPTER TWENTY-EIGHT

D ERO'S EYES GLAZED OVER in concentration.

I tucked my tongue between my teeth and bent my knees before he ordered Masa to paralyze me. My cheek still struck the ground with enough force to make my eyes water.

"I can do this all day long." He puffed from the divider wall, leaning toward me with his teeth bared and his hands gripping the bars.

He couldn't do it all day, and we both knew it. It seemed to take a significant amount of my brother's strength to hold Masa's attention long enough for the dragon to paralyze me in the nuanced ways Dero requested. At first the male Guide had acquiesced easily. He seemed eager for a task that didn't involve shepherding the other three dragons and curious to test the finer controls of his power, but he quickly grew bored and fought Dero like a stubborn vaiya pulling at a lead.

That's what it looked like from the outside, anyway. Masa was just as likely to wander away as stay and listen when Dero attempted to practice on me. From my brother's outbursts of anger and muttering, it sounded like Masa frequently cut off their connection. I remembered how debilitating it had been the few times Nardiri cut me from her mind. Dero endured it daily. And I couldn't figure out why.

He had mentioned that Masa had been the biggest wurm he'd ever seen, and that he'd burrowed mere weeks after they had bonded. Perhaps the less time a Speaker spent with their wurm before their transformation, the less stable their connection? Or maybe Dero couldn't cultivate the bond properly while trying to hold three other dragons at the same time.

I lay on my back, wheezing, as Dero took a break.

"Why do you hate me?" I asked.

He snorted. "What kind of question is that? You are a daeson. Everyone in their right mind hates you."

A sharp twinge ran up my elbow and I winced at the numbing in my arm. "So if I wasn't a daeson, you would embrace me as a brother?"

"You killed Tasie."

I winced. Our sister, Tasie, had drowned shortly after my birth. My mother blamed me, because she had let Tasie touch me. She thought my curse had bled through to my sister and caused her death.

"Do you really believe that?" I asked.

"Aella did. She knew you for the Son of Pau you are."

"It grieved me to hear of her death." I pondered whether I really meant the words or not.

"I'm sure it did." Dero sneered. His face went slack as he attempted to communicate with Masa and I braced myself for another round of paralysis, but Masa shredded their connection and my brother tipped over, gulping, eyes bulging like a fish.

"Just breathe." I muttered, pacing. "It'll pass."

Masa launched off Nasheira's Heart above, his wings battering our hut with wind. I'd asked Dero once where his dragon went when he flew off alone, but he told me his Guide never shared that with him.

I'd finished eating and was gingerly stretching my stiff back when my brother spoke, his words slurred and dazed.

"Did you know she kept all of Tasie's old clothes?"

I turned back to him, frowning but silent.

"When you would cry out in the night and Hasev would run to you and spend *hours* in your company, Aella would unfold Tasie's dresses from beneath her bedroll and make us put them on and dance." His eyes grew unfocused. "Jin enjoyed it. He thinks I was too young to remember, but I do. Aella always wanted another girl after Tasie, but she got you instead, and then she got Jin and me. None of us were ever enough."

Goddess above. "I didn't know, Dero." I swallowed. "I'm sorry."

"You will be," he whispered earnestly.

That night, I woke to the sound of low voices conversing. I'd grown used to Dero murmuring to his dragons under his breath, but this was different. Dero spoke to someone on the other side of the hut wall. When I recognized the deep voice answering him, it brought me fully awake.

"...that we have not always seen eye-to-eye, but you can stop this. You can convince her," Hasev said.

"Do the guards know you're back here?" Dero's words left his lips as bitingly cold as the night air around us.

"I paid the guards four days of rations for a few minutes of your time. You could at least show me the barest respect by listening, boy." Hasev rarely commanded attention, but when he did, he was hard to ignore. It was heartening to hear he hadn't lost his finesse.

My brother muttered, "Say your piece then, so I can sleep."

"You are a Speaker now, Dero," he said softly. "People look to you. Nasheira has chosen you. And you may not like it, but she chose Akrist as well. Both of you. To *lead*. Not to kill each other in some bid to slake Arsu's macabre appetite. This is *murder* you are considering. A high sin."

"You act as if I have a choice," Dero spat. "As if I'm not caged alongside him."

"You wear the mark, Dero. Not her. *You* have the dragons. People only follow Arsu because you stand by her side. What she's doing, butchering boys every month—it's sacrilege. This is not the path Nasheira meant for you to walk, son."

Dero laughed. "A father who happily put his own daeson under the knife, and yet you have the gall to preach to me about crossing blades with him? At least I'll give him a chance to defend himself honourably before sending him to Pau." Dero paused and, though it was too dark to see, I could feel his eyes on me. "That's more than you ever gave him, Father."

"You're right. I was a coward." Hasev's voice broke. "And I have never regretted *anything* in my life as much as that night. Akrist, do you hear me? I am so sorry."

My eyes burned with unexpected tears, and I couldn't answer him. I couldn't think of the full moons without my throat closing and my heart ricocheting between my ribs.

"But I'll be damned if I make the same mistake again, and I'd be no father at all if I let you go through with this, Dero. Do not let Arsu manipulate you. She's a murderer. I fear what she will do to you when you no longer serve her purposes."

"You *fear* for me." He sneered. "Well, you needn't worry, Father. I—" My brother cut off mid-sentence, breath held.

Masa bugled from above and the other three Guides added their alarmed protests.

"What have you done?" Dero whispered.

"What's happening?" I croaked.

My father spoke urgently. "Dero—"

"What have you done?" he roared.

Guards peeled the door flap aside and crowded against our cages. Bright lamps blinded me.

Dragons leaped off the boulder high above us, claws scrabbling on rock, air from their launch pounding around us in deep *thwumps*.

I squinted at my brother through the bars. His eyes had rolled back. Breath came out of him in short, sharp pants.

"What is going on in here, Speaker?" one of the guards asked him uncertainly.

"Get Arsu," he commanded.

The guard dashed out the door. Her partner stayed, gaping with mild horror at Dero twitching like a freshly downed kill on the dirt floor.

Arsu charged in minutes later, clutching the bars. "What is happening? What do you see?" she rasped.

"Two people have stolen vaiyas and are heading away from camp. Masa is on top of them. I—" He hesitated. "It's Jin and Aaron. Shall I take them down?"

A deep shudder ran down my spine at the casualness of those words. *Take them down.* I remembered the spray of blood splattered up the ravine wall, the dismembered limbs, and the wretched screams.

Arsu looked thoughtful. "No. Let them go."

"What?" he spat. "They are traitors! I'm taking them."

"Dero, he is our brother!" I yelled.

"I said *leave* them!" Arsu barked with finality, like she was berating an animal instead of a man.

Dero cried out as his dragon chopped their connection. He writhed and curled away from Arsu as she looked down at him with disgust written plainly on her face. "Get out." she snarled at the guards. "Leave the lanterns."

Shudders wracked my brother. He breathed like a drowning man, all wet gulps with no room for exhalations. Dirt caked the side of his face and his eyes bulged and focused on me through the pain and shock.

Arsu steeped her next words in revulsion. "Get up."

"Leave him." I hissed, crossing the cage as if I could come between them. "You have no idea what it feels like."

The snake blinked once and took me in as if seeing me for the first time. Then she smirked, crouched down and reached her hands through the bars of Dero's enclosure. "Come here." She beckoned.

He heaved himself up and crawled toward her with his teeth clenched, sweat glowing on his pale skin. When he reached her, she took his chin in her hand and used the other to gently sweep away the hair plastered against his forehead.

"Dero," she crooned with hunger in her voice.

His throat worked. "Yes?"

Arsu reefed him toward her and smashed his face against the bars. A wet pop sounded as he hit. Bright blood gushed from his nose and streamed onto the floor between them. "Never contradict me in front of an audience again." She purred into his ear. "Do you understand?"

"Yes," he wailed.

Then she snatched up the lanterns and left us in the dark.

We did not speak. I thought I heard my brother sobbing softly but couldn't be sure. Nausea pricked its cold claws into my stomach as I paced with my heart high in my throat. The visual of Arsu breaking my brother's nose with no expression on her face at all replayed over and over in my mind.

Hasev had come to distract Dero in order to help Jin and Aaron escape. I was glad they were free of this place. But why was Arsu so keen to let them go?

—YARA—

Thank the Goddess that Sun was sleeping, curled onto the dirt floor nearby. I didn't want him to see what I was about to do.

With my pulse already singing in my head, I undid my tunic and shrugged it off. "Do you have a name?" I purred.

The guard turned, took in my bare breasts and froze before licking his lips and swallowing hard. "Now's not the time."

"I disagree." I leaned ahead. "When will you have me all to yourself again? Or can you not perform on short notice?"

Arsu and the second guard had been called away, as Hasev and I had suspected they would be.

He snorted, "Well, when you put it that way." Drawing his knife, he undid his belt and set it aside. Then he raised his tunic, slipped his breechcloth aside and hefted his flaccid penis in his hand. "Perhaps you can warm me up, wurm lover."

"Let me out and I will." I ran a hand over my breasts even as bile burned the back of my mouth. "I've seen you looking. Wouldn't you like a taste?"

"Through the bars is fine." He spat into his hand and stroked himself even as he aimed the knife at my face and it took everything in me to keep my expression inviting. "Be a good girl and don't make me cut you. Is this a fast enough performance for you?" Fully erect, he offered himself through the bars.

"It'll do," I murmured and then I lunged, grabbing his penis and twisting as hard as I could.

He screamed and buckled, bringing the knife down, but the bars between us hindered him, and the blade meant to cut off my hand only sliced my arm.

Before he could withdraw for another stab, I used my whole body to pin his weapon arm against the bars between us and wrenched him harder.

The guard's cursing boiled into an exploding shriek, a babbling repetition of the word "Stop!" He landed a punch to my nose, and then latched onto my hair, but even as my vision blurred with tears and blood gushed from my nostrils, I didn't let go of him. I crushed his genitals until he staggered, his eyes rolled back and his body slumped over, slack and twitching.

Then I grabbed the knife.

Sun blinked at me in the dark, eyes wide.

"I'm coming, love," I grunted, cutting the thick ropes securing the door.

Quickly, I dressed, wrapped the guard's belt around my tunic and tucked his knife at my waist before scooping my baby up and escaping into the night.

And no one chased me. Blood-curdling screams came from Arsu's hut often enough that the guard's cries went unnoticed.

CHAPTER
TWENTY-NINE

DREAD CLUNG TO EVERY corner of my mind, condensing into heavy numbness, leaching away my appetite and spilling out of me as horrific nightmares. Whenever I slept, I dreamed of the ravine massacre. Dero's dragon tore the camp apart while I watched, paralyzed.

Most mornings, we practiced. Dero would hone his dragon's skills, having me lunge and thrust and kick while Masa slowed my movements at the last second. He was planning for our fight to look convincing. No one would know I was being restrained. On the occasions I refused to participate in the fine-tuning of my own demise, Masa would paralyze me until my breathing stopped and I lost consciousness, and when I woke, he'd do it again. The pure panic, the sweeping, raw fear of death, it was the same every time. It never faded or eased.

So, most mornings, I cooperated.

When Masa inevitably grew bored of us, and the other dragons screamed for attention, Dero rested, murmuring placations and clutching his head.

I paced my cage, carefully stretching out my stiff, aching ribs and shaking the feeling back into my limbs. Sometimes Arsu came.

She'd take Dero away and have him perform tasks with his Guides—hunting, surveillance, capturing wild vaiyas—anything to parade him before his adoring audience as a capable, powerful Speaker and not the fractured, tortured prisoner he was.

Many of those hours I spent sitting in the dirt, leaning against the bars and absorbing the sounds of the massive camp outside, the squawking chatter of vaiyas, the constant cacophony of human voices, aeni plying their wares, children squealing and elders chiding them. I strained to hear Yara's voice among them, or Sun's cry. I imagined them safe and well fed and as far from Arsu as possible because it utterly broke me to think of the reality of their situation.

More and more often, Dero spent his evenings away from our enclosure. He'd return late in the night on Arsu's arm. She'd kiss his blackened eyes and swollen nose before locking him in his cage.

"Tell me, does she still call Gevi her mate?" I asked spitefully one night.

"She doesn't love him." He dodged the question and smoothed a hand down the mark on his chest. "She only loves power. You know that."

Two days before the full moons, on a bitterly cold fall night, I awoke with radiant warmth in my mind.

Akrist? Her soft voice hummed through me, fresh, green, and sweet. I bolted upright.

"Nardiri?" I clapped my hands over my mouth to stifle the sound bubbling up my throat, a combination of a laugh and a sob.

Dero lay with his back to me, dimly lit by a strip of white light leaking past the door flap from the nearly full moons.

He looked to be sleeping, or at least feigning sleep. More telling was the silence from above. Masa would have called out an alarm if he sensed Nardiri.

I've missed you so much. I wrapped my arms around myself, chest aching.

We are coming. Her thought was a wisp.

No. The euphoria filling me evaporated in an instant. Panic sloshed in, icy and black. *Arsu will expect it. She'll kill you all.* Breath hung high and shallow in my burning lungs. *If Dero's dragon wakes, he'll hunt you down right now. You have to go back, Nardiri.*

Warmth dribbled out of me. Green peeled away into grey and I scrambled to my feet and pressed against the rough bars of my cage as if I could close the distance between us and restore the connection my dragon struggled to hold from afar. **Do not worry. We are coming.**

Nardiri, I'm begging you. Go back. But she was gone, her clean essence draining out of me like spring water soaking into dirt. I squeezed my eyes closed, pressed my forehead against the bars and prayed. *Oh Nasheira, please. You can have me. If this is the example I'm meant to be, if my death pleases you, so be it, but do not take the rest. Do not make them pay for my mistakes.*

On the eve of the full moons, Dero and I sat staring at each other through the divider wall. His bruised eyes were fading to yellow and his nose was crooked but no longer puffy. My ribs had not fully mended, but the pain had dulled to a persistent ache instead of a knifing agony. Around us, the camp crackled with activity. Dero's dragons circled overhead. Mild air carried the smells of bitter tea, smoked meat, and gifen. Animated chatter and industrious yells clambered over each other. Vaiyas barked bright greeting calls, but none of the excitement quite reached us inside our enclosure.

"You look like you've already lost a fight, brother." I smiled slowly, picking my teeth and pretending not to feel the mounting tension twisting my innards.

Dero's eyes met mine and they were clear—a rare moment when he was totally unencumbered by his dragons. "And you, brother," he drawled. "Look like you're already dead."

We laughed like fools over that, even though it wasn't particularly funny. We snorted until our eyes streamed tears and our faces purpled. And I would never forget that. That unshielded frenetic moment between us. The fact that those would be the last words he ever spoke to me, and the realization—much later on—that Dero had called me brother for the first time.

Our guards brought a basin of water and fresh clothes before sunset. Dero washed and changed. I wasn't allowed. I supposed I looked more like Pau Incarnate if I was filthy and garbed in the sour clothes I'd arrived in nearly a month ago. Instead, my captors tied my wrists, leaving a lead long enough for Dero to pull me along like a vaiya. I blinked as my brother pushed the door flap aside and we ducked outside.

Even muted by the orange glow of a setting sun, the edges of the huts and tents were too bright. The odour of grilled meat and the sizzle of fat overwhelmed me and turned my stomach. As we rounded the corner of the long hut that had been our prison, our path widened and the settlement sprawled before us. I balked at the sheer number of people—at least twice as many as when I'd arrived. The place looked like a crushed ant hill. Bodies swarmed everywhere. Children scuttled between legs, snatching food. Cooks hauled steaming quarters of roasted meat slung on poles over their shoulders. Men in festival regalia with white chalked faces, red-stained chest scars, and bristling feather arm bands haggled with aeni over bowls of gifen, fillets of salted fish, and slices of honeycomb. Women in wide-sleeved pale dresses weighted with intricate beads clattered as they walked. Every time I inhaled, I caught whiffs of fried onions, sharp spices, or body odor. My mind folded in on itself, and I didn't realize I'd stopped walking until Dero tugged on the rope.

Before the crowd swallowed us, the wind shifted and the people closest to us yelped and dove aside as Masa landed behind us with a thud that reverberated through my heels. His intelligent green eyes took in every face in the crowd, reptilian mouth exposing rows of wicked, serrated teeth. His barbed tail lashed overhead and for a sliver of a moment, the dragon made eye contact with me. A weight opened up in my chest, pulling at my ribs until they creaked and I gasped. Then it was gone.

He's testing his control. Apparently satisfied with my reaction, he went back to ignoring me. Two of Dero's other dragons wheeled overhead, dark silhouettes against a red sky, gliding lazily. The third sulked behind us, perched on Nasheira's Heart, her teal wings still shredded from her battle with Nardiri.

A drum beat pounded from afar, sonorous and steady, like a disembodied heartbeat pulling streams of people away from the erratic rock and toward the flats beyond the eastern border. Parent's snatched their children. Aeni hastily packed their goods and rolled up their bright display blankets. People stared at me as they walked, their eyes smouldering with hatred and their lips spewing hot and horrible curses, but none of them dared touch me with Dero at my front and Masa behind us, hissing at the crowd as we passed.

Dust choked the walkways, scuffed up by hundreds of heels. The sky burned blood red, low banks of rippling, grainy clouds reflecting the sunset like a vast glistening body of water, while the muted sage prairie below drank in the light. Each thump of the somber drum plucked at my ribs and nudged my heart higher in my throat. Vaiya flocks clumped together, jostling and hissing with their crests raised as they picked up whiffs of anticipation over the heads of the clotting crowd.

As we closed on the two tall wooden cages I'd passed with Jin nearly a month ago, the thick smell of death took my breath away. Ravens mobbed the tops of the enclosures, feet scrabbling and beaks jabbing. Wisps of hair fluttered in the churn of their black wings. The bodies within were bloated, bare feet dangling, grossly swollen, and purple. Beneath one of the cages, a single boot lay crumpled on the ground.

Mother of Yurrii. I swallowed against the queasy heat rising in me. That would be me soon. I'd hang in a cage, displayed for everyone to see until the wurms tore me limb from limb. I held my breath and stared down at my boots as we passed between the macabre enclosures and the crowd around us spilled into the open prairie.

The gentle dip of the terrain east of the boulder made an ideal, natural stage. Fathers hoisted children onto their shoulders to better see the cleared turf where the drummer struck his ominous beat. Others balanced on the backs of nervous vaiyas. Six huge hearth fires blazed around the circumference of a cleared and raked circle of ground.

My breathing accelerated, and chills swept through my limbs. *One of us will die here. In that circle With a raucous crowd cheering as our blood waters the ground.* And I knew who it would be. Arsu had orchestrated it as precisely as she had Iva's murder. There was no escape from this.

The snake stood beside the drummer. A line of Speakers moved into position to flank her, six on either side, their chests bare except for Nasheira's mark and a single golden scale strapped around each of their necks.

Arsu's black eyes glittered as she took me in. She was dressed in a plain, open-necked tunic and leggings. The only arresting detail of her garb was the thick band of dragon scales she wore around her neck—one of them stained pink. Her brother's sacred necklace. A Speaker's attire, though she bore no holy mark of her own.

"Untie him," she ordered Dero.

Masa pumped his wings behind us as I rubbed my wrists. Hair whipped and clods of grass swirled in the circular clearing as the dragon lifted off to hover over Arsu's line of Speakers. He bugled once, long and loud, and his spectators fell into awed silence as Arsu raised her arms.

"Children of Yurrii," she bellowed and they shouted back and pumped their fists before leaning in for her next words. Wind whipped her hair across her cheeks as she nodded in approval. "We've all gathered here because we've sensed a change in our world. Nasheira is grieved, now more than ever. But she is done waiting for vengeance." Her face sank and she shook her head. "Our Goddess yearns for rightful restoration, and yet our elders make her wait *twelve* years at a time to slake her hunger? *Twelve* years we coddle her daeson before offering them. *Twelve* years we ignore Nasheira's pleas for justice for Yurrii." She paused, inhaled, and then shouted, "It is not enough."

The crowd applauded.

I searched for Yara and Sun amongst the sea of incensed faces.

"It has *never* been enough to wait for the moons to swallow each other. We know that now. Look at how this camp has prospered since we started offering the Goddess proper, *timely* sacrifices." Arsu indicated the Speakers on either side of her. "Look at how she's repaid our loyalty." She nodded at Dero, and Masa tossed his head and trumpeted obediently. "She's blessed us with her Guides!"

The snake waited for the frenzied cheering to thin out before hardening her voice and fixing her cold gaze on me. "But while we have risen to meet the needs of our Goddess, there are those who would shun her instead."

Sour distaste rippled through the crowd. Vaiyas wailed and rolled their eyes.

"Those who would steal what rightfully belongs to Nasheira."

"Wurm Speaker!" Someone shouted.

"A *False* Speaker," Arsu hissed. "Whose lips spew lies."

Her audience roared, all bared teeth and snarling faces.

"A man who forces innocent followers of Nasheira to re-nounce their sacrifices to the Goddess. Who twisted the gifts She gave him, who worships wurms and has *corrupted* one of her holy Guides." She growled. "The very voice of Pau himself." Arsu spat at my feet and her followers went wild.

"He will not corrupt us!" she bellowed over their shrieks. "It ends here. When Yurrii rises on the horizon tonight, good will triumph over evil. We will bring Nasheira the justice she deserves."

The thunder of the crowd was deafening. Masa's wings stirred cyclones of sparks from the whipping fires around us. People shoved and jostled.

Pau is among us. I struggled to breathe.

And then the wind shifted. Masa screamed and surged higher into the sky.

Dero stiffened, his eyes glazing over.

My mind filled with green. *Nardiri.* I choked.

I'm here. She answered with an ear-splitting roar.

The crowd froze. Yells dried out on tongues. Heads craned toward the eastern horizon where my dragon, miraculously whole, rose into the glowing sky, great wings pumping, hide flashing like fire. Celestial. Below her bloomed a churning cloud of dust. Riders on vaiya back towed loaded travois behind them.

My camp.

Dero's dragons shrieked, tucked their wings and dove toward them.

"No!" I howled.

—YARA—

Escaping Arsu's hut had been easy. Escaping her camp proved nearly impossible. Dero's dragons monitored every soul who traversed the borders and they paid particular attention to travellers with babies. One evening, as I considered bolting from the line of huts at the southern edge of the settlement, a woman and child sprinted out into the dusk. They didn't stop when the dragons roared, or when wings whistled overhead.

Dero's Guides raked the woman's back, sending her toppling to the dirt still clutching her screaming child. I pressed Sun against my chest and backed away, unable to take my eyes from the screeching baby, whose mother lay bleeding and squirming in the dirt. They left her there like that. When she tried to crawl away, the dragons snapped at her and licked her blood. Toying with her. They followed her until she dragged herself and her child back toward the huts.

So long as I stayed among crowds, I could evade Arsu. I'd been able to blend in since I was a girl. If I focused on it, if I poured all my energy into making Sun and myself unnoticeable, I looked forgettable enough to slip past every one of Aru's search teams. But I couldn't get to Akrist. Arsu had doubled his guards since I had escaped.

As much as I longed to do that, or slip back to Arsu's hut in the dark of night and slit her throat while she slept, I did neither. If I attempted to rescue Akrist, or slaughter Arsu, I'd be killed and Sun would be sacrificed. So I survived. I sold the guard's knife and belt for food. I kept moving during the day and slept amongst the vaiya flocks at night. I couldn't do anything else. Not until Akrist's dragon came.

On the night of Yurrii's full moon, I followed the crowds. My knees loosened and my chest seized when I saw Akrist and Dero. I poured myself into obscurity and followed as close as I could get. If I could slip a knife from one of the Speaker's belts, if I could get close enough to Arsu as she made her speech to her adoring crowd, I could kill her and we could all flee, but bodies swarmed around us and I couldn't see over them. Elbows pressed into me and heels stamped on my toes. I fought my way to the front of the crowd.

Then Dero's dragons screeched. Nardiri winged toward us and landed. Arsu traded hot words with someone I couldn't see. And a spear sang over my head.

The world exploded into chaos.

I ran. I shielded Sun and sank into the fleeing, screaming crowd. I swam in its chaotic crushing current as best as I could. I thought we'd be crushed underfoot, Sun and I, but even when we were choking in people, I could see the dragons fighting in the patch of blue above.

Then they stopped. With harrowing wails, the Guides broke from each other and hung in the air, stunned. The crowd around me scattered. I tumbled back toward the circle of hearth fires where Akrist had faced Dero, and I saw him on the ground, entangled with his brother and drenched in blood.

Arsu stood between us, just beyond Akrist's sightline. She was aiming a spear at my mate, and well within range to strike a fatal blow.

"Akrist!" I screamed.

CHAPTER THIRTY

"No!" Arsu's yell echoed my own. She clutched Dero's forearm and hissed. "Call your dragons back. Have you no control?"

My brother grunted.

Masa belted out a frustrated shriek and faltered, staggering in the sky before swinging back to his Speaker. The other two shook their heads and banked away from my approaching party, growling deep in their throats. The grounded female wailed forlornly from the rock.

"Pau's people have come to see him die!" Arsu shouted to the stricken crowd. "Let them come. We will show them what true followers of Nasheira look like."

This time, her spectators answered with wilted, uncertain cheers. Parents pulled their children down from their shoulders and clutched them tightly. Several groups sidled back toward the shelter of the camp.

Arsu bent to Dero and whispered, "Rouse the one on the rock."

The female staggered to her feet, spread her tattered wings wide and blasted us with a warning call, narrow green gaze honing in on the movement at the edges of the crowd. Those who had tried to separate from the main mass froze where they stood, exposed.

"*All* devout followers will stay to watch." Arsu said. She left her threat hanging unspoken in the smoke-filled air.

Time passed in ragged breaths and soft whimpers, hemmed in by Dero's dragons, while colour bled out of the sky, and my friends tore towards us, pressing their vaiyas at full speed.

My stomach crashed. Who is protecting the daeson?

We left them well guarded. Do not worry. Nardiri streaked ahead of the charging vaiya flock, flared hard enough to flatten the fires around us, and landed, holding her huge wings widespread. Where her main sail had torn, a line of puckered, even stitches held the membrane together.

Her rider slid down from the harness and strode toward us.

I gaped at the man as he peeled off flight gloves and pressed a wooden visor up into his silver-blond hair before approaching us. "Arsu," he called, drawing a long knife with a wrist lanyard.

Sweet Nasheira, it's Fraesh. Breath bled out of me like someone had punched me. I wanted to dive toward my uncle and push him away as he stalked toward Arsu. I'd lost Iva. I couldn't lose him too. I couldn't lose all these people. *She'll kill him, Nardiri. She'll kill all of us!*

Let her try! I'm stronger than all of them. The male is trying to paralyze you right now, but I'm not letting him. She shrieked a challenge to Masa as he circled high above.

Dero flinched. His hands clenched with the effort of controlling his dragon.

"Healer." Arsu stepped toward Fraesh, her smile slippery and insincere.

"You and Dero have murdered without provocation." Fraesh's voice broke on that last word. "By rights I should carve a brand in your faces right now for every life you've taken."

Arsu tsked. Turning back to the crowd, she shouted. "A Son of Pau calls us murderers with no proof!"

The healer stiffened and bellowed. "This woman and your Speaker have slaughtered innocent people. Children! His dragon laid waste to our camp, unprovoked. They kidnapped our Speaker and his family."

"Your *false* Speaker, his immoral mate, and their beloved *daeson*," Arsu said, and those closest to her raised their spears to prevent Fraesh from coming closer.

"Give us our family," Fraesh yelled. "Or we will fight to free them."

Nardiri folded her wings, revealing what had been hidden in her shadow: eight Speakers armed with spears and daggers, each with a wurm rearing up at their side.

The crowd balked and screamed at the sight of them.

They impressed wurms? My mind reeled. *How?*

Tanar found a knot of wurms far out on the prairie. After he bonded, he came searching for you. He found us after you left and took us back to the wurms.

"He didn't run." I murmured, finding Tanar's red hair among the Speakers who'd come to my defense.

Several vaiyas shrugged out of the bulky travois that had carried the wurms here at speed. Riders tucked low onto their mount's backs, spears ready. More than two dozen of them—every adult from my camp who was old enough to ride. And at their head, controlling his dancing vaiya with ease, was my brother Jin.

I tried to remain calm. "Do not do this," I said, unsure if I was speaking to Arsu or Fraesh. "I will fight. Just Dero and me. There's no need for others to be harmed."

A spear sang over my shoulder and thunked into Fraesh's thigh. He grunted, dropped his knife and sagged to his knees.

I traced the path of the projectile back to a knot of armed men elbowing through the crowd.

Jin screamed and laid into his vaiya's sides, and the other riders howled and charged with him. My Speakers and their wurms tore toward the stampeding crowd.

Masa crashed into Nardiri as she launched.

I dove between Arsu and Fraesh, evading my captors and grabbing Fraesh's fallen knife. I spun to defend him, but most of the snake's Speakers were focused on shielding her. One hurtled toward me and I smashed the butt of the knife into his face. Hot blood spurted from his nose, splattering onto my arm, He dropped to the ground senseless. My wrist tingled from the jarring force.

Fraesh had pulled the spear from his leg when I turned back to hoist him to his feet. Jin's mounted fighters thudded past and crashed into the crowd.

The air thickened with screams. A riderless vaiya crashed into one of the wurms, sending it toppling into the furthest fire. People scattered, scrambling away from the clash of weapons. Others flew into the fray, hurling rocks, slashing at vaiya's legs as they passed, even as the birds bit off fingers and gored attackers. Spears arced high into the sky, whistling as they went. As I scanned the chaos, I recognized my father thrusting a knife into the back of a man trying to peel Jin off his mobbed vaiya. "Mother of Yurrii," I murmured and spun back to Fraesh, but he was gone.

Nardiri screeched.

Red pounded through me. The smell of burning flesh coated my throat as I searched the darkening skies.

Nardiri had seized Masa by the neck, but the smaller females were harrying her, digging into her back and snagging her delicate wings with their tails. Dropping the male, she twisted to shake them off.

Heaviness swamped my chest. I nearly dropped my blade as Dero charged. His knife plunged over my shoulder as I ducked. Crashing into him and holding tight, I slashed at his back before Masa dug his control deeper, and my brother grunted and broke away.

Nardiri! I gulped for air and glanced up, but all of her attention was focused on the two females attacking her. I was on my own.

Dero swiped at my midsection. I sprang back, too slowly. My shirt tore and his blade burned across my belly. Staggering back, buying time, I pressed my palm over my gut. It was a shallow wound, though it stung. I'd never fought a man like this, categorizing his soft spots, areas likely to bleed him out or incapacitate him. Guides, this was my brother!

Dero attacked again, aiming for my exposed side. Masa slowed my arm as I blocked, but I'd embellished in all our practices, dropping things when my fingers weren't yet numb. The trick wouldn't work more than once, but the dragon's casual hold now was weak enough for me to break free. I smashed the flat of my blade into Dero's wrist, deflecting his blow.

He screamed. His weapon spun out of his grip, clattering at my feet. I kicked it into the fire behind me, lunged and sliced Dero's forehead. *The blood will blind him. You can end this without killing him. Get some distance.*

That was the last thing I remember before Masa howled and all of my muscles went slack. My blade slipped from my grip. The wrist lanyard hooked on my seized, crooked fingers and the knife dangled there until I hit the ground. *NARDIRI!* My mind screamed. With my head cocked painfully to the side, I couldn't see the sky, but I heard her desperate gurgles. I felt Dero's dragons snaking around her neck and gouging at her belly as she shared her senses.

Guides, no!

Through the pale grass, I saw vibrant green silhouettes lying slack and twitching; Speakers with wurms worrying them and nudging their chests, downed vaiyas with pinned riders beneath them, legs kicking feebly. The air vibrated with Masa's force. *He's dropped every Speaker and vaiya on the field. Both sides.*

The fighting on the ground stuttered to a stop. Even those who weren't receptive felt the air crackling with energy and turned to us, panting and stunned. Only the wounded wailed, oblivious to it all. Above us, Nardiri fought for her life, outmaneuvered by the two smaller, agile females, and I couldn't reach her mind.

Dero was the only Speaker still standing. He walked toward me, gaze pinned to the weapon snagged in my fingers even as he wiped at the blood running into his left eye from the gash above his brow.

"No!" A voice bellowed from my right. "Dero, don't!" Hasev plowed toward us, a wraith between the hearth fires. He was unarmed.

Dero glanced at our father and then turned back to me.

A projectile zinged past Hasev. Dero heard it coming and turned too late. The lance thunked below his collarbone. Breath barked out of him and he staggered. I saw a flash of red hair from where the spear had launched.

Tanar, the only marked one among us who could hide his receptiveness at will, had aimed well.

All of Dero's dragons screeched. Masa's hold recoiled. Life snapped back into my limbs. The two dragon's clinging to Nardiri wailed and she kicked them away and dove toward the male.

I sat up as Hasev sprinted toward us.

Dero jerked the spear out of his shoulder, lined me up and heaved back to throw. The blood in his eye blinded him to our father's approach.

"No." The word burst out of me, but the weapon had already left Dero's fingertips, bloodied tip rapidly expanding before Hasev pushed me aside. The spear tore into his throat. We fell in a pile, my father sprawling and choking in a widening puddle of his own blood. I don't know if seconds or minutes passed as I stood frozen, watching, helpless, as the light left his eyes and his gagging stopped.

Dero fell to his knees as he realized what he had done. Reeling, I launched toward him, snagging the knife and jamming it against my brother's corded neck.

"When does it stop?" I whispered, the stench of death overwhelming me.

Dero's gaze flicked from our father's body up to his distracted dragons and then back to me. His face relaxed. His eyes cleared. In one fluid motion, he clamped his hands over mine, rammed the blade into his neck and wrenched it sideways. His throat gaped open from windpipe to ear. Blood erupted onto my chest.

"No," I wailed as he crumpled against me. "Oh, Guides, no!"

His dragons screamed, writhing and peeling away from Nardiri.

I held my brother's hand as he clutched at me, sucking wet, rattling breaths.

"Akrist!" someone screamed my name. Yara. Turning toward the sound, I saw Arsu aiming a spear at me, hauling back to throw.

A shadow rippled over us.

Masa hit the ground so hard it shook. His huge wings mantled us as Dero convulsed in my grip. Arsu's spear punctured his wingsail and thunked into the dirt near my foot. The dragon snarled, launched away from us and barrelled into the woman, pinning her.

I expected him to tear her apart, but instead, Masa's tongue flattened across Arsu's stomach, raking upward, tearing her shirt to shreds. She screeched as the dragon's tongue moved toward her chest, up her neck and over her face.

Dero gurgled and blinked. It was all I could do to hold my brother tight as his life spilled out of him and Masa lapped at the wet redness of his newly made Speaker.

The woman's clothes curled away from her like fruit peels. Golden dragon scales scattered around her from the snapped holy necklace. Shredded flaps of skin disintegrated to jittering pink muscle and white tendon. She'd been laid bare from her thighs all the way up her torso and past her shoulders. The skeletal, exaggerated grimace of teeth flashed through a ragged hole where her cheek had been. Masa wasn't marking Arsu, I realized. Dero had said the dragon was angry at her for tearing his brethren out of their cocoons early. He was killing her in the slowest, most painful way possible.

Before he could finish flaying her, Dero went slack in my arms. The vaiyas on the stricken battlefield wailed a death dirge. Something snapped in the air, like a coiled tendon letting go.

Masa shook his head and whimpered forlornly. He looked down at the wriggling bloody body he held and blinked slowly.

The females shuddered and winged away into the moonlit night, and Masa took off and flew away aimlessly. The tattered dragon on the erratic rock slipped off her perch and trailed after him on foot.

Are you hurt? Nardiri landed.

I couldn't answer. Stumbling to my feet and backing away from Dero's body, I gaped at her before blinking down at my blood-soaked shirt. A strange thought struck me. I hadn't been wearing red.

Akrist, are you hurt? She crowed, all frantic yellow and shuddering bloody black wings. Yara crashed into me, asking the same question. My gaze shifted over her white face, her wet eyes. Sun alive and well in her arms. All of it undid me.

Nardiri crouched, cutting us off from the battlefield with sweeping, cupped wings. The deep tones of her half-growling hum pulsed through my aching chest.

"I'm sorry, Yara. I'm so sorry for all of this," I blurted, clutching my mate against me.

Arsu's agonised cries faded into groaning, hitching breaths.

CHAPTER THIRTY-ONE

W E DIDN'T HAVE TIME to comfort each other or mourn, not while Arsu's followers were still scattered among us. I pressed away from Yara and told Nardiri to lift her wings. Although my head swam and my muscles screamed, I didn't lean on my dragon's leg. Rolling my shoulders back, I pointed toward Arsu's wounded Speakers and bellowed to the scant crowd remaining, "Are you with them, or are you with me? Because my dragon does not take kindly to those who would harm us." Arsu—what was left of her—punctuated my words with a rattling cry.

Tanar trotted toward us, blood streaking his face and loyal wurm at his heels. Jin pressed his exhausted vaiya through the ragged crowd. Fraesh rode behind him.

"No one harms them." I barked, jabbing a finger at the downed Speakers before swinging my arm behind me, "Or her. They do not move, they do not breathe, without my permission, understand?"

"Pau's Stones," Tanar blurted as he came to a winded stop.

"Tanar. We'll need junab, lots of it. Sinew for stitching and any healers who are here."

"Good to see you, too." He wiped his nose and swallowed, green gaze fixed on Arsu.

The woman had curled to her side, dirt caking against her bared ribs as she panted between screams.

"She lives." The words dropped from my lips with the hardness of a command. "The healers can numb her pain, but they are not to give her anything to send her to Nasheira early."

Tanar nodded and patted his wurm's head. Someone behind him vomited.

"Tanar." I waited until the red-haired Speaker met my gaze. "Thank you."

He smirked and turned away.

I ordered Arsu moved to a private tent away from the other wounded. The healers, under the direction of Fraesh, scrubbed dirt from the woman's raw torso, slathered her in junab and stitched her cheek back together, tending to her as carefully as they did all the other casualties.

Most of the Children of Yurrii scattered into the night with arms full of plunder. I let them go. Those who decided to stay were put to work. The uninjured scavenged wood to build massive pyres. They tore strips of fabric into bandages and crushed junab into salve until the entire camp smelled of the pungent ointment. We cleared the dead through the night. I made sure Yara was well and then settled her and Sun into a hut; Jin volunteered to watch over them. When they fell asleep, I left them.

The snake and I were the only ones in her tent when she regained consciousness. One of her eyes had swollen shut and the other was a lidless, clouded orb. It rolled toward me when she woke.

"Who's there?" Words fell from her lipless mouth, wet and garbled.

I steepled my twitching hands, pressed them against my lips and inhaled deeply before answering, "Akrist."

"The blanket's hurting me. Take it off." Arsu slurred. Her mess of a chest rapidly expanded and collapsed under the drape of damp, broad bandages.

I didn't answer her, but I hooked a finger under a blood-soaked dressing and peeled it back as she screamed. In the lamplight, the snake's skinned ribs glowed white, and fat loops of glistening intestines poked past her stomach muscles. Saliva flooded my mouth and images flashed in my mind in sharp, stabbing succession. Iva in Na-Jhalar's hut, Hasev's shocked blue-grey eyes searching mine before the light went out of them, Dero's bloody hand clutching mine and then going slack.

I blinked the visions away and focused on the tent walls and the flayed woman before me. Arsu squirmed, pink and raw like a grotesque newborn. She licked her teeth and spoke. "I want Gevi."

I couldn't tell if her bulging clouded eye saw me or not as it searched the room for her mate.

"I want Gevi!" Arsu bawled and her tongue wriggled after she spoke, poking at the stitched hole in her cheek.

I swallowed and ran my thumb over the s-shaped brand on my cheek, the one Arsu had carved with such brutal precision.

"I want Gevi." She blubbered quietly and then her head sagged as she lost consciousness. It was the last thing she ever said.

I watched the laboured rise and fall of Arsu's chest, frowned at her pale ribcage swelling and her abdomen caving in with each inhale. My legs cramped waiting for that last, wretched rattling breath. It didn't come for a very long time, and I did not stand to leave until the keening report of the vaiyas' mourning cry confirmed her death. Leaving the lantern behind, ducking out of the tent, I stretched carefully and squinted up at the deep, dark sky. Dawn bleached the eastern horizon. Nardiri crouched in the trampled grass beyond the smouldering ring fires.

It's done now.

Why did you stay with her? Her eyes bobbed in the dark, two bright grey crescents.

"I wanted to watch her die," I whispered.

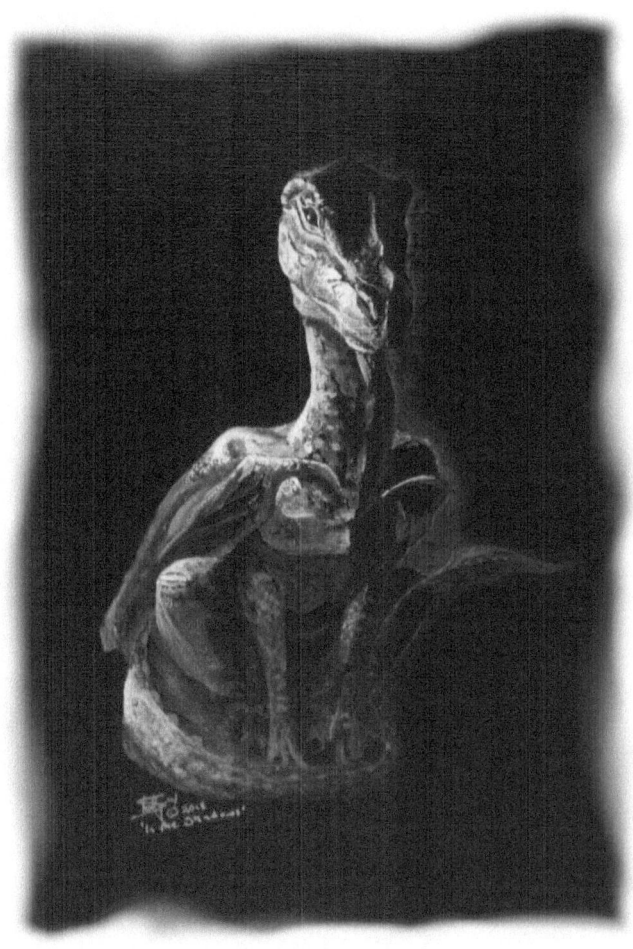

In the Shadows

CHAPTER THIRTY-TWO

THREE WEEKS LATER, WHEN our wounded were well enough to travel, we left the camp at Nasheira's Heart. Many there swore fealty to me, and when I journeyed back to the ravine, I left them with these words: "We are children of Nasheira, every one of us. Do not make your home here if you don't believe that."

Nardiri flew and mated three times that winter.

The first time it happened, she and I were following a winding valley within the southern mountain range. We searched for junab amongst the trees. The ravine grew very little of the shade-loving succulent, but it carpeted the forest floor here, frozen under the snow. Along with the medicinal herb, we searched out old hardwood and planned to carry a bundle of logs home to trade with the aeni, who now used Nasheira's Heart as a central trading post. Nardiri had just braced herself to push down her third tree when she froze and looked skyward.

I straightened. I lowered my axe as I scanned the sky with her. "What?" I whispered.

My dragon kept her head tilted, but her inner lids slid lazily closed and then open as she twitched her tail. *A male. He's alone.* She dropped her green gaze back to me and shook out her wings, raining pine-needles into my hair. *He doesn't know I'm here yet. I've masked myself.*

I circled away from her, stumbling on the partially de-limbed log with my head still tipped to the sky. *He's alone? Could it be Masa?*

Not him, and he's alone. Nardiri snorted indignantly and rolled her shoulder where the pale scars of her battles had faded to milky white. *I don't make the same mistakes twice, Akrist.*

"I'm sorry. I just—" I tripped and my teeth clamped, cutting off the rest of my apology.

Suddenly, you are clumsier than Sun. What's wrong?

I swung the axe awkwardly. *Are you going to fly with him?*

Nardiri regarded me with steady green eyes. She sat and coiled her tail around her feet. *Does that make you nervous?*

"No," I blurted, burying the axe with a thunk into the tree beside me.

Liar. Nervous and jealous, too.

I laughed, sitting down on the log. *Hardly a competition, is it, sweet bird? He's likely ten times my size.*

I only need him for a few minutes. The hungry red emphasis my dragon placed on the word *need* tightened my throat.

Several exhalations puffed into the silence. Alternating clouds of white fog spooled skyward as we scanned the patch of bleached blue above for movement. Snow squeaked under my boot as I twisted my foot.

And then Nardiri's irises contracted, and she tensed. I followed her hungry gaze toward a wedge of dark gold. Far overhead, the form solidified. I couldn't tell from this distance if the male outsized Nardiri or not. His wings tapered thinner and were longer than hers. Sunlight glowed through dappled, unblemished membrane and shone off the scale-studded curves of burnished muscle. A healthy, well-built driftling, nothing like the starved bags of bones Nardiri and I occasionally encountered.

"Well?" I stood.

My dragon shifted from foot to foot, tearing her attention from the dragon banking away from us, to pin me under her green gaze. *I don't need your permission.*

I pursed my lips and shook my head slowly. *No, you don't.*

Take off the harness, please.

I undid the knots in our new harness and pulled the mess of ropes over Nardiri's neck as her breath quickened and she fanned her wings around me. "Be careful." I gulped.

Relax, she admonished in shades of pink and light green. *This will be fun.*

Then my dragon pounded skyward. The trees shuddered, wrapped in the turbulence of her wings, and my heart surged as pine needles and ice rained down around me. She blasted a high, taunting call to the male above.

Primal red washed through me like adrenalin. My arms tensed as Nardiri pumped skyward, tail writhing and limbs tucked.

The male crowed back in happy surprise, hooked into a sharp turn and pushed toward her.

He's slow. Those wings were built for gliding. Nardiri jutted her chin toward her pursuer, blasted another shrieking call, and ascended with quick, assertive beats.

I watched the pair spiral skyward, the male lazily trailing my cavorting dragon as she teased him higher and higher.

Nardiri opened up her sight to me and I was flung from the ground into the thin icy air high above the wrinkling mountain range with the male, crowing and circling below me. His wing membrane darkened to black as laced networks of blood vessels dilated in response to my dragon's calls. A deep, moss green aura clung to him like smoke, curling toward my dragon as she dived.

He's scared of me. Nardiri trumpeted boldly. ***I'm too fast for him, and I'm bigger than—***

My dragon's smug thought cut off mid-dive as the male flipped onto his back, whipped his tail upward and snagged his barbs in Nardiri's own. With their tails caught, both dragons were unbalanced and peeled apart. Nardiri billowed her wings and slowed as she curled upward, but the male zipped into a tight downward loop whose apex positioned him directly over my startled dragon. He dropped and wrapped her in his wings.

"Oh Guides!" I stumbled ahead as they dropped like stones. *Nardiri!*

I'm stuck, she yelped.

"Fight back!" I hollered.

Her tail fluttered like slack fabric as they plummeted. The male hooked his mid-wing claws together beneath Nardiri's chest, locking her in his embrace. His tail twined with hers and peeled it aside. They coupled while they fell.

Nardiri's red thrashing thoughts smoothed abruptly to a billowing, blind green. She hummed as the ground arced towards them.

I staggered in the current of her jarring emotional shift and slammed through the woods to follow the pair's dive. *Break out of it. You're falling!* I lost sight of them. Her thoughts cut off from my head with a tension that nearly dropped me.

"Nardiri!" I screamed. Treetops bounced overhead as I ran. I broke into another clearing just in time to see the male unfurl his wings, his back legs still gripping my dragon as he held her away from the skimming trees. Pulling her upward, he waited until Nardiri got her wings under her, thrust into her once more, and pulled away with a satisfied trill.

"Sweet Nasheira." I dropped to my knees, gulping.

I liked that. Nardiri shook out her shoulders, settled into a glide, and clicked her teeth. ***Very much.***

The next two shared experiences were equally intense. Fielding the primal wash of emotion broadcasting from a fertile dragon as she flew with a male nearly overwhelmed me. The gutting mix of rapture and raw fear as he captured and entangled with her in a diving embrace, the vital moment, when the pair uncoupled and banked away from each other, so close to the ground their wings carved grooves in the snow; all of it ticked by in swift slow-motion and left me wrung out.

Nardiri didn't need to tell me when she was ready to lay eggs. The irritated hardness in her eyes, the way she held her jaw dropped slightly open and twitched her tail, even while she slept, advertised her broodiness well enough.

She was utterly unapproachable for the three days it took to clutch her eighteen eggs on the sandy south shore of the half-frozen canyon lake. We did not have the privilege of admiring the cluster of creamy, oblong eggs for long. With frost still licking the ground each early spring morning, my dragon made numerous trips to the grasslands above in order to blanket the eggs in a thick layer of damp vegetation.

By the time she finished fussing with the arrangement of her nest, scattering branches, covering it with gobs of mud she had gouged from the lake, and grading the edges with her tail, the site looked rather mundane. Only a slight mound, artfully groomed to follow the lay of the land around it, betrayed the nest's whereabouts.

When Nardiri had finished fussing, she left us. I tracked her as she blooded, killed, and consumed two oxen. Smugly, she flew back to us, wheeled and set down in the middle of the icy lake. She rolled luxuriously for a few minutes before shaking out her wings and returning to me.

We can go now.

I grinned, and tentatively reached out to pat her snout.

Where are we going?

Nardiri shook her head, her beamed crest cutting through the air with a low whoosh. She blinked at me and then yawned so widely that her jaw popped. ***Anywhere,*** she answered in lazy tones of content green.

Speakers came to us from all over as word spread. Rowin often flew with Nardiri and me when he wasn't busy hunting with Tanar. I never thought I'd trust my child with the man who'd tried to murder me, but Tanar's had changed. He rarely spoke to himself anymore. When he smiled, it wasn't a pinched sneer, but an expression that softened all the sharp angles on his face, like how he'd smiled at Xen when we were young. He still had moments of madness, but they happened less often and were not as severe. We were there to help him through them.

During our travels, Rowin and I visited the camp at Nasheira's Heart for receptive newcomers and consulted aeni passing through about camp movements. When we found a potential candidate who was agreeable to bearing Nasheira's mark—and most were—we laid out our conditions.

Speakers were not marked by Nardiri unless they first agreed to leave their life behind and fly immediately to the ravine with us. They swore to stay and work until they earned a dragon. And they pledged to keep their new home's location a secret. I knew it would all crumble once we had a sky full of bonded dragons and Speakers, but it was all I could do to protect my own while providing Nardiri with enough candidates for her eggs.

The mark was only the first trial our new Speakers faced. The second was crossing the threshold of a Guide's nest when we'd all been raised to fear treading on such sacred ground.

I hoped that seeing the eggs promised to them might ease my candidates' fears and asked Nardiri if it were safe to uncover her nest during the day. She was amenable, as long as we buried them again. But, the sight of those cylindrical, golden shells huddled like dimpled boulders in the brown grass—and Nardiri sprawled at the nest's far edge—seemed to shake my unbonded Speakers even more.

"Wouldn't it be faster to impress a wild wurm?" a young aeni woman asked. I recognized her as the Speaker we'd rescued from an altercation in the caldera valley to the south. She toed the border of the nest beside me, her gaze flashing up to mine, one eye brown and one blue.

"They bond stronger when they're young." I smiled. "That's the running theory, anyway.

She snorted and stepped into the spongy grass first, before any of the nervous group behind her could beat her to it.

"Go on." I grinned at the rest of them, waving them forward.

The aeni shook her head, tugging at the white streak in her black hair. She shot a hard glance at a disinterested Nardiri, before peering back over her shoulder at me. "You sure she doesn't mind?" she gulped.

"Does she look like she does?" I chuckled.

Venda shuffled over the edge of the nest to stand beside the aeni girl. "Come on. Let's show the rest how it's done." She clutched the young woman's hand in her knobby fingers, and tugged her by the arm. "That one in the middle." She stabbed a finger toward the centre of the nest, turned back and bunched her dark cheeks into a toothless grin. "That one's mine." Without hesitation, she marched the aeni woman into the midst of the golden eggs and pressed her palm flat on a speckled shell. "Oh yes. That's the one all right. Which one's yours, girl?"

The aeni shrugged and turned a slow circle before leaning into an upturned egg and touching it hesitantly. The rest of the group poured reverently into Nardiri's nest with their fingers pressed to their foreheads. Once they'd touched an egg, claimed it as their own, I knew they wouldn't turn away. Some of them clutched at the scars on their chests. Many of them cried and prayed. Faced with palpable proof of my promise, every candidate fell head over heels for my dragon's unborn hatchlings.

CHAPTER-THIRTY-THREE

T HREE MONTHS AFTER NARDIRI laid her eggs, Rowin bounded into our cave, brown hair pasted across his sweaty forehead. Sun squealed at the sight of him, pressing to a stand and beating his fists in the air.

Rowin grinned and mussed his little brother's hair. Then he fished a scrap of smooth pechi bark and a stick of charcoal from his belt pouch. He hastily drew an oval with a jagged line through it, and it took me a moment to decipher the meaning.

Eggs opening.

"'Owin!" Sun grabbed at his pant leg and would have toppled over if Rowin hadn't caught him.

Nardiri, it's time.

We had cleared a row of three ground-level caverns several days ago and constructed a v-trap funnelling toward their openings. It had been simple for Nardiri to drive a small herd of oxen up the valley into the mouth of our trap, but harder to press the stampeding animals into the caves without them jamming in the narrows. We managed. Without Nardiri, we would never have been able to set the large boulders across the entrances to hold the herd within.

We'd chosen slabs of stone that left enough of a gap at the top to dump water bags into the shallow troughs Nardiri had carved within, and we'd gathered countless bundles of green grass from the prairie above. For the past two days, my candidates had tended to the corralled oxen almost as much as their eggs.

I'll move the stones at your word. Nardiri answered. I heard her swoop down from her perch on the cliff above.

"Yara?" I hollered back into the cave, scooping up Sun.

My mate strode toward me, curls bobbing and a slow, widening smile easing onto her face. "It's time?"

I nodded as I shifted Sun onto her hip, leaned into her and kissed her hair.

She pressed to her toes and pulled me into a hurried kiss. "Be careful."

Sun blew a wet bubble past his pursed lips. I leaned in to kiss his damp, downy hair before kneeling before Rowin.

"Stay here with Uncle Jin and Aaron and protect them?" The thought of unbonded, ravenous wurms anywhere near my family momentarily took my breath away.

Rowin nodded sulkily.

Call them, Nardiri. Any who aren't already there. I need all the candidates at the nest now.

My dragon bugled. The sound reverberated through the valley as she held the note and ended it with an excited trill. ***This is fun! Do you think I am the first dragon who's ever watched her own eggs hatch?***

I grinned at her excitement and jogged toward the lake shore. Glancing over my shoulder to the cave corrals, I took in Nardiri crouched in front of the stones. She tossed her head and trumpeted again, bouncing from foot to foot.

Their hunger is much stronger than it was yesterday.

As I crossed the band of grass between the caves and the soft soil of the nest's border, my mouth went dry. The eggs, over five feet tall, looked much the same as they had all summer, some of them angled upward, others reclined heavily on their sides. The whole nesting site looked as if it was in the throes of a localised earthshake. Eggs jerked and shuddered. Candidates skidded through sloughing, half-rotted grass. Some of them used their hands to dig, freeing partially exposed eggs. Others simply stood watching, wide-eyed and immobilized.

I was the only one here to help. It wasn't safe for anyone unmarked and I refused to expose Tanar, Oric, and my other bonded Speakers to the possibility of an accidental second bonding. I'd seen what it had done to Dero, how his dragons had torn his mind apart. I wasn't sure if the number of bonds or the youth of the dragons had been the cause, but I wasn't about to test theories. I also wasn't sure how the Speakers' wurms would react to newborn kin. It seemed safer to keep the nesting site as empty as possible.

As the eggs pitched and rocked, I clapped the backs of several of the gape-mouthed candidates around me. The young aeni woman with the mismatched eyes pursed her trembling lips when I reached her. She stood alone.

"Were you afraid, Speaker, when you imprinted your wurm?" Her voice wobbled.

"Terrified."

A tendon twitched at her throat. "How did you stop yourself from fleeing?"

"I was tied." I flinched. *In a pool of my own blood.* "As utterly terrifying as it is before a wurm impresses, I promise you, it's equally euphoric afterwards."

She nodded, but she was looking at the nest, not me.

I cleared my throat. "You'll need to expose your chest."

A hard laugh barked out of her. "I forgot." She yanked her patchwork tunic over her head, set it on the ground and drew a shuddering breath. "Mirala," she whispered so quietly, I nearly missed it.

"What?"

"My name, Speaker. Mirala. I'm giving you my name... in case."

I leaned closer and laid my hand on her shoulder. "Mirala, they won't hurt you." *Sweet Nasheira, please let that be true.*

"What if none of them chooses me?" The second-most fear on all of my candidate's minds. Twenty-five candidates. Eighteen eggs.

"Then Nasheira values you for your patience. There's plenty of nests in the wild, and Nardiri will brood again."

An egg in front of us shifted. I spun to the next Speaker.

"Remember to expose your chests!" I bellowed.

I found Venda next.

Tossing her braid behind her back, the old woman faced me with bright eyes.

"You seem unafraid." A smile twitched my lips despite my heart pounding in my head.

"Phht." Venda waved her arms. "I'm too old to run around like a vaiya chick." She prodded a finger between her sagging breasts. Nardiri's mark crossed her heart like a flag. "I've got to conserve my energy. Only got so much allotted for one day, and I'm planning to bounce your Sun on my knee later."

"You're all brave." I raised my eyebrows and scanned the candidates. Guides, I was so proud of them.

She screwed up her face and jabbed a finger at the bare-chested men and women shaking out their hands and bouncing on the balls of their feet. "Think they're gonna sprint right on in and steal my dragon. I've sung to him in the egg already. He'll find me."

I laughed shakily, encouraged by her confidence.

A thunk and a dry crack erupted from the centre of the nest, snuffing out every other sound. We stood rooted to our spots as two more splintering snaps hammered in quick succession. One of the slanted eggs in the middle fissured at its end. Gold shards expanded away from each other like clay baking in the sun. The egg dimpled and then bloomed. Leathery membrane split and two slimy feelers slipped hesitantly over the sharp edges. The egg beside it burst open violently.

A few candidates squealed. The second wurm uncoiled like a pasty leaf and curled toward the sound, sampling the air with twitching teeth and furiously wriggling feelers. And then the stench hit us, acrid, oily and clinging to the backs of our throats. Everyone was familiar with the scent of wurms by now, but this was thicker, stronger.

My heart hammered behind my temples. The first flood of adrenalin splashed through my rib cage, sloshing in my stomach and warming my limbs.

The candidate behind me gagged. Jolting toward the sound, the wurm crashed into the first egg and it toppled sideways. The hatchling within oozed out and latched onto its sibling.

Out of the corner of my eye, I saw three Speakers backing away from the enmeshed wurms. One tripped over the other, recovered and sprinted toward the caves. His two compatriots staggered and then turned to follow.

"No, you don't," Venda mumbled. She pressed past me. I gaped, watching her braid wobble as she shuffled toward the wurms. "Stop that, you two!" she shouted at them.

The two hatchling's heads flicked toward her voice. A woman who had been about to follow the retreating Speakers paused to watch Venda.

"No dragon of mine's gonna behave so badly."

The pair of wurms shot toward the old woman. She stepped to the side, but one of them caught her arm as it lunged past and sent her reeling onto her stomach. The second latched onto her back and pressed her deep into the vegetation, stifling her startled cry.

"No!" I barked and realised my mistake when the wurm that missed Venda reeled toward me. Turning, I sprinted toward the closest candidate.

I didn't stop running until the dry chuff at my heels receded. When I looked back, the wurm had found Mirala. It enveloped her chest as her eyes popped and spit flew past her lips.

More eggs burst open as Venda's wurm yarded the old woman onto her back and dabbed at her chest. The nest looked like a burst pustule, teaming with maggots.

I tried to swallow my panic.

And that's when the laughter started—elated, and entirely out of place. I swallowed and staggered toward the foreign sound. Mirala had her arms wrapped around the wurm at her chest. It curled in her lap.

"She's mine. She's hungry!" She sobbed with bright eyes.

"Sweet Nasheira!" Venda cackled. "You're a clumsy one, aren't you?"

Her wurm tugged at her arm. She sat up and gazed reverently at it.

Divert the unpaired. Nardiri's order pressed through the rushing noise between my ears. ***They're following the noise.***

"O-over here!" I stammered, stamping and waving my arms at the trio of hatchlings snaking toward Venda and Mirala. The candidates opposite from me broke into a jog and repeated my shout.

Wurms spilled out of crushed shells and tumbled toward our voices like white water as we darted through the nest. Shocked, silver laughter multiplied in our ears as dragon hatchlings impressed and merged into beautiful sentience. Our gutted silence dissolved into industrious, bright orders as bonded pairs stood and used their wurms to direct the straggling hatchlings toward waiting candidates.

When it was done, I fell to my knees amongst the shattered shells, panting, cheeks wet with overwhelmed tears.

I'm releasing some of the oxen. I'll bring them to you. You're all a mess. Nardiri said.

I grinned, wiping my nose on my arm. My hand shook as I shaded my eyes to squint toward my cave—the entrance was just visible from where I stood. Yara stood at the cave mouth, clutching Sun and Rowin. Jin, Aaron, and Fraesh stood beside them. All of them waved enthusiastically.

And for the first time in my life, I was not afraid of what the future held.

The End

THANK YOU

First and foremost, thank you to Colin, Liam and Finn for giving me so much time to play with words. To my Writer's Alliance crew, bless you for being the first to heroically wade through those words in their rough form. Al Hess, Jennifer Lane and Ravaena Hart, your help was immeasurable and immense. To my editors Allison Alexander and Emma Skrumeda, your incredible vision took my story from a watery idea to a poignant, vibrant tale in ways I could never have imagined on my own. Lastly, to everyone at Mythos and Ink Publishing, thank you for loving my story enough to take a chance on me. Even though you've since closed your doors, you've all made a lifelong dream come true.

GLOSSARY

Aaron: Jin's mate.

Aella: Akrist, Dero, Jin and Tasie's mother. Hasev's mate.

Aeni: Smaller nomadic counterpart to the larger camps. They never settle in one area and are excellent mapmakers and scouts. Individuals never reveal their names, except to their closest kin. Individually, to strangers, they are all called ani.

Akrist: Hasev and Aella's eldest son (daeson), Speaker, outcast, and Yara's mate, bonded with Nardiri.

Ana: Storyteller. Caretaker of the daeson camp.

Ani: Placeholder name for all aeni as they only share their true names with their closest kin.

Amar: Youngest speaker Nardiri marks, from Venda's camp.

Arsu: Na-Jhalar's older sister, who orchestrated Iva's murder and Akrist's sacrifice in order to seize leadership. Gevi's mate, mother to daeson Sivi (deceased).

Baline: Fraesh and Iva's eldest daughter, once chani to Na-Jhalar, mother to Galeed.

Barth: Hunter in Akrist's camp, father to daeson Gideous (deceased).

Bury Bug: Parasite similar to a tick. It embeds itself between the scales of both vaiyas and dragons.

Celi: Fraesh and Iva's youngest daughter, once chani to Na-Jhalar.

Chani: Concubine to a Speaker. Their families are well provided for. Chani are not allowed alone in another's company while they hold their title. Technically, they are allowed to step down from their role, but few do so for fear they will be cast out.

Creb: Hunter in Akrist's camp.

Daeson: Title of the eldest son in a family. It means *damned son* in the old language.

Darvie: Hunter in Akrist's camp, father to daeson Enso (deceased).

Dero: Akrist's youngest brother. Arsu's stout follower. Hasev and Aella's son. Sibling to Tasie, Akrist, and Jin.

Elder: An older member of a camp, chosen to act as one of several councillors to the Speaker. The position is not guaranteed to all older members of a camp. For example, if a man abandons care for his daeson, he revokes his future elder position as well as losing hunter shares.

Enna: Yara's mother.

Fey: Orphan daeson who was sacrificed with Akrist. Deceased.

Fraesh: Akrist's uncle. Healer for his camp. Iva's mate, Celi and Baline's father.

Galeed: Baline's son.

Gevi: Arsu's mate. Father to daeson Sivi.

Gideous: Barth's daeson. Sacrificed with Akrist. Deceased.

Gifen: Narcotic plant. Leaves are chewed to release their bitter juice. Used for pleasure and also medically to dull pain.

Guides: Dragons. Nasheira's angels sent to guide her people out of the wastelands and toward hunting grounds. They choose leaders (Speakers) in Nasheira's name by marking chosen individuals with a complex scar across their chest.

Harek: A pig-like animal with plated armour, similar to that of an armadillo.

Hasev: Tasie, Akrist, Dero, and Jin's father. Aella's mate. Iva's brother.

Healer: This camp member is skilled at midwifery, herbalism, undertaking, and tattooing. Healers preserve and pass on knowledge of medicinal plants, keep a history of daeson births in a camp, prepare bodies for cremation, and provide the rare blue ink used to tattoo a woman after she's born her eldest son.

Henri: Daeson who was sacrificed with Akrist. Deceased.

Iva: Akrist's camp's storyteller. Fraesh's mate. Mother to Baline and Celi. Hasev's sister. Akrist's aunt and mentor. Murdered by Na-Jhalar and Arsu.

Jule: Orphan daeson who was sacrificed with Akrist. Deceased.

Jin: Akrist's middle brother and confidant. Hasev and Aella's son. Aaron's mate. Siblings: Tasie, Akrist, Dero.

Junab: A low growing succulent. Its leaves are crushed and used as an effective (but smelly) antibacterial ointment.

Kiro: A sweet-smelling grass used for incense and bedding.

Masa: Bonded dragon.

Mirala: Aeni Speaker.

Na: Prefix in front of a name that signifies that person is a Speaker (e.g. Na-Jhalar).

Na-Jhalar: Speaker for Akrist's camp. Younger brother of Arsu. Once kept Celi, Baline ,and Yara as chani. Galeed's father. Possibly Sun's father. Deceased.

Nardiri: Dragon bonded to Akrist. She announced her name upon emerging from her cocoon.

Nasheira: Goddess of Akrist's world. Her Son's Pau and Yurrii feature in the creation legend. Dragons or Guides are believed to be her living emissaries.

Nella: Hunter in Akrist's camp.

Oric: One of the Speakers Akrist and Nardiri mark.

Pau: The Goddess Nasheira's eldest son who murdered his younger brother Yurrii and entombed him in a moon. Wurms are believed to be a living symbol of his evil incarnate. The largest moon is named after him.

Pechi: Type of deciduous tree, similar to a poplar.

Rowin: A daeson who survived sacrifice. Bought from Aeni slavers by Nardiri and the first daeson rescued by Akrist. He doesn't speak—except during his night terrors.

Serin: Girl in Ana's camp with forged daeson tattoo.

Sivi: Arsu's and Gevi's daeson, died in infancy, most likely from emotional neglect.

Speaker: An individual marked by the Guides to lead a camp. They frequently have prophetic visions and always have 'Na' added to their name to signify Nasheira has chosen them to speak for her people.

Storyteller: Keeper of a camp's history and legends. With no written language, history is passed on orally, through song and storytelling. Ideal storyteller apprentices must be well-spoken with excellent memories, and natural people skills as they are often emotional councillors as well. In camps with no Speakers, leadership often falls to the storyteller.

Sun: Akrist and Yara's son—although Na-Jhalar is possibly Sun's biological father.

Tanar: Akrist's childhood friend and the daeson who abandoned Akrist to escape with infant daeson Xen. As a crazed, starved outcast, he later reunites with Akrist in the cave where Nardiri has cocooned.

Tasie: Akrist's older sister who died in a flood after Akrist was born. Aella blames him for her death. Sibling to Akrist, Jin, and Dero.

Tavi: A popular game played with two pieces—one dragon and one wurm—per player. Players take turns guessing which hand their opposition holds the dragon piece in and win a round if they guess correctly.

Ula: A tree that produces berries poisonous to humans, but irresistible to vaiyas.

Vaiya: Pack animal, like a large bird, but scaled instead of feathered. They are intelligent and can be taught to speak.

Vala: One of the vaiyas in the flock Akrist tended as a boy.

Vax: The patriarch vaiya in the flock Akrist tended as a boy, and his most loyal friend. Deceased.

Vell: One of the vaiyas in the flock Akrist tended as a boy.

Venda: The oldest Speaker that Akrist and Nardiri mark. She comes from the same camp as Amar.

Voti: One of the vaiyas in the flock Akrist tended as a boy.

Wurm: Blind, subterranean predator and scavenger shaped like a maggot, but with teeth and face tentacles. Wurms are larger than humans and are a symbol of Nasheira's eldest son, Pau, the first daeson.

Xen: A daeson baby who Tanar secretly cared for as a boy. Tanar escaped with Xen in Akrist's childhood, stealing all the food and supplies they cached together and abandoning Akrist before their sacrifice.

Yara: Akrist's mate. Sun's mother. Enna's daughter. Was once a chani to Na-Jhalar.

Yurrii: The goddess Nasheira's youngest son, murdered by his brother, represented incarnate in dragon form. The smallest moon is named after him.

Emotions Colour Chart

Colour Intensity	Pink	Red	Orange	Yellow	Yellow-Green
Light	distracted, bored	cranky, upset	nervous	unsure, confused, surprised	interested
Medium	irritated	frustrated, angry	anxious, worried	startled, afraid	intrigued
Dark	apathetic, contemptuous	furious, bitter, enraged	frantic	terrified	amazed, fixated, astonished
Grey to Black	hysterical	hysterical	hysterical	hysterical	hysterical

Colour Intensity	Green	Green-Blue	Blue	Blue-Purple	Purple
Light	satisfied	content, calm	hurt	disappointed	averse
Medium	happy, overjoyed, excited	relaxed	sad	distraught	disgusted
Dark	thrilled, exuberant, obsessed	numb, dis- connected, unmoored	depressed	anguished, ashamed	disdainful, scornful
Grey to Black	hysterical	hysterical	hysterical	hysterical	hysterical

REVIEWS MAKE A DIFFERENCE

DID YOU KNOW THAT one of the best ways you can support an author is to leave a book review? All it costs is a few minutes of your time! If you liked this book, please consider leaving a review on the website of your favourite bookseller.

An Interview
with the
Author

WHAT HAS LIVING IN AKRIST'S HEAD FOR TWO BOOKS BEEN LIKE?

I'VE BEEN LIVING IN Akrist's head for decades, and—let's be honest—the guy's got some issues, right? How could he not? He's lived through unimaginable trauma, but he's one of those incredibly resilient people who keeps on living and trying. He doesn't lose his empathy even while struggling with the massive aftereffects of what life has dished out for him. He never fully heals, but he doesn't stop growing either. I'm inspired by that. Trauma—what little I've experienced—tends to shut me down.

It's been amazing watching Akrist transform from a timid daeson boy into a leader I'd be proud to follow anywhere. That said, I'm pretty sure I wouldn't last a day in his world. There were many times in the series, living in his head, where I thought, "Yeah, I'd be dead about ten times over by now." Akrist has a much stronger will to survive than I do! I'd lay down and give up far sooner.

WHO'S YOUR FAVOURITE CHARACTER FROM THE MARKED SON SERIES?

Vax. Oh, poor Vax. Don't hate me, y'all.

I tried to find *any* possible way for that wonderful bird to live, but just couldn't picture a scenario where Akrist's most loyal friend would ever let him come to harm. He'd give his life without hesitation to save Akrist. And there's no way Akrist's camp wasn't going to sacrifice him. Sorry, Sweet Bird.

My second favourite would be a tie between Nardiri and Tanar, because they are both wonderfully colourful characters for entirely different reasons, and they both challenge Akrist in their own ways.

WHICH WAS MORE DIFFICULT—WRITING

BOOK

ONE OR TWO? WHY?

Oh, book two, for sure. New readers have to be able to jump in without getting disoriented, and readers who enjoyed book one are expecting a decent sequel. Book two wraps up all of the character arcs for the whole series and I always doubt my ability to nail the landing when it comes to endings. Also, it's hard to leave these characters after hanging out with them for so long. Perhaps there's another story in this world percolating in my brain...

WHAT IS YOUR CREATIVE PROCESS? HOW DO YOU GET FROM A BLANK PAGE TO A FINISHED NOVEL?

My current creative process is much different than it used to be. For *Under the Lesser Moon* and *Voice of the Banished*, I wrote the whole series out in one drawn-out, meandering mess of a story. I didn't outline, I just wandered wherever the story took me. Turns out, this method took me down a lot of dead ends that no one else really needed to travel down with me—except my poor critique partners and editors. Those first drafts helped me to worldbuild and get to know my characters, though, so in a way, they were a *sort* of outline. After that, with the help of my lovely editing team, I built some solid outlines and rewrote both manuscripts almost from scratch. Each draft had two or three rounds of edits after that to tweak plot, pacing, and development. Then beta readers, some more tweaks, and a proofread. The end product readers receive is the result of a lot of talented people working really hard to make me look good. I'd never be able to produce such well-polished stories on my own!

I am somewhat teachable, though. Now, when I'm starting with a blank page, I don't word-vomit as much. I start with a solid outline to map where I want to go. It helps keep me on track and makes my creative process less painful and time-consuming. As always, my process is a work in progress. I rely a lot on feedback from my critique partners and my editors.

WHAT IS THE MOST DIFFICULT THING ABOUT BEING A WRITER?

It can be really lonely. Most of the process is just sit my butt in the chair and write. It takes a lot of time away from my hubby and kids, which is unfair to them—I suck at work/life balance. Being an author is also a bit like living in a time warp, because books take so long to write, edit, proofread, design, and print. By the time readers are getting hyped about my book, I'm thinking, "Yeah, I've already read this several hundred times and it's been living with me for years. I don't even know what I think about it anymore!" I've got to say, that's also one of the best things about being a writer too: seeing other people get excited about a world that didn't exist until I typed it all out. Having writer friends and editors who are passionate enough about it to put a lot of elbow grease into making it the best it can be. And new readers will always be discovering my stories for the first time, no matter how old the books get. That's pretty darned gratifying.

WHAT'S YOUR ADVICE ABOUT WORK-ING WITH AN EDITOR?

Every edit letter is going to sting, no matter how many you get, or how gently-worded they are. And you know what? That's okay. Expect the sting. Read your edits. Breathe. Come back to them in an hour, or a day, or a week when the stinging has faded, and *then* read objectively. Editors are incredible people who dedicate their time to make your writing the best it can possibly be. They pour almost as many hours into your book as you do, and they have your best interests at heart. So, do your best to take their advice to heart. They know their stuff.

That said, if you have a particular edit that just doesn't sit well with you, and no matter how you approach it, it doesn't *feel* right for your story, remember that you know your world better than anyone else. You've lived in your characters' heads. It's okay to stand up for them when you really need to.

WHAT DO YOU LIKE ABOUT WORKING WITH SMALL PRESSES?

I love working with a team that is as excited about my project as I am. Most small presses aren't in this for the money. They truly want to see good books find good homes. I love that I get a lot of input into my cover design and layout, and I love being able to email and video chat with staff that I know. Small presses are like walking into your locally owned, independent bookstore and *knowing* that you're going to find treasure there that you can't discover anywhere else.

HOW HAVE YOU CHANGED AS AN AUTHOR SINCE WRITING YOUR FIRST BOOK?

I am more confident in my ability as an author. I've seen proof that readers out there enjoy what I'm writing, and of course I'm motivated by that! Before my first book was accepted, I went through a long spell where I wondered if I was wasting all this time in front of a computer for nothing. I had no way to gauge if I was any good at writing or if it was a hobby that I should give up. Now, I have more fun with the whole process from drafting to querying to publishing, and I'm hoping I've learned to roll with the punches. The publishing industry is always changing in unexpected ways. I'm hoping it keeps me adaptable and flexible and always growing.

WHAT ARE SOME OF YOUR FAVOURITE WORLDBUILDING RESOURCES?

Right now, I'm loving *Making Myths and Magic: A Field Guide to Writing Sci-Fi and Fantasy Novels* by Yours Truly and Allison Alexander. It's been such a fun book to research and co-write, and if I can remember to implement even a smidgeon of what we packed into those pages into my own writing, my worldbuilding will improve vastly.

WHO'S A FICTIONAL CHARACTER YOU'D WANT FOR A BEST FRIEND?

I think I'd choose Inigo Montoya from *The Princess Bride*. He's focused on a long term goal. He's honourable and treats his friends with respect. He doesn't mind getting drunk every now and then, but when it comes to killing six-fingered men, he's all business. Plus, I have no idea about the ins and outs of Bonetti's Defense, Capa Ferro, and Agrippa. I respect a guy who's spent a lifetime dedicating himself to studying one skill, and I think an expert fencer would come in handy if we ever got mugged. Mostly, I respect Inigo because, when his whole life shifts—he's had his revenge killing Count Rugen, and the moment his *entire* life has led up to is just done—he doesn't shy away from the idea of taking up piracy, just to keep him busy. I don't think life would ever be boring as his best friend. But honestly, Fezzik deserves the role more than I do.

WHAT'S A BOOK YOU LOVE THAT DE-SERVES MORE READERS?

Jennifer Lane's *Of Metal and Earth* is a story about seven ordinary lives changed by their ownership of a little Green Jeep. It's such a fresh and nostalgic read. Jennifer does an incredible job of breathing life into each character and letting us in on their personal journey as the Jeep pushes each of them to tackle life from a different angle. Like a restored car, take your time enjoying this read, because they just don't make them like this anymore! Jennifer is an incredible writer who deserves more eyes on her work.

You may also enjoy…

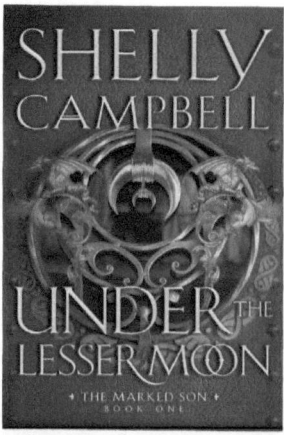
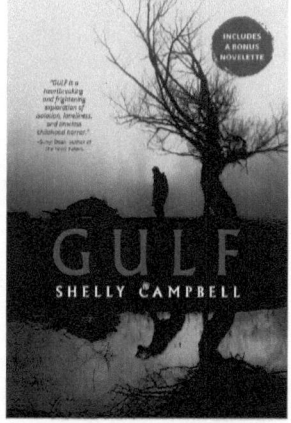

www.ingramcontent.com/pod-product-compliance
Lightning Source LLC
Chambersburg PA
CBHW051315190726
48290CB00001B/159